RUNAWAY

Acclaim for Anne Laughlin's Work

"*Veritas* is a fun, well-paced and intriguing mystery with all the components every reader of classic and competent cozies seeks. Satisfying and solid."—*Lambda Literary Review*

"Anne Laughlin's *Veritas* is a gripping murder mystery packed with suspense and intrigue. Laughlin's prose is natural and engaging whether she's writing about the politics of academia, Beth and Sally's multilayered romance, or the intricacies of a murder mystery. Named a Lambda Literary Foundation Emerging Writer in 2008, *Veritas* proves Laughlin worthy of the honor."—*AfterEllen.com*

"*Veritas* by Anne Laughlin is, simply put, a good read. It's serious without taking itself seriously. It has humour without being silly. It is sensuous and written with clarity and maturity."—*Kissed by Venus*

Visit us at www.boldstrokesbooks.com

By the Author

Veritas

Runaway

RUNAWAY

by

Anne Laughlin

2012

RUNAWAY

ISBN 10: 1-60282-649-8
ISBN 13: 978-1-60282-649-6

This Trade Paperback Original Is Published By
Bold Strokes Books, Inc.
P.O. Box 249
Valley Falls, NY 12185

First Edition: March 2012

Credits
Editor: Cindy Cresap
Production Design: Susan Ramundo
Cover Design By Sheri (graphicartist2020@hotmail.com)

Acknowledgments

With every book I've written, there comes a point about halfway through the process when I throw up my hands and wonder why I'm torturing myself. I imagine every writer has a crew to help pull her out of these pitiful periods, and mine is made up of: Linda Braasch, Joan Larkin, Liz Laughlin, Rita Balzotti, and Michelle Sandford.

Thanks also to Kelley Eskridge and Nicola Griffith for insightful feedback. My editor, Cindy Cresap, helped me tuck in the corners and smooth the sheets.

I can't thank Linda enough, but I'll never stop trying. Learning to write and learning to love were made possible with her in my life. I really have no ambitions beyond that.

Dedication

For Joan Larkin

Prologue

It was her sixteenth birthday, but no one in camp mentioned it, not even her father. The birthday meant she was eligible to take guard duty on the perimeter of the camp. She waited all day for a sign from him that she'd been given a duty shift, but none came until eleven thirty, a half hour after she went to bed. He tossed a rifle onto her cot and ordered her to get ready. She was in uniform under the blanket, worrying he'd forgotten her altogether.

He led her into the vast woods that surrounded their camp, past the dozen shacks that held the camp's families. Each shack had a tiny window and a door; otherwise you'd never know they were built for humans. She lived in a larger cabin with her father, the Colonel. All the windows in the shacks were now dark, for the Colonel strictly enforced eleven p.m. lights-out.

She kept her flashlight trained on his boots as she marched behind him. They were the same style of boots he wore in Vietnam. There he had been a colonel. Here he was God.

As they neared the camp's western perimeter, she saw Trevor Martin snap to attention and shoulder his rifle. Trevor was a few years older than she was and a suck-up to her father. Trevor had announced to her last week he intended to ask the Colonel for permission to marry her. She wasn't really surprised by his intentions. It was a move so transparent as to be laughable. The problem was the Colonel would probably approve the marriage, and she would have to comply. Even if her mother were alive, she wouldn't have run interference for her. After treating her as a soldier her entire life, the Colonel seemed suddenly aware his daughter was female, something that clearly didn't sit well with him. She wasn't sure how it sat with her either.

The Colonel stopped in front of Trevor and stood with his hands on his hips, looking around the dark and dense woods. Then he stared straight at him.

"Report."

"All quiet, sir. Electronic fencing is operational."

"Very good, Corporal. You're relieved."

The Colonel turned to her. "Do you know what to do?"

She also stood at attention. "Yes, sir."

She took the radio off her belt and called in to Douglas Anders over at the eastern perimeter.

"Hey, birthday girl," he said. "Welcome to your first guard duty."

She looked up at her father, nervous that Douglas said something so personal. Her father wore the same stony expression as always.

"Roger that," she said, her voice a little creaky. "I'll check back in at 0100."

She put the radio back on her belt and resumed attention.

"Is there something going on between you and Anders?" the Colonel said.

"No, sir."

He looked around the area, silent for a moment before looking back at her.

"Carry on. You'll be relieved at 0800." He turned and marched back the way he came, with Trevor trotting behind him.

Very slowly, she relaxed her stance and put her rifle butt on the ground. She listened as closely as she could. The woods were very dark, but there was noise all around—a constant rustling of leaves, droning insects, acorns and branches falling. She heard a plane overhead, a sound that made her heart pick up its pace as she peered into the dark sky hoping to see it. What did a plane look like up close? What would it be like to fly in one? The only place she'd been outside of camp was to the nearest Idaho town, and those trips were infrequent. She'd concentrate on taking in every detail, every person, place, and thing that existed outside the remote camp she lived in.

Once enough time had passed for her father and Trevor to be back in camp, she put her plan into place. With her rifle hanging from her shoulder, she climbed a tree twenty feet from her guard post and jumped over the electronic fence. The tree had been picked out some weeks before, during one of her many reconnaissance missions through the woods. There was usually some part of each day that allowed her to slip away from the center of camp when her duties were done, the Colonel occupied elsewhere, and the attentions of all the men, women, and children on their own concerns. She began to realize if she planned carefully, she had a decent chance of making her escape, and beyond that she couldn't begin to imagine. She reasoned if she could make it out of camp alive, chances were she'd figure out what to do next.

She ran straight west as fast as she could, stumbling over and over again on the branches littering the forest floor. Along the way, she pulled a small knapsack from the hollow of a tree. It contained a change of underwear, a bit of food, and a loaded pistol she'd stolen from the armory. The Colonel had not trained his soldiers on side arms, those being the privilege of rank. But she understood the basics. She knew enough.

She checked her bearings on the small compass she'd found among her father's things. It should be another mile or so to the county road that led into town. She couldn't afford to walk along the road once she got there. She would be hunted, and if she were found, he'd try to kill her. She was sure of that. She had a better chance if she crossed the road and continued into the woods as far as she could get before she had to rest.

When she neared the road, she stepped forward as silently as she could, sensing rather than seeing the break in the trees. A steep embankment led from the edge of the trees to the roadbed, and as she broke through into the clear space, she heard a car coming, moving fast. She wondered for a moment whether she should run up and flag it down, plead with whoever was driving to help her, to save her from her father and all the adults in the camp who wouldn't let her leave. She was a prisoner, she wanted to say. But she didn't trust whomever it was she might flag down. They might take her to the authorities, and they would bring her back to the Colonel.

She crouched in the clearing just before the embankment, feeling exposed in the moonlight. Outside the deep forest the silence was nearly complete. Just as she reached for her canteen she heard someone scrambling down the embankment, hitting the bottom about fifty yards north and running full speed toward her—the figure indistinct, but instantly recognizable. She swung her rifle around and assumed a prone position, wondering if the gun held one of the Colonel's tracking devices, then realizing with shame that of course it was the radio that had a tracking device, and how could she have been so stupid? Then her father began shooting. Two bullets hit just to her right. A third was on its way when her shot found its mark. She could see the look of shock in his mean eyes as he dropped to the ground. She'd always been a much better shot than him.

CHAPTER ONE

Jan Roberts stood in front of her bedroom mirror and smoothed the front of her high-collared, button-down shirt, tucking it into her charcoal trousers and zipping up. She knew she looked sharp. When she felt this good, the glow seemed to transfer out; her black hair was shinier, her cheekbones rosier, her athletic frame fluid and stronger. Behind her, the woman lying in her bed was up on one elbow, watching her every move. Jan returned to the bedside to kiss the soft curls springing every which way from the top of Gwen's head.

"I'll need to leave in a minute to make it to work on time," Jan said. "You can relax and just lock the door behind you when you leave. Take as much time as you want." Gwen didn't respond.

Jan gathered her keys and wallet from the top of her dresser and put her Glock and its holster onto her belt. She turned toward the bed as she pulled her suit jacket on.

"Gwen?"

Gwen was now on her back, her hands laced together on her stomach. A stream of western light from the late afternoon sun fell across her naked body.

"Why don't you just leave the money by my purse?" she said to the ceiling.

Jan stood still. "What?"

"That's how people generally pay for a sex date, isn't it?"

"This is not a sex date," Jan said, trying not to sound defensive. "What are you talking about?"

"Let's see. You called me at noon to ask whether I could come by before you left for work. I arrived at 3:00 and by 3:05, I was naked in your bed. It's now 4:00 and you're running out the door. What would you call it?"

Jan sighed and leaned over, pulling her pants leg up and strapping her backup gun to her ankle. She thought about shooting her way out of the room, so uncomfortable did the conversation feel. She looked at Gwen: her long body was lovely, her intelligent, pretty face marked only by the furrow in her brow.

"You could have said no," Jan said.

Gwen closed her eyes for a moment. "Excellent suggestion. This was hardly worth the cab ride over. In fact, I could have had the cabbie wait for me on the street."

Jan felt the familiar pressure start to build in her chest. Her body was sounding alarm bells, warning her of another impending loss.

"Tell me what you want me to do. Please."

Gwen sat up and put her feet to the floor, staring at them for a moment before looking at Jan. "I don't think so."

"Does that mean we're not going to see each other anymore?"

"If I thought you really cared one way or the other, I'd say I'm sorry."

"But I do care." Jan knelt in front of Gwen and tried to take her hands. Gwen pulled them away.

"That's the first I've heard of it. You're a complete mystery to me."

"I thought you liked a little mystery," Jan said, trying out a smile. It didn't seem to do any good.

"I like mystery in books. Not in lovers. I'm not interested in tweezing out everything I need to know to have a real relationship with you."

Jan stood and turned away, fighting off a familiar shame. She couldn't seem to hold on to a woman for more than a month. It felt like holding a moth in her cupped hands.

"Just lock the door handle on the way out," she said.

She quickly left the apartment, feeling a little sick, like she did every time women broke things off with her because she wasn't who they wanted her to be. They didn't know she wasn't even who she said she was.

❖

The Java Bucket was like a hundred other coffee shops that had opened in Chicago over the last decade or so, the main thing recommending it being its closeness to home and the fact that her partner, Peet, could usually find a parking spot when she came to meet Jan there. She took a seat near the window at the rear of the shop, the same table she and Peet sat at nearly every day.

The barista put her Americano on the table.

"How you doing today?" Elise was a quintessential urban coffee shop worker—tattooed, pierced, funky, and cute. Jan enjoyed flirting with her, but today she found it hard to keep her smile in place.

"I'm good."

"Right." Elise seemed unconvinced. "Do you need a pastry?"

"No, it's not that bad."

Elise stared at Jan for a moment and then moved back to her counter. She returned with a cupcake on a plate.

"Just in case," she said. "It's on the house." Elise squeezed Jan's shoulder and left her alone.

Jan saw Peet walk in. She would be hard to miss—nearly six feet tall and solidly built from her broad shoulders down through her sturdy, powerful legs. Her bright blond hair was cut in a modified Dutch Boy, which is what Peet looked like—a Dutch boy. Or a big ole lesbian, which is what Jan assumed she was until she met Peet's husband, Kevin, and their three kids. Jan knew that everyone who met Peet also thought she was a lesbian, and Peet let them think what they wanted. She was solid in every way.

"I'm grabbing mine to go," Peet said. "We need to get to the office."

"What's up?"

"Boss called. He wants to brief us on something before he leaves for the day."

Jan sipped her coffee and frowned. "Why doesn't he just tell us over the phone?"

"He likes to look you in the eye, Jan. It's his management style."

Jan wondered if Peet was serious about defending their boss, Victor "Little Junior" Begala. Six months ago, LJ had lured Peet away from the Chicago Police Department Homicide Division to join Titan Security and Investigations. Jan thought six months was long enough for her to realize that LJ had his head up his ass.

"I'll tell you what his management style is," she said. "Take credit for everything and never get your hands dirty. He's a lazy, selfish bastard."

Peet did not respond at first. The silence felt uncomfortable. "All I know is that I have better pay and benefits than I did with the police, I see my kids more, and I'm a little tired of hearing all the complaints from you."

Jan sank a bit lower in her chair. She thought Peet liked her. She needed Peet to like her.

Peet looked at the time on her cell phone. "I'm headed to the car. You coming with?"

She looked at Jan as if they'd just been talking about the Bears game. If she was angry or annoyed, it didn't show. Jan followed Peet out to her Volvo and got in, staying quiet as they headed toward the TSI offices in the River West area. Then the damn silence felt too uncomfortable. What if Peet requested a new partner?

"Do you think I'm a complainer?" Jan asked.

Peet smiled. "Half the time, I don't know what to think of you. You're a great investigator, but your attitude is kind of fucked up. Frankly, it's a drag to listen to your bitching, which has gotten worse, by the way."

Peet turned into the company parking lot behind a turn-of-the-century factory that had been converted into lofts and offices. They got out of the car and Jan stood still for a moment.

"You can smell the chocolate factory tonight," Jan said.

"I hate that. It gives me a sweet tooth all shift."

"Yeah, me too." When they reached the building, Jan stopped just outside the front. "Wait up, Peet. I want to say something."

"What's that?"

"Just that if you want a new partner, I'd understand."

"Oh, Christ. Did I say I wanted a new partner? You're a great partner. I just don't like negativity. There are a bunch of coppers like that—all wrapped up in their attitude. It's all about how people are trying to fuck them over. I think you've got a hell of a lot more going on for you than those guys." Peet turned and went into the building. Jan wanted to kick her ass and hug her at the same time.

LJ's office was on the second floor. They trotted up the old wooden staircase rather than wait for the creaky elevator. Most of the administrative and executive offices were on one side of the second floor, with the investigation division at the other. LJ had the northeast corner office with a view of the river and a good slice of Chicago skyline. His assistant, Vivian, was packing her things to leave for the day as Jan and Peet approached. She looked exactly like the kind of woman LJ would want outside his office, young, curvy, dressed to kill. That she was ten times smarter than LJ was something he wasn't clever enough to realize. Vivian must have found some way to make the job worthwhile, though Jan couldn't imagine what it might be.

Vivian saw them coming. "He's waiting for you."

She made Jan as nervous as a fourteen-year-old boy, as if she were about to reach out and smother Jan with her breasts. She was so richly voluptuous and sure of herself that Jan felt ill-equipped to deal with her. It was like having Mae West as your office manager. If Vivian ever let her into her bed, Jan thought she could probably satisfy her. But she'd want to bring in her special toolbox and leave nothing to chance.

They walked into LJ's office.

"There you are," he said as if they were an hour late and not fifteen minutes early for their shift. "Sit down, already. We've got a lot to go over."

LJ was a block of a man, broad-shouldered and muscular, but starting to fill out. Middle age and sloth were going to force him into a new wardrobe soon.

He turned to Peet. He always addressed her when the three of them met, had done so ever since Peet joined the company. It was clear he thought Peet's background with the homicide police gave her more stature than Jan would ever have.

"What's up, boss?" Peet asked.

"A buddy of mine sent a guy to us. Some North Shore executive whose daughter is missing. I need you to go up there right away to interview the parents."

He passed a piece of paper across the desk.

"How long has she been missing? How old is she?" Jan asked.

"She's sixteen and she's been gone at least twenty-four hours," he said. "That's about all I know, other than he sounds like the sort of guy who needs to make things happen fast."

"Well, it's his daughter missing," Peet said. "I think any parent would sound frantic."

"No, it's not like that, exactly. It's more like he's just pissed that she's gone."

"Has the girl run away before?" Jan asked.

LJ looked at her as if she were a little slow. "Didn't I just say I don't know anything else? You have to go up there and ask them. And find the girl, pronto. This guy is the CEO of some electronics manufacturer up there. If we impress him here we might pick up his worker comp business."

Jan looked at the man's name and address. Alan Harrington on Willow Road in Winnetka, one of the wealthy suburbs north of the city. Jan had worked quite a few missing teen cases in that area, and she wondered about the number of kids from there that she found on the city streets, dirty and drug-addled and still resistant to going back to a comfortable home. She understood running away from something bad, but her conception of a bad living situation was light years away from that of an upper middle class suburban kid.

"We're still on for following the Wilson husband tonight?" Jan said.

Their plan for the evening had been to catch up on paperwork and then head out to the Lincoln Park address of Ron and Paula Wilson. Paula Wilson wanted proof that her husband was leaving their bed in the middle of the night to go have sex with another woman. She'd confronted him about his absences, but he said he had insomnia and driving was the only thing that made him feel sleepy. As if he were a baby. Jan and Peet spent four nights at the outset watching the house from the street, but he never went out. Peet thought Paula Wilson was paranoid. Jan thought Ron Wilson was just laying low.

LJ was standing now, clearly anxious to be on his way. "Let's hope he heads out tonight. The wife has been calling me to complain, like it's our fault the man's not sneaking out to get a little."

"Maybe he's not," Peet said. "He comes home every night for dinner, walks the dog, plays with the kids. I'm not convinced he's cheating on her."

"We'll give it a few more days and then tell her to let it go. Now get out of here. The traffic on ninety-four is going to be a bear."

❖

Not everyone who lived in Winnetka was rich. Just a huge majority of them. The Harrington house was on the east side of Sheridan Road, just yards from Lake Michigan. It was built to look like an English manor home—quaint and enormous at the same time. Peet pulled into the semi-circular drive and parked behind a landscaping truck. A small army of gardeners was blasting the oak leaves blanketing the lawn, shouldering their leaf blowers as if they were weapons. Jan pulled the bell by the enormous wood door.

A woman in her early forties answered. She was thin in an anorexic-chic way, her angles and bones shown off in a heather gray knit sweater dress. She had a shawl scarf over her shoulders and pearl earrings on. She'd pulled her thick hair into a ponytail so tight it was stretching her skin away from her eyes. Either that or she'd had some very bad plastic surgery.

"Mrs. Harrington?" Peet said. "I'm Peet O'Malley and this is Jan Roberts. We're both senior investigators at Titan Security. You were expecting us?"

"Yes, of course. Please come in."

They followed her into a living room to the right of the front entryway. It was enormous, sumptuously decorated, and looked barely lived in. Jan sat in an uncomfortable Windsor chair. Peet took the other end of the plush sofa from Mrs. Harrington.

Mrs. Harrington leaned over and pulled a long brocaded cord that hung from the wall. "My husband stepped out for just a moment but will join us soon," she said. She seemed to have a slight lisp. "May I offer you something to drink?"

"No, don't get up," Jan said. "We're perfectly fine."

A uniformed maid entered the room.

"It's no trouble, I assure you," Mrs. Harrington said. "What would you like?"

"Coffee," said Peet.

"Coffee," said Jan. "With cream."

"Bring the coffee service, Eva."

Peet opened her notebook and began. "Mrs. Harrington, we'd like to begin with some preliminaries before your husband arrives, if that's all right with you."

"Certainly."

"Let's start with a photograph of your daughter that we can take with us."

Mrs. Harrington picked up her phone and went through a number of screens before handing it to Peet.

"This is the photo I gave the police this morning. It's Maddy, just a few weeks ago. We'd promised her a new car for the school year, and this is just after her father had given her the keys."

The girl standing next to the new Honda squinted as she faced the sun. Her blond hair was long and limp, her T-shirt and jeans standard teenage issue, though not as dressy as many girls would have chosen, and they hung loosely on her slender figure. She wore black Converse sneakers. She was dressed like a boy, but was unmistakably a girl, a slouchy, unhappy girl.

"If you could print this for us?" Peet said.

"I can e-mail this to you," Mrs. Harrington said.

"Even better. Now, when did you discover that Maddy was missing?"

"This morning when our housekeeper asked whether she was here. Her bed didn't look like it had been slept in, and we realized that neither of us had seen her since the night before last."

"Are you saying that she may have gone missing as long as forty-eight hours ago?" Jan said.

"It's hard to know exactly. Today is Tuesday, so it was this morning when Eva said something about not knowing that Maddy was out of town. I asked her what she was talking about, and she said she didn't think anything about it yesterday because maybe Maddy had fallen asleep in front of the TV. She only watches in the dead of night, when no one else is awake. When Eva saw the untouched bed again this morning, she was curious. That's when it occurred to me that I couldn't remember actually seeing Maddy for a little while."

"Is there a reason that wouldn't have set off alarm bells earlier?" Peet said.

"Do you have children?" Mrs. Harrington asked, looking as if she seriously doubted Peet was mother material.

"I have three," Peet said. "Two teenagers."

"Then you know how hard it is to keep up with them. My husband and I have crazy schedules. But we mostly stay on top of it."

"Tell me everything you did today after Eva pointed out the made bed," Peet said.

"Well, I called Alan first, not that I really expected him to know anything. His company is in the middle of a product launch, which means he is not aware of anything but that. He couldn't remember when he'd last seen Maddy, but he didn't think he saw her yesterday."

"Are there any other children at home?"

"Our son, Justin, is at Dartmouth. There's no one else."

The maid came in with a gleaming silver tray, and there was a lot of clattering of cups and saucers and passing around of plates before they got back to business. Jan ate a tiny cake while Peet continued the questioning.

"Mrs. Harrington, at what point did you call the police? What made you realize that your daughter was gone? She could have made her own bed, for instance."

Eva was just leaving the room with the empty tray. She turned and said, "No, she couldn't. That bed was made the way I make a bed. Maddy hasn't slept in it for two days, and that's the truth."

"Thank you, Eva. That will be all." Mrs. Harrington sipped her coffee and continued. "After Eva told me this, I went up to Maddy's room. I knew she was gone as soon as I saw her laptop was missing."

"Couldn't she have taken that with her as a normal thing? Some people don't go anywhere without one," said Jan.

"She has one of those pad things that she carries with her everywhere. She uses her laptop at home. Both machines are gone."

"Did you contact the school?"

"Of course. I called them before I called the police. They said Maddy wasn't in classes on Monday and they had called us to report her absence. They left a message on our home machine, but I usually forget to check. We're always on our cells," Mrs. Harrington said as she glanced at her iPhone.

"What have you noticed about Maddy's behavior, Mrs. Harrington?" Peet asked. "Any recent changes? Moodiness? Withdrawal? Maybe a new set of friends?"

Mrs. Harrington appeared to give the question no thought at all. "Change? No, Maddy stays pretty much the same. She comes home from school and makes a snack and then sits in front of her computer. There's been no change."

"She doesn't hang out with any school friends?" Jan said.

"None that she's ever brought here. She doesn't even talk about any friends."

"You're saying that Maddy doesn't have any friends at all?"

"I'm saying that she doesn't have friends that she actually sees. They're all on the computer. You know how they are. Everything is online. You could live alone on a mountaintop and still have friends."

"Are you around when she comes home?"

"No, not usually. But when I come home I ask her about her day and she always says the same thing. 'What's new?' 'Nothing.' 'What did you do today?' 'Nothing.'" Mrs. Harrington cast her head to the side in an odd gesture, like she was posing for a photographer. "I'd be bored to death if I had her life."

Jan flipped to a new page in her notebook. "We'll check in with the Winnetka Police, but it's my experience that police don't do much when it comes to teenage runaways. Abductions are another matter. Is there any reason to believe your daughter was kidnapped?"

Mrs. Harrington was about to answer when the front door opened and they turned to see a giant man walk into the house with a giant dog. The dog continued slowly into the living room with his head down, as if he were a child forced to say hello to his parents' guests. He bumped his head against Jan's legs and she gently pushed his slobbery snout away from her dress pants. She was unmoved by his charm.

"Don't mind Sanderson," Mrs. Harrington said. "He's harmless."

Not to my clothes he's not, thought Jan. She hated when people said things like that. *Don't mind my screeching child. Don't mind my barking dog. Don't mind me while I talk really loudly on the phone in the bookstore.*

Harrington was at least six feet six inches tall and built like a football player.

"Alan, these are the investigators you had sent over. They want to know if it's possible that Maddy's been kidnapped. I'd say you'd know more about that than me."

"I think you could say that about most anything," he said. He looked at Jan and Peet in that way that said "Why was I sent two women?" They'd both seen that look plenty of times before.

"Mr. Harrington, have you any reason to believe Maddy was abducted?" Peet asked.

He moved to the drinks cart near the bay window looking over the expansive side lawn. It was nearly dark and the leaf blowers were silent. Apparently, the gardeners had decamped. He poured himself a neat Scotch.

"It's certainly possible. I have money, although not the kind you think of in kidnapping cases. But it's like I told the police this morning. If she were abducted, wouldn't we have heard something by now?"

"Probably. It all depends on why she was taken. If it were money or something else from you, you'd probably have heard of their demands by now. If it's for some other reason . . ." Jan didn't want to spell out the alternatives.

Mrs. Harrington glared at her husband. "If anything happens to her it's your fault."

"Shut up, Lynette. We don't need your histrionics now, for God's sake." He poured another drink. "Can I get you gals anything? No?" He knocked back the drink and put the glass down. "I think what you're asking me is whether I have any enemies."

"That's right. Anyone at all, even if you don't think they'd go this far," Peet said.

Harrington stared at his wife accusingly. She stared back at him. They seemed to be wrapped in loathing.

"I think we can eliminate me as a suspect," Mrs. Harrington said to her husband, "as much as I know you'd like to see me hauled away. I did not abduct my own daughter. In case you'd forgotten, we all live together." Mrs. Harrington leaned back against the sofa, a furrow in her brow forming, despite the g-force strength of her ponytail.

"Do you want to retain us to attempt to locate Maddy?" Peet asked.

"Yes," said Mrs. Harrington.

"I want her found," Mr. Harrington said, "but I also want some idea of what it will cost."

"Do you have a budget in mind for how much you'll spend to find your daughter, Mr. Harrington?" Peet said, her tone pointedly neutral.

"God, you're unbelievable," said Mrs. Harrington.

Harrington ignored his wife. "I'll take the billing up with your superiors. You two need to get to work finding Maddy."

He made it sound like Jan and Peet were dillydallying. "We need you to compile a list of all of Maddy's friends. Give us as much contact information as you can. I also need to talk to your son. It's her friends and her brother who probably know what's going on with her," Jan said.

Mrs. Harrington looked up from the pad of paper she was jotting on. "Are you implying that I don't know what is happening with my own daughter?"

Jan could see that Peet was trying to restrain herself. Mr. Harrington, however, felt no such reticence.

"I don't think we need waste our time with implications, Lynette. Let's just come right out and say it. You don't."

Jan jumped in. "It's hardly unusual, Mrs. Harrington, for parents to not know what their teenage children are really up to."

Mrs. Harrington looked worried. Mr. Harrington took a peek at his watch.

Jan went on. "We also need her cell phone records. You can probably go right online and download the detail from her most recent bills."

"Actually, we won't be able to do that," Harrington said. "Maddy set up and paid for stuff like that with her own credit card, and I paid the credit card bill each month."

"Then print out the detail on the credit card statement and we'll take it from there. Don't cancel the card, whatever you do. It will give us some valuable information if she continues to use it," Jan said. "I'll also need the account number and password for your Internet service provider. We should be able to get some information on Maddy's recent Web activity."

"I'll write down the name of friends I can think of, but there won't be many," Mrs. Harrington said.

"Please be as thorough as you can be."

"Of course."

Harrington looked at his watch again and put his empty glass down. "Listen, why don't we do this? You gals get on your way so you can start tracking Maddy down. We'll put the information together that you've asked for and call you when we've got it, probably tomorrow sometime.

Jan rose and stepped in closer to him. "Actually, Mr. Harrington, here's what we're going to do. You'll assemble that information while we go take a look at Maddy's room."

Mr. Harrington opened his mouth and his wife stopped him with a hand in the air. "We'll get it for you," she said. "I'll take you to her room while my husband gets you the other information."

Mr. Harrington moved back to the drinks cart and turned his back on them. Jan couldn't remember meeting a bigger prick, and she'd met her share of them.

Mrs. Harrington led them upstairs and down a long hallway. Jan lost track of the number of bedrooms along the way. Maddy's was the last one.

"Is your room also on this level?" Jan asked.

"Yes, it's at the opposite end of the hall. Why do you ask?"

"I'm wondering if you would have heard her leaving at night. Do you recall waking up to any noise?"

Mrs. Harrington shrugged. "I wear earplugs because of my husband's incessant snoring. But Maddy could have slipped away and I wouldn't have heard it, with or without the earplugs."

She opened a door next to Maddy's room, which led to carpeted stairs leading down to the back of the house. A perfect teenage escape route.

"Isn't it just as likely that she left during the day?" asked Peet. "She could have taken off when you thought she was going to school."

"She could have gone at any time, and it would probably have been a while before we noticed."

Jan and Peet looked at each other as Mrs. Harrington walked into Maddy's room. She'd spoken as if it were perfectly normal for a family to not have any idea where their sixteen-year-old daughter was.

"I'll leave you to it," Mrs. Harrington said. "The police have been through it already. You won't find anything here to help you."

They remained silent until Mrs. Harrington left the room.

"What a piece of work," Peet said. "That poor kid is probably a thousand miles away by now. Who wouldn't run away from parents like that?"

Jan, for one. They looked around Maddy's room, which was bigger than the living room in Jan's condo. She thought Peet sounded naïve about what constituted bad parenting, especially as a former police officer. You'd think one night on the beat would be enough to make the Harringtons look like Ozzie and Harriet. One night in the camp she'd grown up in would make the Harringtons' home look like Shangri-La.

Maddy's room looked like it belonged to a forty-year-old neat freak, which Jan recognized as a pretty good description of herself. There wasn't a single thing out of place. There were no posters on the wall, no hint of any teenage passion. Instead, there were a series of mountain landscapes, professionally painted, framed, and hung, almost certainly not of Maddy's choosing. A large desk and high-end ergonomic chair took up one corner of the room, and Jan imagined those might have been picked out by Maddy. The desktop was completely bare, except for a printer cord and a blank memo pad.

"I'll take the closet," Jan said. She opened a door and stared at the huge walk-in closet. It was more than half empty, and Jan thought about the jeans and T-shirt that Maddy wore in the photo they'd been shown. The girl was not a clotheshorse. A few dresses hung toward the back, behind a row of flannel and oxford cloth shirts. Several pairs of blue and black jeans were ironed and hung next to the shirts. A built-in dresser took up the end wall of the closet, one drawer filled with folded underwear and socks, two others devoted to short and long sleeve T-shirts. None of the shirts were decorated with band names or slogans or causes. They were all plain and stacked together according to color. A shoe rack ran the length of the floor along the long closet wall, but Maddy didn't have a thing for shoes either. There were cowboy boots, hiking boots, and snow boots, tennis shoes and soccer shoes, and a pair of dress shoes that had a fur of dust on them.

Jan felt in every drawer, every nook and cranny, and found nothing else. The overhead rack that ran along each wall was completely bare. She needed to ask if it had once held luggage.

She stepped back into the room to see Peet going through the drawers of Maddy's computer desk. "There's nothing in the closet except clothes," she said. "It's almost like a guest had hung their clothes there. Nothing personal at all."

"Nothing in the desk either. Some school records, a few letters from a grandma, office supplies. That's it."

"Let's ask the parents about the grandma. Maybe they didn't think to call her. Maybe she's hiding Maddy from them."

Next to the desk were a printer, a shredder, and a couple of scanners.

"I wonder if she operated paperlessly?" Jan said. "Maybe she scanned everything and then shredded it." She looked at the shredder bin, but it was empty also.

"If there was anything in this room before she left, it's gone now. But I get the feeling there wasn't much to begin with," Peet said.

"I hope we find out more when we look at her computer activity. Otherwise, there isn't squat to go on."

Peet took a look in the closet. "This is kind of creeping me out. It's like this kid is a guest in her own house. Do you know what a teenager's room is supposed to look like?"

"What? Because I don't have kids I'm not supposed to know what they're like?" Jan failed again to keep the defensive tone out of her voice and hated hearing it there. "I was a teenager too, you know."

Peet raised her hands, palms forward. "Jan, that was a rhetorical question. You don't need to get huffy."

Jan felt huffy. She felt like she probably knew more about Maddy than Peet did, or her parents. She felt a connection with a kid who ran away and didn't leave a trace. She brushed by Peet and headed to the stairs in back.

"Let's get that info from them and get the hell out of here," she said.

The rear stairway took them soundlessly to the first level and out into a kitchen/great room area. Mrs. Harrington stood at the breakfast bar writing on a notepad.

"I'm trying to get this information all in one place for you."

"Thanks," Peet said. "I'm just curious whether Maddy has always been so neat?"

"Neat? I'd call it more neurotic. She hated anything out of place. Hated clutter. Drove us all crazy, really. If you put a cup of coffee down, thinking you might get another cup in a minute, there was no chance it wouldn't end up in the dishwasher if Maddy walked through the room."

"Hey, I'd love it if my kids were neurotic like that."

Mrs. Harrington looked at Peet again with doubt on her face. Something about Peet and motherhood wasn't computing for her, which Jan thought was funny as hell. Peet's kids were all happy at home.

"It drove her brother wild. His room looked like a hurricane hit it."

"They're pretty different from each other, I take it," Jan said.

"Night and day." It was pretty clear which child Mrs. Harrington favored. She stared out the windows looking over the backyard. It was dark, but the deck and garage were lit up. Jan saw a car pulling out of the garage. "My husband is going back to work." She turned back to the counter and picked up the slip of paper. "Here's the information you asked for. I hope it's helpful."

Jan looked it over. There were three names and numbers on the list, including Justin Harrington's, along with Maddy's telephone number and e-mail address, and a network log-in. "We'll need a router log-in as well if we're going to find out what she's been looking at on the Internet. I should have mentioned that before."

Mrs. Harrington looked exasperated, as if there were no end to the demands on her. "I don't even know what that is. I'll have to have my husband help with that."

"And an e-mail to you or your husband from Maddy," Peet said. "We need her IP address as well."

"Yes, yes. I promise we'll do what we can."

"We saw letters to Maddy from her grandmother. Are the two of them close?"

"They were, but all of Maddy's grandparents are now dead."

"How about any other relatives she's close to?"

"There's no one. I'm an only child, and my husband's family isn't close."

"Close as in tight, or do you mean they live far away?" Jan asked.

"Both, I'd say."

She led them to the front door. Jan watched her face recompose itself into a concerned mother expression. She thought she'd seen better acting by Peet's eight-year-old daughter.

"One last thing," Jan said. "Did Maddy have any luggage in her bedroom closet?"

"Luggage? No, that was kept downstairs and there's nothing missing. But she has a backpack. You know, the large kind for when you're camping. She kept that in her room."

"It's gone now."

Mrs. Harrington looked stricken. "So she has run away?"

"It looks that way. Now we go find her."

Chapter Two

Jan and Peet were back on Willow Road before either said a word. Jan stared out the passenger window, lost in thought.

"Okay, let's hear it," Peet said.

"What?" She turned to Peet. "What's there to say? The Harringtons are jerks and their daughter's a runaway. We do our job; that's all."

Peet's knuckles were white on the steering wheel. "Jerks? No. A jerk is someone who spills beer on you at Wrigley Field and then laughs about it. These people are criminal, as far as I'm concerned. You probably had a better upbringing than Maddy did."

"What's that supposed to mean?" Jan felt a flush climb up her face.

"You grew up in the system, right? Out west? I'm just saying you probably got more love and caring there than Maddy Harrington has."

Jan stared back out the window. "It was a group home. An orphanage, not a foster home with a brood of happy, mismatched kids."

"Sorry."

"Think Oliver Twist and you're halfway there."

"Sorry. I shouldn't have said that. I just can't imagine parents who don't notice when their daughter's been gone for two nights."

Jan shrugged. "At least we have one motive for Maddy running away. I doubt it's the whole story." She wanted the conversation steered away from her own childhood. She'd known when Peet became her partner that she'd have to say something about her past. Peet was too curious and chatty to not ask questions and expect answers. Jan told her the same story she'd been telling since she was sixteen—parents killed, no relatives, the group home. It usually shut people up. She'd never had to flesh out the details because most didn't probe too deeply. She rebuffed, ignored, or abandoned those that persisted. The lie was much easier and safer than the truth. She didn't think she had the ability to describe her childhood.

Though she tried to avoid remembering her life in the camp, she knew it was impossible. Just as it became impossible for her to stop thinking of a life outside the camp once she started to realize one might exist. In the two years prior to her escape, Jan had discovered ways to slip beyond the camp's perimeter and explore the woods beyond. Timing and stealth were all she needed. She discovered a ranch four miles north of the camp, and in the ranch she found her hope. It was a small homestead run by a large family, and Jan would spend every moment she could tucked up next to a boulder on a ridge overlooking it. She watched men, women, and children doing chores, sitting together on the porch of the house, entertaining guests, hugging and kissing, coming and going from the property as they pleased. She knew she had to have some of that, any bit of it, in her life. She would somehow find a way to get it.

Peet pulled into the parking lot of the Winnetka police station. It was past seven o'clock and they didn't expect to see the detectives who'd taken the call from Mrs. Harrington, but they needed to let the department know as soon as possible that they'd been hired to find Maddy. The police would be only too happy to share information and offload as much of the work as they could on to the private investigators.

The desk sergeant made a call to the back of the shop and pointed them toward some folding chairs lined up along a wall. He never said a word directly to them. Jan hated the scorn that some police felt toward private investigators, the kind she now saw on the sergeant's face. She started to say something to him, but Peet took her arm and pulled her over to the waiting area.

"It's not worth it," Peet said. "We want them to cooperate."

"We're surrounded by assholes," Jan said. She put her elbows to her knees and stared at the floor while they waited. Within a few minutes, a very short and very sharply dressed detective came to get them. If Winnetka had a minimum height requirement for its officers, this man had found a way around it. Peet towered over him as they shook hands.

"Donald Hoch. Glad to meet you both," he said. He led them down a hall and into his private office. It was small but painted a tasteful cream color and furnished in wood and leather. A new computer sat on his desk.

"I talked to Mrs. Harrington this morning. Frankly, I'm glad they've called you in on this. We're getting a late start if the girl's really been gone two days."

"She's likely to be far away by now," Peet agreed.

"Or she may be right here, just seeing whether her parents care enough to try to find her," Jan added.

"That too." Hoch pulled a slim file off a stack on his desk and opened it.

"She's never been in trouble with us. Her teachers say she's a good student, especially in the sciences, but not really working to her potential. They describe her as withdrawn. I haven't met the father, but they seem like the kind of parents a kid would run away from."

"Exactly. Do you intend to keep trying to track her down?" Jan asked.

"We don't want to duplicate your steps or get in your way," Peet said. "I used to be on the job. I know what a pain PIs can be."

"Oh yeah? Where did you work?"

"Chicago. Homicide."

Jan knew Peet always worked this in for a reason. Cops were cops and the brotherhood ran deep. It pissed Jan off as a general rule, but she couldn't deny the benefits. Peet often got information much more quickly from the police than she did. As Peet and Detective Hoch talked for a bit about cops they knew, what their shops were like, and who had the best benefits, Jan wondered where Maddy Harrington had disappeared.

"Let me give you the bullet points," Hoch was saying. He pushed a piece of paper across the desk. "Here's her complete physical description. Pretty nondescript, no tattoos, piercings, scars. But that's according to her parents. She may have tattoos and piercings in places they don't see anymore. We've put out a BOLO on her car. The vehicle identification information is included here. We've gotten nothing back on any of it. We put her name and description in the NCIC, so we will be contacted if she's picked up for any reason."

"I'm not familiar with all of the hangouts in Winnetka," Peet said. "Tell me where the drug activity takes place."

"That's back on your turf," Hoch said. "The kids here buy their drugs in the city. Clubs on the north side for meth and coke, West Side for heroin, though there isn't a big heroin problem around here."

Hoch stood to end the meeting.

"If you find her you can call me and I'll arrange to have her picked up. Other than that, I'm not sure our department will put much in the way of resources into this. You're right about that."

❖

Peet drove back toward the city while Jan took out her phone and looked at the list of Maddy's friends Mrs. Harrington had given them. None of the names had phone numbers.

"This is pathetic."

"I think it's sad," Peet said. "My kids live for their friends. They're everything to them."

Jan had a few friends growing up in the camp. There was only one who Jan found interesting—Holly Alvarez. She was beautiful and lively and willing to question the Colonel's authority once in a while, which Jan found thrilling. As they grew older, Jan found thoughts of Holly thrilling in an entirely different way. She squirmed in her seat and felt nervous whenever they sat close. But when Holly was sixteen, the Colonel approved a match between Holly and a boy in the camp, the son of one of his close lieutenants. The ceremony would not take place until her eighteenth birthday, as was custom, but from that moment on, Holly was lost to Jan, and so was any remaining reason for Jan to stay in camp. She remembered seeing Holly the day before she escaped. She was tempted to tell Holly of her plans and urge her to come with. But then Holly looked up from the bread she was kneading in the cook tent. She looked right through Jan, as if she weren't standing six feet in front of her, as if she didn't exist.

Jan dialed directory assistance and tracked down some numbers for families with the same last names as those on the list. By the time they'd reached the city, she'd left half a dozen messages. She was about to call Maddy's brother when Peet took the Irving Park exit off the expressway.

"I thought we were going back to the office," Jan said.

"How about we grab a bite at my house? We have to eat somewhere, and I have a sudden urge to see my kids."

Jan agreed, but reluctantly. She always felt overwhelmed by the normalcy in Peet's house. At least, it's what she supposed was normal family life. Mom and Dad still in love after twenty years of marriage, sweet teenagers, an adorable eight-year-old. A dog. They lived in Kevin's old family home, a rambling frame structure in the city's Old Irving Park neighborhood. Everything about it made her feel anxious.

They entered the huge kitchen that Kevin had remodeled the year before. Kevin and eight-year-old Lily stood at the kitchen island, decorating sugar cookies. When Jan and Peet came through the kitchen door, Lily ran over and took Jan's arm, tugging her over to the cookies. Kevin kissed Peet and then gave Jan a kiss on the cheek.

"Sorry to barge in unannounced," Jan said. "It was her idea."

"Hey, we're thrilled," Kevin said. "Can you eat something? We just finished off a pizza, but I can scramble some eggs or make a sandwich."

Peet shrugged off her jacket and sat at the kitchen table. "Eggs would be great, hon." She pulled out her phone and started texting. "Sit down, Jan. I'm just telling Sandy to come downstairs."

"It's our new version of an intercom system," Kevin said. He looked over at Peet. "Kevin Junior's out tonight."

"I know that." Peet sounded impatient and Kevin's eyebrow went up a tad.

She waved her hand in front her, like she was swatting a fly. "We just had a meeting with some parents who had no idea what their kids were up to," she said. "I don't want Jan to think we're anything like that."

"No danger there," Jan said.

Peet's daughter Sandy came into the room, phone in hand, and Jan stood to accept her hug. Sandy hugged Peet even though they'd seen each other a few hours earlier. There was an awful lot of hugging here. "I wanted to ask you something," Peet said, pulling out a chair for Sandy. "What would you think of a high school junior who doesn't have any friends?"

"Who are you talking about?" Sandy asked.

"No one you know. A runaway Jan and I are trying to find."

"A girl?" Kevin asked.

"Yeah. From Winnetka."

"That's scary," he said. "Not the Winnetka part. The girl all alone on the streets part."

"It is," Jan said.

"And she didn't have any friends?" Sandy asked. "What's wrong with her?"

"I don't know that there was anything wrong with her. She looks pretty much like everyone else, but I don't know how she acted around other people. Her parents said that she spent all her time on her computer."

"It's weird to not have any friends," Sandy said. "I wonder whether she didn't have any friends because she was on the computer all the time, or whether she was on the computer all the time because she didn't have any friends. You see what I mean?"

"I'll be her friend," Lily said. She looked so earnest that Jan couldn't help smiling. Sometimes she thought Peet's kids were from central casting. Kevin put a plate of eggs in front of her. He was also from central casting—a handsome firefighter secure enough to marry a woman who looked like she could carry him out of a burning building. They probably had great sex too.

They were silent for a long time as they headed back to the office. Peet snuck a look at Jan.

"There's a new firefighter at Kevin's station," Peet said, startling Jan. She'd been staring out the window, feeling bad about Gwen.

"And?"

"I've met her. She's just your type."

"How do you know what my type is? I don't even know what my type is. Is it because she's a lesbian, ergo I'll be attracted to her?"

"She's not clingy."

"How do you know whether this woman's clingy or not?"

"I asked her." Peet said this as if it were a good thing.

"Do you mean you asked her during a conversation about me?"

"Yeah. It came up. She said she hated clinginess in others so she wasn't that way herself."

"Goddamnit, Peet. You know I hate this. What's the matter with you?"

"Come on. What can it hurt? You're so stubborn about this."

Jan knew exactly what it could hurt—whatever good opinion Peet might have of her. The whole scenario had a sense of inevitability to it, just as it had a few hours earlier with Gwen. If she were to sleep with the firefighter there would be greater ramifications than usual when things didn't work out between them. The firefighter would tell Kevin. Kevin would tell Peet. Peet would look at Jan in a new way and…what? Maybe it would be good for Peet to know Jan wasn't the kind of person who could have the ideal home life she and Kevin had. Maybe then she'd stop trying to set her up with people.

"No," Jan said. "I don't do blind dates. It's not like I need help, you know."

"Then why haven't I seen you with any girlfriends?" Peet was turning into the office parking lot.

"I'm telling you to back off. You have no business in my sex life. Period."

Peet looked surprised by Jan's anger, but completely unfazed.

"Why are you pissed? I'm your partner. Don't you think I want to see you happy?"

"What makes you think I'm not happy?" Jan was practically screeching. She threw open her car door and then slammed it shut behind her. She didn't miss seeing the grin on Peet's face.

She led the way into the building and past the first floor security division. It seemed a lifetime ago that she left security and moved upstairs to investigations. She started as a twenty-year-old guard on the graveyard shift. Ten years later, armed with a college degree and a record of heads-up service, she got her shot in the newly formed investigations division. It didn't take long for her to outshine the former detectives who trained her. Peet was the only former police officer Jan felt might be her match in private investigations.

When they reached their desks they saw Don Detmer standing by the door of the break room, holding a cup of coffee. He was also an ex-cop, but not in Peet's league. He had left the sheriff's department after putting in his twenty and seemed to view TSI as a hobby. Jan couldn't imagine what he was doing in the office after hours. He bitched so loudly about working evenings that he managed to be assigned only the type of work that could be done during the day or from home—skip tracing, mainly. He had a particularly hangdog look on his chubby face.

"What are you doing here?" Jan asked him.

"The only time I could talk to a witness is tonight, and I forgot the fucking file."

"You look like you're ready to kill yourself," Peet said. They went into the break room and poured themselves coffee from the fresh pot. "But since you made coffee, you must be intending to live."

Don sat at the small table and looked at them. "You guys haven't heard yet, have you?"

"Heard what?" Jan said.

"LJ and his old man sold the company."

"What?" Peet said. She went pale.

Don looked smug at having delivered the bad news. "Vivian told Collins and Collins told me."

David Collins was another TSI investigator. He'd recently started dating Vivian and apparently not yet discovered her darker side. He was going to have to answer for breaking her confidence, Jan thought.

"I don't understand," Peet said. "How could we not have heard about this? Wouldn't we have seen people poking around?"

Don sighed. "I don't know how the fuck they do these things. It's probably all Web conferences and secure websites and crap like that. Plus, what do they need to look at? They're not really buying the building or us. They're buying the client base. They'll probably fire us and bring in all their European James Bond types."

"They're European?" Jan asked.

"I don't know. Global something something."

Jan was wondering if this didn't start having the ring of truth to it. If Collins was using a company name, it indicated a level of detail not found in the usual office rumor. She left the break room and headed to her cubicle.

"Where are you going?" Peet asked.

"Let's look it up." She fired up her computer and did searches on "Global Security Company," wading through a lot of muck before seeing a reference to a London firm called Chartered Global Security, an international security and investigations firm with offices in quite a few US cities. A news release from London announced the planned acquisition of a small Midwestern company intended to be another step toward expanded penetration of the United States market.

Peet was reading the screen with her. "God, it's true. Shit."

Jan knew Peet would be worrying about her job. They needed it to pay for college for their kids, and TSI paid surprisingly well. Jan was worried for a different reason. She didn't know much of the work world beyond TSI. The thought of looking for a job made it a little harder to breathe.

"You gotta wonder when the hell they were going to tell us," Don said. "If you just found it in the computer in a minute and a half, others will too."

Jan looked up at Peet. "It doesn't mean they'll be firing us. They're not going to replace everyone in the company."

Don shuffled away, looking grim at the idea of losing his job, or worse, having to work harder if he kept it.

"They'll definitely weed out some people. They always do," Peet said.

"Then let's not give them any reason to pick us. Let's do our jobs."

Jan pulled the Harringtons' list out of her pocket. It was past ten p.m. on the east coast, much too early for a college student to be in bed; she called Maddy's brother at Dartmouth. He picked up on the first ring, and Jan could hear bar noise in the background.

"Yo," he said. It was a bad sign when a white boy in a loud bar answered with "yo." She hoped Justin Harrington cared that his sister was missing. Jan started to fill him in.

"Wait, are you telling me that no one knows where Maddy is?" Justin sounded serious. The background noise grew softer. "Hang on a sec. I'm walking outside."

Jan looked at her watch again. They'd have to leave the office soon for the Wilsons' weenie watch, as Peet called it. Justin came back on the line.

"Who are you again?" he asked.

"Your parents hired me today to help track down your little sister. She's been missing for two days."

"Two days? God, they're unbelievable."

"So she's not there with you."

"No way. She wouldn't come to me. We're not that close."

"Has your sister run away before?"

"Not since she was really little. Like seven or so. The police found her late at night hiding in a big box behind the grocery store. She'd set up her things in there like she was planning to stay for a while."

Jan thought about that. Was it normal childhood adventure stuff? Or was Maddy running from something even then?

"I get the feeling that you and Maddy might both have some problems with your folks. Can you tell me about that? It might help me find her."

Jan heard Justin light a cigarette and take his time exhaling. "I don't know if you'd call it a problem. Basically, they leave us alone to do what we want to do, which is cool with me."

"How about Maddy?"

"It's hard to say with her. The main reason we're not close is that she doesn't tell me anything, and I'd be surprised if there's anyone she shares stuff with. She's a complete enigma."

"Even when she was little? She must have played games or had friends or something."

"Yeah, when she was real little. Mom would have her go to play groups and stuff. She played soccer the last few years and she was really good at that. I don't know if she hung out with those girls or not. I never saw them at the house."

"So was she a loner? Or was she unpopular with kids for some reason?"

Justin gave it some thought. "I just think she was too fucking serious about everything. It's kind of creepy, actually."

"Like how? I'm not sure I know what you mean."

Justin paused again. "It's kind of weird, but right before I left for school, Maddy and I had one of the few real conversations we've had in the last several years. We were reading the paper in the kitchen, the folks were gone, of course, and she suddenly blew her stack at some article. I asked her what the matter was and all she said at first was that she could hardly stand living in this country anymore."

"What?"

"I know. It wasn't the first political thing I've ever heard her say, but this time she was really hot. She went on a rant about not being truly free and government regulation and stuff like that."

"Like a conservative?"

"I'm a conservative, but I'd say it was more like a paranoid. Then she started going on about Ayn Rand's books and *Atlas Shrugged* and that whole Objectivist spiel. I tried to discuss it with her, but she wasn't interested in a debate. She talked right over me. I finally just got up and left."

Jan didn't know the Objectivist spiel or who Ayn Rand was, but it sounded like something she could look up on the Internet.

"Justin, do you know if your sister was doing drugs or running with a crowd, or anything that could help us track her down?"

"No, she didn't do drugs. At least she didn't the one time I offered to share a joint with her. She called me an idiot and a degenerate." Jan could hear him taking another drag on his cigarette. "As you can see, we aren't close."

"Sounds like Maddy may be hard to be close to."

"I feel sorry for her in a way. I mean, she's always been so alone that she just doesn't know how to act with people. If she's out there on her own, she could get in trouble pretty quick."

Jan thought the same thing.

❖

The CarMax manager handed Maddy a cashier's check for $20,000.

"I'd feel better if one of your parents were here," he said. He was a pudgy, sweaty old man. Maddy couldn't wait to get away from him.

"I owned the car, not them. It doesn't really matter how you feel."

She tucked the check in a pocket of her backpack, hunched it onto one shoulder, and strapped a heavy computer bag across the other. She left without thanking him or saying good-bye. Fuck him, anyway. He'd made the whole process of selling the car an exercise in patience, and she had little of that to spare.

Once on the Metra train into Chicago, she pulled out a pay-as-you-go cell phone, one of several she'd bought. She planned to use them and toss them, not giving anyone the opportunity to track her down through a signal. She sent a text to David. He was already downtown, waiting for her at the train station. She pulled her ball cap lower over her eyes and relaxed into her seat, watching the familiar suburban landscape flash by. It would be all new scenery after this.

David. She would recognize him, though they'd never met in person. They'd started video chatting a few months ago after discovering each other in the comments section of a conservative political blog. Both were too radical in their ideas for the forum, so they took their conversations private. Now she was running away with him. She wasn't nervous, but she'd be pissed off if he turned out to be another All Talk, No Action sort of guy. It was easy for people to talk about going off-grid, but few had the guts to do it.

She found him outside of Union Station, leaning against an old pickup truck parked in a tow away zone. It was early evening and getting dark, the fall air cooler every day. He was dressed in flannel shirt and jeans, no jacket, and she was surprised at how tall and thin he was. She'd only ever seen him from the neck up. He looked more like a boy her age than a man of twenty-five. He stepped toward her and shook her hand.

"You definitely do not look eighteen," he said. "Have you been lying to me?"

"I'm eighteen. I can't help it if I look young. Dude, you look about twelve."

David grinned. "I'll show you my ID if you show me yours."

Maddy reached for her backpack and pulled out the check. "Here's what I'll show you."

He took the check and looked it over. "Cool. This is going to help a lot."

"Do we have to get that cashed here?"

David slipped the check in his shirt pocket. "Nah. It's made out to cash. They'll take it at my bank in Michigan."

"We're all set then. Let's get the hell out of here. Where are we going first?"

David put her bags behind the seats in the truck.

"First we go back up to my house. You can stay in my basement while we're getting all our shit together."

"When will we leave for Idaho?"

He glanced at her as he entered the ramp to the expressway. "No cold feet for you, I see."

"Hell no. The sooner the better."

"We still have some things to do here. We'll lay it all out for you, but most of it you already know. We'll close on the land this week and then we're there."

Maddy sat back and took a deep breath. It was all happening fast, but it felt exactly right. She wanted something real. David thought like she did; tired of all the endless bullshit all around them, in everything they heard on the news or read in the media or listened to spewing out of the mouths of idiotic, corrupt politicians. To live in a meaningful way, they were going to have to leave a meaningless society.

David pulled into traffic on the Dan Ryan Expressway for the five-hour drive to southeastern Michigan. "We'll be out there before you know it."

"God, this is so great," she said. "I feel free."

❖

Jan and Peet parked three houses down from where Ron and Paula Wilson lived in the eastern part of Lincoln Park, one of the city's priciest neighborhoods. Jan thought she was spending entirely too much of her shift in neighborhoods she never had a prayer of living in. The wood cabin she grew up in was smaller than the tree house she'd seen in the backyard of the Harrington house. A nice tree house would suit her just fine. She could hang a "Keep Out" sign at the entrance, flipping it around on occasion to say "Girls Only," then flipping it back again. That would feel about right.

Paula Wilson was a trader, the kind whose income zoomed up and down, but mostly up. Her moods seemed to do the same. The idea that her husband of five years was cheating on her made her especially volatile, and she was determined to catch him out. It was the most common and the most boring work they did as investigators.

Jan sipped her coffee and read from the Wikipedia entry she'd printed out on Objectivism. "Okay, Ayn Rand wrote some books and people went all cultish about them."

"What books?"

"*Atlas Shrugged* and *The Fountainhead*."

"Oh, yeah. I think Kevin Junior read *The Fountainhead*. Why do we care about this?"

"Maddy's brother said she got very excited talking about Rand's philosophy. Objectivism. Maybe it will help explain why she left."

"You're not around teenagers much," Peet said. "They are totally into something one minute, and just as you start understanding what they're talking about, they're on to the next thing."

"Still." Jan read on. "Says here that Rand's philosophy, in essence, is the concept of man as a heroic being, with his own happiness as the moral purpose of his life, with productive achievement as his noblest activity, and reason as his only absolute."

"It sounds lonely," Peet said.

Jan thought it sounded like her father. He pursued his own vision and sense of moral purpose. No question about that. And he insisted to all those in his camp that their thinking be in line with his. In fact, he preferred they not do much thinking at all. Those that openly questioned him were punished. He'd built a set of stocks that he rolled out into the center of camp whenever he felt the need to remind people of how things worked.

Jan kept reading. "'The only social system consistent with this morality is full respect for individual rights, embodied in pure laissez-faire capitalism.' Now that sounds pretty conservative, if you ask me. Justin said she was ranting about the government."

Peet touched Jan on her arm. "Put the philosophy away. Looks like Ron Wilson is in search of earthier pleasures."

Jan looked up to see Wilson's BMW pull out of his side drive. Peet waited until he got to the end of the street and turned before she put the car in gear and sped up to follow him. They hung well behind as he led them right into Boystown.

Peet said, "I wonder if Paula Wilson will be relieved if the other woman is a man?"

"Ten dollars says he's going to Steamy," Jan said.

"Nah. I think he's going to Hydrate. Doesn't look like the type who'd go to the baths."

"Like you'd know," Jan said. "Do you think you can line up The Village People and pick out the steam bath type?"

Peet stuck her tongue out at her, which made Jan laugh.

"The point is that this is the fastest way to get what he wants. If he only has an hour or so, the baths are a surefire place to get sex," Jan said.

Wilson slowed down as he neared Steamy, an old, nondescript brick building with no signage on the front other than its address. It could have been anything. Wilson was looking for parking, so Peet pulled to the curb across the street from the place, into a hydrant spot. Jan got out her camera and climbed into the backseat. She took several shots as he approached the building.

She knew she wouldn't get any successful photos of Wilson inside the bathhouse. They might not throw her out, but neither her camera nor her female body would be welcome. She tried to guess how long a bathhouse for women would stay open. She might appreciate the convenience of one. When she felt the need for some companionship, she found picking up women annoyingly time-consuming, even tedious.

"I think he'll be less than an hour. It's unlikely he'll have a man hanging on him when he walks out," Jan said.

"If he doesn't, we'll still have the time stamps on the photos to show he was in there a while," Peet said. "How do you think Paula is going to take it?"

"I don't know. Why doesn't he tell her, for Christ sake? It's a shitty thing to do to the wife, and a worse thing to do to himself."

Jan grabbed her laptop from the front seat and uploaded the first photos. She e-mailed them to Paula, who always had her BlackBerry in her hand. Jan knew she'd get the message almost as soon as it was sent.

Then they waited. Jan watched the parade of gay men walk up and down the street, the beautiful fall weather bringing more out than perhaps there would normally be on a Tuesday night. But there was always action on Halsted Street. Men knew exactly where to come to find the bars, the restaurants, the steam baths, all the places that threw them together and spit them out in different combinations every night. The mayor had installed tall metal pylons decorated with rainbow colors that marked this stretch of Halsted as Boystown, as if to contain the energy within geographical boundaries.

She thought of the time she lived on the streets in LA, the land of the runaway teen. She was more naïve by far than any of the others she met there. They talked of their shitty homes and schools and the parents they fought with and their pain in the ass little brothers and sisters. Many were running from abuse. But they all knew a hell of a lot more than Jan did about living on the streets. She was taken in by Fagin-like dealers and thieves who taught her skills unusual even for her unorthodox education. Among the many things she learned about from scratch was sex—how to have it, who she wanted to have it with (girls), and how to steer clear of the predators. There were plenty of girls willing to show her the ropes, sometimes literally. But no part of those experiences had the quality of freedom and celebration she saw in the way the boys walked around Boystown.

She heard a text message come in. It was from Paula Wilson, releasing them from duty. She understood the situation and the photo and wasn't that surprised. She was just relieved to finally know. Jan called her to make sure she didn't need anything else and moved back into the front seat of the car while she listened to Paula talk. And talk. When she was finally able to hang up, Peet was just pulling up to Jan's building.

"Is she pretty upset?" Peet asked.

"It sounds like she's trying to decide which is more humiliating—losing him to a man or to a woman." Jan got out of the car with the camera. "I'll write the report. You going straight home?"

"I've got to tell Kev about this job thing."

"Try not to worry about it, Peet. There's nothing that's going to be helped by you worrying."

"Thank you, o wise one. I have a feeling tomorrow will be an interesting day at Titan Security and Investigations."

"Yeah, I'll see you there." Jan slapped the top of the car as Peet pulled away. She headed for her building's garage, and a few minutes later she was in her Jeep on Lake Shore Drive. It was one in the morning, still plenty of time to see if anyone on the West Side of the city might recognize a photo of Maddy Harrington.

❖

Jan knew that if you were white and needed to get hold of some heroin, the easiest place to find it was west on Augusta or Division or the streets in between. When you slowed down as you drove by the corner stores, you'd be recognized for what you were—one of society's privileged who had willingly given up every advantage for the rush of smack. You would not be well respected.

Jan didn't know Maddy Harrington. Her instincts told her it was unlikely she was a heroin addict, but it was always possible. She drove slowly, looking for the dealers, the retailers on the streets, some of whom she would recognize from past searches for teenagers. She never had any trouble here. In fact, she found them to be pretty cooperative. The last thing they wanted was underage runaway white kids hanging around their corners or in their basements. It only brought the heat on. If Maddy had been hanging around there, someone would give her up.

Along Augusta Boulevard the streetlights glowed in between the piercing blue lights perched high on steel poles that marked the area as a police watch zone. The police lights provided no added security for the citizens of the neighborhood, but they did manage to make it really difficult to sell property there. Jan came to a familiar corner and parked in front of a liquor store. The surrounding area was residential, mainly brick two and three unit buildings and small houses. Neighborhood Watch signs were on the front windows of nearly every house, and most intersections held a large sign announcing that the area was drug and violence free. Talk about your misleading advertising. If Jan stood at one of those signs for an hour, she'd see countless drug deals and probably at least one act of violence.

A group of young men stood around the store entrance. They parted just enough to give her a narrow path to the door. She knew at least one of them would be holding, carrying out the retail heroin business that was the lowest rung in whatever gang they were with. One of them stopped her with a pull on her jacket sleeve.

"You were here last year looking for some chick. Ain't that right?"

"That's right. Now I'm looking for another. Same thing. Suburban girl, high school age."

"You got a picture?"

The group huddled around as Jan showed them the photo of Maddy.

"I can't tell one white chick from another," one of them said. They all laughed, but she thought it might be true. They only saw these girls for a moment, unless they became regular customers. And by then they didn't look very much like Maddy.

"No, I ain't seen her," said one. The others agreed.

Jan went into the store and turned to the caged cash register to her left. A Middle Eastern man sat at the counter, part of a trend throughout the West Side of Korean shop owners selling out of the neighborhoods. Jan didn't know what that was all about. Maybe the Koreans were fed up. Maybe the Middle Easterners were from the war zone and a West Side corner shop felt like a peaceful place. She put the photo of Maddy on the carousel and the man twirled it around.

"You seen her?" she asked.

"No."

"At least pretend like you're looking at the photo."

"Haven't seen her."

She took the photo and returned to the group of boys.

"Any luck, lady?" It was the one that had recognized her.

"Nope. Does he speak much English?"

"Oh yeah. He's always saying, 'I call police!'"

"Yeah. Or 'I got gun!'"

"Right. But if you ask him for change for a twenty, he don't know what you're talking about."

Jan grinned at them. She handed her card around. "If any of you see my girl, be sure to give me a call. I pay for information."

She left them on the corner, keeping their eyes peeled for business.

Chapter Three

Jan was pouring her first cup of coffee in the break room when Peet walked in. She normally looked like she'd just woken from a particularly refreshing nap, but today she seemed tired. Jan could count on one hand the number of times she'd taken a nap herself. They'd all been frightening experiences. When she'd wake up, it felt as if she'd just fought her way to the surface of deep water with rocks in every pocket. When her eyes finally opened from these "death naps," the feeling that she'd just escaped something dire would shroud her. She didn't need therapy to figure out what that was all about.

Peet sipped some coffee. "I told Kevin about the takeover."

"You make it sound like a coup d'état. Maybe these new people will be better to work for than LJ is."

"That's presuming I'll be working for them. I've only been here a few months. I'll be the first to go."

"This isn't a union shop, Peet. They'll keep their best performers."

"If they keep any of us."

Jan was surprised at how pessimistic Peet was. "I bet Kevin told you not to worry," Jan said.

"He did. He always says it will be okay, as if saying so makes it true."

"But things are always okay for you guys. Let's see what happens before we get in the soup line."

David Collins walked into the break room, carrying his Chicago Bears mug. He also looked haggard.

"Long night with Vivian?" Jan teased him.

"Shut it, Roberts."

"You may be interested to know that Don Detmer told us about the sale of the company and that he heard the news from you. I'm thinking your testicles are in peril if Vivian finds out you blabbed her secret."

Collins topped off his coffee. "I wouldn't worry about mine, Roberts. They have more brass than yours ever will. I'd worry about our jobs, though. The new owners have just arrived."

"What?" Peet asked.

"A group just went into the main conference room. Big Junior's even sitting in. They're about to close the deal." Collins started to walk out the door. "It's really not much of a secret now, is it?"

Jan and Peet went back to their desks.

"This is fucking unbelievable," Peet said. "You'd think they'd talk to us before parading the new owners through the office. That's really disrespectful."

"Maybe now you know what I mean about LJ. He's a joke."

She saw that Peet was genuinely upset. "You stay put. I'll go on a reconnaissance mission. It will look stupid if we both go."

Jan crossed to the other side of the office and stood by Vivian's desk. The conference room was filled with people in suits, all of them taking laptops and files out of their briefcases. Junior Begala sat at the head of the table with LJ and their lawyer, while at the other end sat a larger contingent, presumably representing the buyers. Jan's eyes locked on one of them, a beautiful woman with long dark hair, shot through with a startling streak of white. She looked to be Jan's age, and there the similarities ended. This woman was elegant, beautifully dressed, and composed. Confident. Jan couldn't look away, even when the woman lifted her head and looked her up and down, a slight smile turning up one side of her mouth. Then she turned back to her computer screen and Jan felt heat rush through her body. She was completely turned on.

"Who's that woman?" Jan asked Vivian.

"That's Catherine Engstrom. She's the VP of something or other of CGS. Kind of a barracuda."

No shit, thought Jan. She continued to look into the conference room, but Catherine didn't look at her again. She'd never had a reaction like that to a woman. There would normally be a lot more direct stimuli occurring before Jan had this sort of physical response. Interesting, but potentially disastrous.

"They're supposed to let everyone know about the sale as soon as they close. I think they're sending out an e-mail," Vivian said. "Because they're classy like that."

Jan went back to her desk and found Peet sitting in her chair, staring straight ahead.

"Collins is right. The buyers are here. There's a bunch of suits in the conference room. Vivian said they're sending an e-mail to let us know what was happening."

Peet stayed quiet. Jan couldn't think of what to say to make her feel better, so she sat quietly with her. She looked up at the sound of heels clacking toward them on the tiled hallway outside the break room. Catherine Engstrom stopped and stood at the door to the room, not far from Peet and Jan, and looked at them with a question on her face.

"Can I help you?" Peet asked.

"I'm looking for some tea, actually," she said, British accented, bright. "I was directed here." It didn't surprise Jan that Catherine's voice crossed over her body like the low notes of a cello. She felt the vibration that it left. She sat there speechless.

"Let me show you." Peet got up and headed toward the break room while Catherine looked at Jan. When Jan got up the nerve to meet her eyes, it was every bit as bad as it had been on the other side of the office. Catherine broke the eye contact and followed Peet into the break room. They emerged a few minutes later, each with a mug.

"And this is my partner, Jan Roberts," Peet said. "She's been with the company a long time, our top investigator. Jan, this is Catherine Engstrom."

Catherine's handshake was warm and firm and extremely businesslike.

"You're here to buy the company, aren't you?" Peet asked.

Catherine laughed. "It's so true that Americans are direct. It's startling, I must say, but a wonderful time saver."

"Is that a yes?" Jan asked. She kept her eyes on Catherine's forehead, not trusting her powers of speech if she looked into her eyes. Ridiculous.

"Yes, it is. Though I wish the word hadn't leaked out before we had a chance to properly announce it to the employees."

"What happens next?" Peet asked.

"Nothing that you'll notice. We'll assess for a while, finding ways we can improve things for you here. It will be some time before you see any changes."

Jan felt Peet stiffen beside her.

"Does that include layoffs?" Peet said.

Catherine touched Peet on the shoulder. Lucky Peet.

"We hope to avoid those altogether. And certainly we don't want to let our best people go. From what the Begalas have said, you have nothing to worry about."

Jan wasn't sure she was being included in that reassurance, but she couldn't open her mouth again to ask.

"I'd better get back to that meeting. It was so nice to meet you both." Catherine walked away, moving through the space as if she'd always owned it.

"Feel better?" Jan asked.

"Yeah, I do." Peet sat back down. "Sounds like we're in good shape."

Jan watched Catherine walk down the hall. She wasn't sure she was in good shape at all.

Maddy fought to keep her eyes open. She and David had arrived at his house at four in the morning, his overheating truck turning their five-hour trip into ten. He seemed to want to talk the whole time. She just wanted to sleep. She'd spent her first nights away from her family sleeping in the Honda, parked on a street two suburbs away from Winnetka. Another night in a vehicle was too much.

She shouldn't have been surprised at what a talker David was. He monopolized their video chats, unaware that Maddy was continuing her own work while he went on and on. He would detail his vision for their new society, as he grandly called it, while she programmed the intranet site they would use to coordinate the move to Idaho and stay in touch with his contacts in Michigan. He placed a high premium on secure communications, though she couldn't see who would be interested in their group. She didn't mind all of David's talk because she agreed with what he said. She just thought people in general talked too much.

When they reached David's town, Maggie stared out the window at the stretches of abandoned homes and businesses. She'd driven through some pretty depressing parts of Chicago, but nothing quite so dead and beyond resurrection as this. The For Sale signs on the houses were as weathered as the houses themselves. She felt her spirits flag. Maybe she was just tired.

David pulled into the gravel driveway of a rundown ranch house, jumped out of the truck, and grabbed Maddy's bags from the back. He seemed to have limitless energy.

"We're having a planning meeting in a few hours," he said. "You should get some sleep."

Maddy was staring at the house. She'd never seen anything like it in Winnetka. It looked abandoned, dead. She wondered if he was squatting. "How long have you lived here?" she asked.

"I was raised in this house. It was my grandparents' place, but they both died a few years ago. The mortgage is paid off, but at this point, you couldn't give it away."

He led her into the dark house and straight down to the basement. As she walked behind him through the living room, she thought it smelled like an old person's place. She used to visit some elderly shut-ins with her grandmother, and she'd get scolded when she scrunched up her face at the smell. Apparently, David hadn't done much to the place since his people died.

He showed her to a dark corner of the basement, her "quarters," and pointed out the sink, shower, and toilet, all open to the rest of the room. The musty smell was strong. She worried that the mattress thrown on the floor would be damp.

"Sleep well, my sister," David said, clapping her on the shoulder. "I'm so glad you're here."

"Well, thanks."

"I'm serious. You are my ideological soul mate. No one else understands what we're really trying to do. I'm thinking of having you write something up, a manifesto of sorts, because you've got the ability to sum things up brilliantly."

"I write code, David, not words."

He smiled at her. "We're all going to be multitasking. Going beyond our comfort level in so many ways. But we can talk about all that when we're better rested."

Maddy fell on the mattress fully clothed and slept deeply.

She woke in the morning to hear David calling for her to come upstairs. She used the toilet, worried he'd come down to get her and see her with her pants down. When she got upstairs, she found a group huddled with him around the kitchen table, all of them staring at her as she entered. These were the people she'd be living with, she thought, and found it less reassuring than the look of the mattress downstairs. She felt like the newest house member in a reality show, forced to live with people with wildly different backgrounds from hers.

"Good morning," David said, sounding cheery and hopped up, hopefully just on caffeine. "Grab a cup and join us. I'll introduce you."

Maddy slipped into a folding chair next to David. The table was meant to seat four, but now there were seven squashed together and Maddy felt claustrophobic. She drank her coffee and took quick glances around. She hadn't seen much of anything when they arrived in the middle of the night. She hadn't seen that the walls of the kitchen were pink, that the floor seemed to have every other tile missing. The window over the sink was largely obscured by swaths of duct tape holding the glass together.

"We're having this special meeting so I can introduce you all to Maddy and we can get on to the next stage of our planning. Maddy and I had a hard night's travel, and though I might normally ask you to go easy on a sleep-deprived newbie, she's twice as smart as all of us put together so I know she can take care of herself."

There were two women in the group, both about the same age as David. The one sitting next to her was stocky and pierced at eyebrow, nose, and lip. She looked tough as hell.

"What the fuck, David. This girl looks twelve years old."

"I'm not twelve," Maddy said matter-of-factly. "I'm eighteen."

"Right. And I'm Lady Gaga," the tough one said.

One of the men snorted. He was skinny and had big veins popping out all over his arms. His sky blue shirt said "Warren" over the shirt pocket. "Well, you ain't no lady, Kristi."

Kristi reached over and whacked him on the arm, but they were all laughing. Maddy resented the closeness of the others, but desperately wanted to be accepted. As always, she felt clueless as to how to go about making friends.

"Listen, I know I look young. But I'm old enough. And I know a shitload about computers," Maddy said.

"Why do we need computers? We're going to be in the middle of fucking Idaho. Do you think they're going to have Wi-Fi or something?" This came from another of the guys, dressed in camouflage. His head was shaved and she could see a jagged scar running along his skull. It was red and angry looking.

"Ed, I know you're concentrating on all the hunting and fishing we're going to be able to do out there, but you've got to remember that we'll need security and communication capabilities. Smoke signals and guard duty just aren't going to cut it," David said.

"I guess. It just seems everything is getting real complicated. We're twice as big now as when we first started talking about this."

David looked satisfied at that. "Yes, we are. And that's a good thing. Everyone at this table is bringing something unique—some skill or ability that contributes to the life of the camp. Maddy here is bringing some awesome computer skills."

The room was quiet. Kristi got up and brought the coffee pot over and poured for everyone. She looked Maddy in the eye and gestured to her with the pot. Maddy lifted her cup for a refill.

"I'm Kristi," she said. "And the only thing I do with computers is play games."

She sat back down and looked happy to have cleared that up.

David reached around and pulled an envelope out of his rear pocket. "Here's what else Maddy's bringing to the table."

He took out the $20,000 check and placed it carefully on the table.

"This puts us over the top for our down payment so we can go ahead and purchase the land. It's all going to happen for real." A big smile crossed his bony face. "Do any of you have a problem with Maddy joining us?"

All eyes were on the check and all mouths stayed shut.

"All right, then!" David shouted, slapping the top of the check with a loud whap. "Let's get ready for Idaho!"

Maddy looked around as the others erupted in whoops and high fives. The other woman in the room, a pretty blonde, launched herself into David's arms and gave him a big kiss. Then she turned to Maddy and stuck out her hand.

"I'm Diane," she said. "And we're really happy you're going with us."

Maddy stood as the others came up to shake or give her a hug. Kristi bumped her fist against Maddy's and grinned. The last of the group, a handsome boy named Tom, pumped her hand.

"I know some about programming. Maybe we can talk about what you'll be working on."

She saw David give her an encouraging look. "Sure," she said. "I'd love to work with you."

There was a first time for everything, they say.

❖

The school principal, Mr. MacBride, was a six-foot-five beanpole. His Adam's apple stuck out like a chicken wing. Jan and Peet looked up at him standing in his office.

"Of course, I want to do what I can," he said. "I'm afraid I don't know Maddy at all, which some people take to mean she simply hasn't gotten into trouble. But, really, by junior year I usually know students for one reason or another—grades, clubs they're in, athletics, something. But I actually couldn't have picked Maddy out."

"It's a huge school," Jan said. "I'm not sure what you're saying necessarily means anything."

"True," MacBride said. "But we do know she's not really involved in any activities. I've looked at her record. Her grades are average, mostly Bs and Cs, but all As in math. Teacher comments tend to run along the line of 'not performing to potential,' and 'very quiet student.'"

"That jibes with what we've heard," Peet said. "Can we get a copy of that record? The parents will authorize it if you need to get permission."

Jan and Peet each took an office to interview teachers and students who knew Maddy. Jan was in the vice principal's office, staring at a family photo on the desk when she heard a soft knock at the open door.

"I'm Natalie Towne, Maddy's social sciences teacher."

Natalie Towne was teacher crush material. She was youthful and elegant and had Jan ever been a high school student with a teacher like this, she'd have had a major thing for her.

Natalie handed her a report as she took a seat in front of the desk.

"What's this?" Jan said.

"A recent research paper Maddy wrote. When I heard she was missing and that investigators would be here to talk to us, I read it over again."

Jan leafed through the pages. They were heavily marked with red ink.

"It doesn't look like she did very well on it."

Natalie leaned back in the chair and crossed her legs. They were excellent legs, covered to the knee with a tailored skirt. Then she uncrossed her legs and moved her chair forward and Jan lost her view. She turned back to the paper.

"Actually, she did very well on it. This copy is my own and I marked it up last night as I was reading."

"Okay. Why don't you tell me why you brought it in?"

"Can I ask whether you have any idea what's happened to Maddy?"

Jan saw the look of concern on Natalie's face, more genuine than she'd seen from Maddy's parents.

"I'm afraid we don't know at this point."

"This is the first year I've had Maddy in class and school just started a couple of months ago. I don't know her well. But she turned this paper in last week and it alarmed me. Maybe I should have said something to her parents about it."

Finally, Jan thought. Maybe someone knows something about this kid.

"First of all," Natalie said, "the paper is huge. I asked for fifteen pages and she gave me thirty. Kids don't do that. But she wrote very passionately on the subject of the new wave of right-wing insurgency groups."

"As in the militias? That sort of thing?"

"Yes, in general. Less on the military aspect than on the desire of the these groups to live free of government interference."

Like the Objectivists, Jan thought. Like her own father. She felt a sucking sensation, like being pulled into quicksand.

"The thing that struck me about the paper wasn't the subject matter. That's interesting and timely and a good topic for research. It really was more about how she wrote about it."

Natalie reached over to the paper in Jan's hands and flipped through to the last page.

"Her summary describes her state of mind best, I think. It's what alarmed me when I heard she was missing."

Jan read the last paragraph of the paper.

"The range of opinions expressed by these conservative groups is very broad. As broad as America itself. Some are hateful, bigoted, and unrepentant. Some are crazed by religion. But some just want to be left alone, to live as true Americans—in the pursuit of happiness. To live free of unnecessary and ridiculous regulation. To leave the

truly talented unfettered so that they can soar. When those that crave that freedom are robbed by their government of the ability to experience it, they are morally obligated to leave that government in order to form their own more perfect society. Of course, this is viewed by the media and the average stupefied American as extremist. They can't understand those who are not content with the lowest common denominator. But their opinion does not matter to the gifted who seek to live with like-minded individuals. They will be living in a world apart."

Jan was silent for a moment. "She sounds much older than sixteen," she said.

"She's a good writer," Natalie said. "But her black and white thinking gives away her age. You remember that, don't you? If you could only have this or that, your life would be perfect. This is the right way; yours is the wrong way. It's all absolutes and very few shades of gray."

The idea that a sixteen-year-old would want to live away from the world seemed insane to Jan. It was precisely what she'd escaped from.

"I have no idea if this has anything to do with Maddy's disappearance, but I wanted to let you know about it," Natalie said.

"So you think Maddy may have run away to live with like-minded individuals, as she puts it?"

"I don't know. I've marked the areas in the paper where she advocates her position. See what you think."

Jan looked at her notebook. "I've heard the book *Atlas Shrugged* mentioned. Do you have any thoughts on why that book would be important to Maddy?"

"You don't need to know much about the plot of the novel to see why, and Maddy does reference it in her paper, which isn't really appropriate in a research thesis. *Atlas Shrugged* is a novel. Rand portrays the government as a collection of dunderheads hell-bent on punishing people for their creativity and production, especially if an idea or invention improves the lives of others. The government in her novel will find a way to rob you of any motivation to implement it."

"She's clearly anti-government, then."

"Yes, but we have to remember the context. *Atlas Shrugged* depicts a government that has powers ours does not, that takes steps toward socialism and communism that ours never has. It's a fictional US government, and it's in response to this fictional government that the hero of the book, John Galt, sets up a new society in a remote area of the country. It's a society where the individual will be freely rewarded for the work they produce and not concerned with what a government decides is in the best interest of the masses."

"But she's too young to have been thwarted yet. Or even to see yet whether she has ideas good enough to be suppressed."

"True, though she's very intelligent and I don't doubt she has confidence in her ideas. That comes through in her writing. But I don't think she has a very clear idea of what she's running to."

"I'm sure she doesn't. I appreciate you reaching out to us about this."

Natalie tore a corner off Maddy's paper and wrote her number down.

"Please call me if you want to talk this over further. I'm really concerned about Maddy."

Jan gave her one of her cards and watched as Natalie walked out of the office on her excellent legs. Nice, but not Catherine Engstrom nice.

The next person up came complete with whistle around the neck, athletic shorts, polo shirt with the high school logo on the front, and...*Yep*, Jan thought, *lesbian hair*.

"I'm Yvonne Kuterasaminsky." The woman smiled. "Call me Coach. It's easier."

Jan grinned and closed the office door. Coach said with a chuckle, "Usually when a door closes around here, someone's getting an ass-kicking. Am I in trouble?"

"No ass-kicking today. I'm looking into Maddy Harrington's disappearance."

Coach nodded and sighed. "It's never a good thing when they take off, you know? I mean, even when it turns out they're okay and no real harm done, it's still bad that something made them leave in the first place."

"Any idea what might have made Maddy leave?"

"None," Coach said. "I only know her on the soccer field. And she's not even on the team now. She was with me for two seasons and then she didn't come out this year. Not sure why…she really seemed to enjoy the game. She played well and she played all-out."

Interesting, Jan thought. So Maddy wasn't just all about computers.

"How was she with her teammates?"

"Here's the thing. She was a good scorer and not selfish, and it's difficult to find both in a player. She usually scored every game. And all the girls would come up and congratulate her, but it wasn't the big hug and bump." Coach shook her head. "Girls that age, well, they hang all over each other. They're devoted to each other. Maddy didn't seem to have any of that."

"Were they mean to her?" Jan asked.

Coach thought a moment. "No. It was more that they never included her. And she didn't try."

Jan thought about that later as she waited for Peet outside the high school. She stood in the crisp air of a beautiful fall day and tried to understand what could drive a lonely girl toward the same forces that Jan had shot her way out of. But her job was to find her, not to analyze her.

Peet joined her out front.

"I just got a call from Vivian. I guess the deal has closed and we're supposed to be at the office by four for a company-wide meeting."

Jan's first thought was not annoyance but excitement that she'd see Catherine again.

Jan and Peet joined the large group of employees gathered in the first floor security division of TSI. Catherine entered the room with father and son Begala, and the crowd fell silent. She waited a beat before beginning.

"Good afternoon to all of you. My name is Catherine Engstrom, and I am Vice President of Corporate Development of Chartered Global Security. I know that the rumors are flying, and I'm here to give you the information you need and put your minds at rest. We are a fifty-year-old company based in London, specialists in all forms of services related to security and investigations, with offices in a growing number of US cities. We acquired Titan Security and Investigation today, which gives us a very strong presence in Chicago, and therefore in the heart of the country. The ownership transfer is complete, so as of the present moment, we are your new employer.

"Now, many people panic when they hear their company has been sold. There will be some changes, of course. We'll need to conform your computer systems to ours, for instance, and we'll need to make sure there is some uniformity in procedures, benefits, that sort of thing. All of these details will be carefully explained to you as we move forward. I will be here on-site overseeing these processes, and Mr. Begala Junior will also be on hand to assist in this transfer.

"I want to make it clear, however, that we do not plan any wholesale layoffs. If there is an obvious redundancy, we will find you another job within the company."

Jan leaned over and whispered to Peet. "There you go. That sounds pretty safe." But Peet stared intently at Catherine, as if trying to divine some hidden meaning behind her words. Jan found it unnerving to have Peet so unsettled. She felt unsettled as well, but less about any change in her job situation than in the simple physical reaction she was having to Catherine. Another part was frustration. Catherine was completely out of Jan's league. She lived in London, an eight-hour plane ride away. And if that weren't enough, she was her new boss and a relationship would be very frowned upon. All of these things made Jan want her more, as if the number of obstacles increased the desire, independent of the object of desire herself.

CHAPTER FOUR

Jan slipped out of the meeting and into the back lot. Her Jeep was close to the door, her reserved parking a privilege of her long employment and rank as a senior investigator. These were the things she had to show for years of piecing a life together, working diligently on countless cases of workers comp fraud, employee theft, cheating spouses, missing deadbeats, and runaway children. At sixteen, Jan had started a completely new life. She had to think of a new name—Jan Roberts was the first that came to mind—and then build a new identity with the help of some experts in such documentation she'd met through her LA contacts. Always at the back of her mind was the worry that someone from the camp or law enforcement was hunting her down for shooting her father. For twenty years, her work at Titan had enabled her to live essentially like everyone else, which was what she longed to be. Titan was her sturdy link to normalcy. Any talk of changing up that system made her brain shut down.

She headed to her favorite bar.

The bars in Boystown weren't close to the office, but they were where she liked to go for a beer. Her friend James hung out at Sidetrack; that's where she knew people and where she felt comfortable. The clientele was almost entirely gay men and that suited Jan just fine. She generally got herself in trouble with women. She had enough trouble right now.

James was sitting on a barstool near the window looking out over Halsted Street. He was tall, nearly bald, neatly bearded, turtlenecked. The last bit of his martini was disappearing down his throat as she walked toward him. He pulled out the barstool next to him with the tip of his Italian shoe.

"Here, darling, take a load off," James said, then, to the bartender, "Cory, please, it's an emergency. Bring this girl a beer. And a tini for me."

Cory brought a bottle of Bud and a glass. Jan poured her beer and drank before the glass was full.

"Tell me everything you know," he said, leaning on his elbow, staring right into her eyes. She knew he'd listen for as long as she wanted to talk. This didn't overly burden him since she never talked much.

"Our company was sold today. I had no idea it was going to happen."

"Oh, dear." James said. "Cory, we need a shot for the lady. Stat."

"I don't want a shot. I have to go back to work."

She drank the shot of bourbon anyway.

"Well, at least that means there's work to go to. They wouldn't lay you off. Not their super secret agent.

"Maybe it's time for me to move on."

James looked at her a bit. "It doesn't really sound like that's what you want."

"If they lay off any investigators, I'll give up my spot before I see Peet lose hers. Anyway, a new part of the country might be a good idea. A change of scenery." Jan drank some more and finished pouring the bottle into her glass.

"You just bought the condo last year. You'll get killed if you sell it now."

She waved her hand, swatting away his concern.

"Is it something about the new owners? Are they homophobes? Are they going to make you wear ugly uniforms?"

Jan laughed. "That's it. They're going to make all the investigators wear uniforms. Pink ones." She drank again. "No, I don't know that there's anything wrong with the new people. They arrived here today, bought the company, and told us about it after the fact. They're headquartered in London, and they left an executive here in charge of the transition."

"British?"

"Yes."

"Male or female?"

"Female."

"Hot?"

"Gorgeous."

"Oh, dear Lord. Why are you thinking of leaving?"

"It just doesn't feel right. They may want to change everything. I'll give it a few days before I decide anything."

James shook his head. "Waiting a few days probably seems like long, judicious pondering to you, but try to take your time. This is a really big decision. As long as they're not laying you off, you have time to see whether you like working for them or not. Remember, the job market is really, really horrible. Right? Why do you think I'm sitting here drinking martinis before five o'clock?"

"Because you're a lush?" Jan smiled.

"There's that."

Jan's phone rang and she saw it was Peet.

"What's up?"

"I just heard from the Winnetka PD. Maddy's car was sold two days ago at a CarMax in the northern burbs."

"Did they confirm it was Maddy who sold it?"

"Yeah. They have a copy of her driver's license."

"How much did she get?"

"About twenty thousand. Now she has money to hold her for a while. And I just ran her credit card again. There's been no activity."

"Confirms she's a runaway," Jan said.

"She may not have had a gun to her head, but we don't know if she's being coerced or how much she's under someone's influence. She's only a kid, Jan."

"I know that. You know that. Maddy probably doesn't feel that way, and we know her parents don't."

"We've got to find a place to start. I'll go check the bus and train stations," Peet said.

"And I'll get started on her Web activity. Has Harrington gotten back to you with their router information?"

"I left a note at the office with the password to the router."

"Okay. I'm on my way there."

She finished her beer and said good-bye to James. She did know one thing. She didn't want to make any decisions about her job until she'd found Maddy Harrington and made sure she was safe. Every kid deserved that much.

Now that it was after five, the offices and desks upstairs were nearly empty. On her side of the floor there were a couple of people in the small conference room with Dave Collins. It looked like he was taking a statement. Jan stopped by her desk to start up her computer and then went into the break room to make a pot of coffee. She heard the sharp tap of high heels behind her.

"Hello," Catherine said brightly.

Jan nodded hello and watched the coffeemaker, not trusting herself to speak. She thought her voice might squeak. The brown liquid seemed to be trickling down like sap from a maple tree.

Catherine rinsed her mug out at the sink and then came by to stand and watch the coffeemaker also.

"I noticed you had to leave the meeting early," Catherine said.

"I'm working on a case." That came out all right, Jan thought.

"Please tell me about it. I'm interested in what sorts of things the investigators handle here."

Catherine stood with her body angled toward Jan, holding her empty mug in her hand as if it were a glass of champagne and she was at a cocktail party. It was annoying as hell, and completely intoxicating. Jan wanted to say nothing to her new boss, but everything to this beautiful woman.

She took the empty mug from Catherine's hand and poured the fresh coffee into it, then handed it back handle first. "I'm working a missing teen case, very new, with lots of information still to gather and assess. In other words, I'm pretty busy."

Catherine sipped the black coffee and peered at Jan over her mug. "I can see you approach your work very seriously. Do you plan to be here for a while this evening?"

Jan focused on blending a huge amount of sugar and creamer in her coffee. Was Catherine flirting with her?

"I suppose I don't really think or care about the overtime right now," Jan said. "Time is of the essence in a case like this. Her parents are getting daily reports on our progress and our charges." Jan struggled to keep her tone business-like.

"Of course." Catherine stepped aside as Jan walked out of the room, and then followed her to her desk. "I think what I meant to ask is how you approach a case such as this. I don't care about the overtime either."

Jan sat at her desk and looked up at Catherine. "I think I'd better get back to it. I have to check out what websites the missing girl was visiting before she left."

"Ah. Now you're within my realm," Catherine said.

"What do you mean?"

"I have a background in computers. It's one of the things I think you'll like in working for a bigger company. We'll have the personnel and equipment to help you track down information in a fraction of the time it probably takes you now."

Jan shrugged. "We do okay the way things are."

Catherine looked amused. "You aren't going to say something about good old shoe leather and gut instinct, are you?"

"We're not hayseeds here, you know."

"Of course not. I'm so sorry if I sounded like I thought you were."

Catherine looked amused still, but her eyes were kind. Jan found it confusing. She turned from Catherine and put her hand on her computer mouse, waking up the screen and opening her remote access software.

"May I ask how you're going about this search? Perhaps there's a way I can help."

Now Jan began to sag a bit. One thing she loved about working for TSI was the nearly total autonomy she enjoyed. The last thing LJ wanted to know about was the details of their investigative process, unless he could use it to look good in front of someone. If she was going to have to detail her work to her new bosses, perhaps it was time to move on.

"I'm about to access Maddy's home router and wireless network. I'll log in remotely from here and access the websites she visited while she was on that network," Jan said.

She typed in the IP address of Maddy's computer and the screen filled with Web addresses. Jan peered at the long list, with words like "militia," "Michigan," "patriot," and most disturbingly, "Idaho" popping up throughout. These could all have been a part of Maddy's recent research on right-wing militias. Or they could be a clue as to where she was now. The words seemed like little bombs going off on the screen, so loaded in meaning were they to Jan. Catherine leaned over her shoulder, pointing a finger at a Web address for a Michigan militia group.

"Why was she on these websites? They're a little scary."

"I don't know at this point, other than her social studies teacher showed me a paper Maddy wrote on right-wing militias."

Jan pulled her chair closer to the computer, farther from Catherine. No good would come of touching.

"Listen, I need to get back to work here. If you want to be briefed on this case I'd be happy to do that, but at a different time. I hope you understand." Jan addressed the screen as she talked, with Catherine still behind her, her hips just behind Jan's shoulders. Catherine placed a warm hand on top of Jan's right shoulder and gave it a gentle squeeze.

"Of course. I do apologize. I see that you're getting the information much as I would and I'm properly impressed."

Jan looked up at her, waiting to see if she had more to say. Catherine stared down at her, as if waiting to see if she would speak. The silence lengthened.

"Well, I'll see you around," Jan said.

"Right. Good luck, then."

Jan watched her walk down the hallway, unable to look away She couldn't help it. Naturally, Catherine turned back and caught Jan staring. Her smile was just a little wicked.

Hours after David sent the crew out the door, Maddy sat at the rickety kitchen table working on her computer. He had handed lists and cash to everyone but Maddy, telling them to pick up the items they'd need to make their start to Idaho. Some of the items they'd truck out west, some they would purchase when they got there. They had it all planned out to the last literal nut and bolt. Now David was out running errands and the house was silent.

Maddy worked on the database she'd developed that would keep track of provisions, a budgeting system that would keep the money handlers accountable, and an intranet that would keep their communications with the outside world secure. She was proud of her work. She knew what programming to steal from other bits of software and what to make uniquely her own. She loved being in total control of the software world she lived in. What she didn't have control of was the people David had chosen to make the move to Idaho with them. They'd all been friends of his for years, schoolmates who had long run as a pack. There was no question that David was their leader. Maddy assumed they were skeptical about her, despite their warm welcome. But she was skeptical of them in turn. She doubted that any of the people she'd met that morning had the same purity of purpose she and David did about making their new society work. For the most part, they looked like they didn't have much else going on in their lives rather than being on fire with a vision of a new way to live. It didn't matter how big their new place was in Idaho. If she didn't like her compatriots, it was going to feel like close quarters.

David was trying to run a tight ship, though. He made it clear he wanted everything organized and everyone trained before they made their start out west.

"What do you mean trained?" Maddy asked.

"Basic training," he said. "Boot camp."

"What are you talking about? You never mentioned any boot camp."

In the hours they spent talking and writing to each other, every bit of philosophy was explored on the question of starting their own society. They had made fun of the many groups spread throughout the country that called themselves militias, which seemed to them to be a lot of grown men playing at soldiers. They scoffed at religious cults, were appalled by racist clans, and had no interest in tax protesters or political parties. Their vision was simply to live as they wanted to without any interference.

"We're working with a local militia that's been around a long time. We've got to know what we're doing out there, Maddy. We're doing a basic training weekend that's going to kick your ass."

"Wait a second. Is that the group that thinks bombing Congress is a good idea?" Maddy narrowed her eyes and closed the lid on her laptop.

"We don't need to agree with them in order to take advantage of their military training. Ed and Warren have already been through the two-day camp, and I'll tell you, it's useful stuff. And I think I've convinced six of his guys to go with us."

"What?" The people she'd met at that morning's meeting didn't seem like intellectual giants, but she allowed for the fact that she didn't know them at all. She was willing to assume David had picked them for a reason. But militia were bad news. She'd read their "manifestos" on the Internet and didn't doubt that at some point they would find a reason to fire at real targets.

David riffled through a stack of papers on the table and pulled out a real estate brochure. He opened it to a survey of the land they were buying in northern Idaho. "This is one hundred and sixty acres, Maddy. Do you think that seven of us are going to be able to maintain and secure that amount of land?"

Maddy gazed at the survey and turned the page to look at a map of the surrounding area. It was incomprehensibly huge. The main thing they'd been looking for in land was that it be remote, fed by a river or four-season stream, have good solar exposure, and plenty of pasture land for the animals they planned to raise. As they researched available property, David was saving money, acquiring funds from others, laying the groundwork for actually going off-grid, and starting up something new and separate from everything Maddy had known. It all had to be as close to perfect as possible from the moment they left the Midwest.

She shrugged. "I thought you said we'd be growing the group slowly. You've just doubled it."

David looked intently into Maddy's eyes. "You're just going to have to trust me on some of this. You'll see when you go off to boot camp how useful these guys will be. They're workhorses, and they know all kinds of survival stuff. I might be able to survive a Detroit mugging, but face-to-face with a bear, and I'm in deep trouble."

Maddy stared at her screen as the computer compiled her software. It was just as well that she wasn't out and about with the others, just in case her parents had actually done something like call the police when they realized that she'd disappeared. It was possible they'd been roused from their parental lethargy by now. The last thing she wanted was to be picked up as a runaway minor by the police. How embarrassing that would be.

Jan sat at her desk and read through the websites Maddy had been visiting. Every militia and political group had its own website, and each of those had dozens of links to other militias. There seemed to be an endless chain of connection between groups that all believed the government was their enemy. They believed it operated illegally. They believed they would be stripped of their civil liberties. And they believed, above all, that they would go down fighting when the time came.

She fought off the flashbacks to the camp she grew up in, but it was a useless battle. The similarities were so strong, the rhetoric she read identical for the most part with what she had to listen to every Saturday evening in camp, over twenty years earlier, when her father would hold "community meetings."

"All of you are safe and living free because I had the foresight to protect us from the coming events that will tear this country apart. There are threats out there that you can't even begin to imagine."

He would pace back and forth in front of the mess hall, looking like he was briefing a room of soldiers. Everyone in camp was expected to attend.

"It is a commonly accepted fact now that the United Nations has amassed an enormous army for the sole purpose of invading our rich nation and eliminating its borders."

There was a cabal of communists/socialists/Wall Street tycoons/the United Nations who was running the country in order to strip citizens of their wages, impose evermore crippling taxes, and generally undermine American values. There were hordes of immigrants and people from countries we hadn't even heard of poised to invade our cities and take all our jobs. The nuclear holocaust was upon us.

The list went on and on. The fact that the same paranoid theories still existed didn't surprise Jan. In fact, the only difference she saw was the frequent racism and ultra-conservative Christianity espoused by many of the groups freely posting their views on the Internet. Her father considered himself a righteous leader, and he hated everyone not under his control, no matter what their religion or skin color.

By far the biggest difference between then and now was the role the Internet played in linking the various ideologues together. Maybe there had been other camps nearby in Idaho where people felt as fervently as her father did and they just didn't know it. Perhaps they could have had friendships with other groups, seen other ways to live, had some form of society outside the clearing they'd made for themselves in the middle of nowhere.

If she hadn't stumbled on the ranch she regularly spied on, she'd never have known what a "normal" family was. One summer day, she watched as the entire family drove away from the ranch with luggage strapped to the top of their station wagon and she guessed they wouldn't be coming back soon. She slipped through an unlocked back window and studied the home's interior much as an alien would after opening a time capsule. Next to an overstuffed chair in the living room was a stack of magazines. Jan grabbed a fistful from the bottom of the pile and ran from the house. She buried them by her favorite thinking tree and unearthed them one by one, studying them carefully. Like the moment when *The Wizard of Oz* changes from black and white to Technicolor, a new world opened to Jan.

There were a few adults in camp who had talked to her about what life was like for them before they came to Idaho. The stories and photos in the magazines made her realize she'd still had only the smallest glimpse of the world around her. From then on, she found ways to pilfer discarded newspapers and magazines from the ranch.

For the first time in ages, Jan wondered if her father were alive. She wasn't absolutely sure where her bullet had hit him. She'd aimed for his chest, but he was zigzagging toward her when she'd fired. The shot didn't necessarily kill him. It took him down, which is what she wanted. If he wasn't dead, was he still in Idaho? Still in the middle of nowhere? Did a middle of nowhere still exist in this day and age?

Jan clicked through the pages of one particularly polished website offering registration for militia training weekends held throughout the year. Some were general and geared to recruit-level participants. Others were highly specialized. Advanced Scout, Art of Camouflage, Tracking and Counter-Tracking, Advanced Urban Escape and Evasion, Off-Grid Medical Care, and on and on. There were several sniper courses. She could easily see why a teenager would think this all sounded pretty exciting. Jan guessed she had a better chance of finding Maddy in Michigan than in the Chicago area. If she was as disdainful of the government as her paper implied, then it made sense she'd run toward the people who at least loosely agreed with her views. There wasn't anything else Jan could find that hinted at where she might be.

Jan parked in front of the Vin en Rose, a storefront bar tucked into the middle of a row of small businesses on a residential block. It had a smoked glass window and a neon sign: two female symbols and two wine glasses linked together in a chain. Inside was an array of tables in front and a glittering bar stretching along the back wall. It was fairly early on a Friday night. A group of four women sat at the only occupied table, and a few women were at the bar, one of whom sat away from the others. She was perched sideways on her tall chair with a book in hand and her long legs crossed at the knee. Jan saw the white streak in her hair and thought that either Susan Sontag had come back to life to drink in the Vin en Rose, or Catherine had found the only remaining lesbian bar in Chicago. One seemed as unlikely as the other. Before she could dodge back out the door, she heard Catherine's unmistakable low voice.

"Jan!"

There was no escape. Jan crossed the room toward the bar, feeling as if she were being pulled in by a fishing rod with heavy tackle. Catherine reached her hand out and pulled Jan the rest of the way in.

"My God, I was beginning to wonder if there were any lesbians in this town," Catherine said. There was a nearly empty bottle of wine on the bar in front of her "I should have guessed that the only interesting woman to walk through the door would be you."

Jan glanced around to check whom Catherine was comparing her to. The others looked like perfectly respectable lesbians to her.

"Have a drink and keep me company. I've about worn out Diane here."

Jan glanced at Diane behind the bar, whom she'd known for years. Diane raised her eyebrows almost imperceptibly.

"Beer?" Diane said.

"Yeah. And whatever Catherine's having."

Catherine smiled broadly and turned to Diane. "Just a glass this time, thank you."

Jan pulled the barstool next to Catherine out of the way and stood, thinking she was either the luckiest or unluckiest woman in the world. She resigned herself to seeing which it would be.

"I was just on my way home and thought I'd stop in for a drink," she said. "The last person in the world I expected to see is my new boss."

"Please do not utter the word 'boss.' I loathe it. Anyway, I didn't come in here to talk about work."

Jan took a long drink from the cold glass of beer Diane set in front of her. Catherine was wearing the clothes she had on at the office, but now her suit jacket was draped along the back of her chair and the silk blouse was unbuttoned low enough to show a bit of cleavage. Catherine appeared to be in her mid-forties, but her breasts appeared to be in their mid-twenties. Jan wondered if she'd have the opportunity to examine whether that was the result of good genes, good lingerie, or good plastic surgery.

Then she took another long drink. "What did you come in here for?" she said.

"Hmm. How should I answer that?" Catherine poured the last of the wine from her bottle and sipped. "I could say that this is close to where I'm staying, but I'm in a downtown hotel."

"Then you must have read about this place in your book," Jan said, pointing to the travel guide in front of her.

"You're exactly right, and now both of our secrets are out."

Jan's glass stopped midair. "What secret are you talking about?"

Catherine smiled. "That you're gay, of course. But I'm dying to hear about your other secrets."

"I don't make a secret of my sexuality," Jan said. "But I don't advertise it, either."

"Clearly, you don't need to."

Jan thought she heard Diane snort as she rubbed down the bar nearby.

"Now tell me all about yourself."

"What would you like to know?" Jan said. The woman was her boss, no matter what she might say, and she was also obviously flirting. Jan wasn't sure how to play it.

"Whether you're attached, of course. Surely you must be."

"No, not attached."

"That's excellent," Catherine said, waiting for more. Jan sipped her beer. "Let me ask you something a little more open-ended, and see if I can get more than five words at a time out of you."

"You don't like the silent type?" Jan said. That was flirting, she cautioned herself.

"Oh, I do. I'm just so terribly sick of my own voice right now. All those meetings today."

"Ask away, then. I'll try to help you out."

Catherine drank more. She may have been tipsy. It was hard to tell from her throaty voice and precise diction. But there was the empty bottle of wine.

"Tell me how you spend your time. When you're not investigating missing persons and the like."

Jan hated being asked to describe what her life was like. She found it strangely depressing when she put it in words. "You'll be happy to know that you've inherited a workaholic."

"You Americans seem to revel in working too hard."

"I'd say that's one of those myths that isn't based on reality. I see a lot of people who find all kinds of ways to work as little as possible."

"But you're not one of them. In fact, I suspect you're unlike most people," Catherine said.

"You've known me less than a day. How could you say that?" Jan turned to her beer.

"I'm sorry," Catherine said, looking sincerely concerned. "Did I insult you somehow? I just meant that in the best way. You're clearly, at least to me, a person of integrity. Of all the people I met today at TSI, you're the only one who seemed more concerned about doing the job than keeping a job."

Jan shrugged. There wasn't much to say to that. They were silent for a moment.

"So go on," Catherine said. "You can't work twenty-four seven. Not really."

Jan sighed. "Let's see. I work out at the gym."

"Yes. I can see that you do."

Where to go with this, Jan wondered. Catherine wasn't shy; that was obvious. It didn't really matter what they were talking about. The words were the thin veneer covering the single question on both of their minds. Would they or wouldn't they have sex?

"And I read. See friends. Drink some."

"Here's to that." Catherine beamed. She took up her glass and touched it to Jan's. "And here's to a very mysterious woman."

"I'm not mysterious. I just don't have much to tell you."

"Yet. I have a feeling we'll be getting to know each other better."

Jan was usually not much intrigued by obvious flirtation, or by women who came on too strongly. She preferred the feeling of control when she picked a person to pursue. She felt freer to also choose to leave when their time together was up. The fact that Catherine was flirting and coming on to her strongly didn't dampen her interest in the least, which was a first. She worried about that.

"Tell me about yourself," Jan said. "Fair's fair."

Catherine's knees brushed along Jan's thighs as she swiveled her barstool toward her. Jan backed away and sat down.

"Let's see. Raised in London, mum and dad both doctors. Didn't see much of them, but we were happy enough. My sister, Elaine, is married and lives near Brighton, poor thing. I went to Cambridge and did a masters in information technology and economics."

Catherine seemed to change her mind about what she was about to say and stopped talking.

"Did you go to work for CGS right after school?" Jan asked.

"No, actually. I worked for the government for quite a long time."

Jan waited for more. She thought Catherine looked a little less sure of herself than she had moments before. She put her hand lightly on Catherine's forearm. She felt it jump.

"You don't have to tell me anything, you know. We're just making small talk."

"Is that what we're doing?" Catherine asked. "I was rather hoping it was something a bit more."

Jan stared at her lips as she spoke, concentrating more on how they looked than what they were saying. They were luscious lips and she watched them curl into a smile

"Tell me what you think we're doing," Catherine said. She reached over to take Jan's hand.

"A second ago I would have said we were talking. Now I'd say we're playing with fire." Jan wrapped her thumb around the top of Catherine's hand and lightly rubbed; she could see the little hitch in her breath. Catherine's eyes glittered as she leaned closer to Jan.

"Because I'm technically your boss? I think Americans are much more hung up on what two consenting adults do than even the British. If we were in France, our clothes would already be off."

Jan looked around the room. "Well, I'm not French. But I'm not concerned about you being my boss either. Not if you're not. Anyway, you live in London, right?"

"Yes." Catherine now had a hand on Jan's thigh, matching the rubbing motion Jan was making on her other hand. It had taken nothing more than the sight of Catherine to flip the switch on Jan's libido and start the march of caution out the door. Now she was unbelievably turned on. All that rubbing

"So you'll be gone soon and we can't really get into too much trouble."

"Well, I'd like to get into a little trouble," Catherine said.

Catherine leaned in for a kiss. As Jan met her lips her thinking stopped, mercifully, and her tongue found Catherine's. A first kiss was often such an awkward thing. When teeth clanked and heads moved the wrong way and tongues felt more at war than love, Jan often felt her desire slip away. But Catherine's mouth pressed into hers as if precision fit for it; the kiss felt like the flame of a match strike—instantly flaring and white hot. When Jan pulled away at last, she kept Catherine's face in her hands and whispered, "My car. Your hotel."

"Yes. And quickly."

❖

Catherine was staying at the Ritz-Carlton, an uber-luxury hotel in the heart of Chicago's Magnificent Mile. Jan fought her way through the Friday night traffic on Michigan Avenue, trying to concentrate while Catherine's hand moved up and down her thigh.

"We'll get in an accident if you keep that up."

Catherine's laugh was musical, like her voice. The cello, the bow, the thrum. Jan began to turn left on Pearson Street, completely missing the sign warning that left turns were on the arrow only. Pedestrians poured into the Pearson crosswalk, stranding her in the intersection as a cavalry of cars barreled toward them on Michigan. Horns erupted as she blocked their passage.

Catherine removed her hand. "Perhaps you're right. I'll restrain myself."

The Ritz valet took her keys and Jan followed Catherine through one lobby, up an elevator, through another enormous and lavish lobby and up a second elevator. She trailed her silently down a long hall. The journey seemed to take forever. Her mind sagged into the certainty that the excitement of what was happening now would soon be replaced with sorrow when Catherine backed away. Not tonight, necessarily, but as soon as she found that Jan was…what? That Jan was Jan. Or that Jan wasn't Jan. She'd always assumed that letting anyone know she wasn't Jan would be a surefire end to any relationship, budding or otherwise. But being Jan seemed to do the trick all on its own.

The hotel room looked directly east over Lake Michigan, the carnival lights of Navy Pier drawing Jan's eye from the dark, endless water. As she stood at the window, Catherine approached her from behind and wrapped her arms around her waist.

"I fear you've gone from feeling to thinking," she said. "I can see it in your forehead. No good comes from thinking in these situations, you know."

She slowly turned Jan around and laced her hands behind her neck. "My mind is quite blank at the moment."

How wonderful that must be, thought Jan. Then she leaned in and kissed Catherine, determined to kick-start the arousal that she'd lost somewhere during the long journey from car to room. The kiss deepened as she cradled Catherine's head, held her close with the other hand low on her hip. They were in no hurry to move.

She had no memory of kisses like this. She'd kissed many women, usually with great pleasure, but always with some impatience to move things along to the next step. She felt she could kiss Catherine all night. But soon their bodies demanded more. She took her by the hand to the enormous bed, already turned down for the night. She unwrapped one of the chocolates lying atop the pillows, put it in Catherine's mouth, and started undressing her. Catherine made mewling sounds as Jan worked her way down, freeing the beautiful breasts from her bra (good genes), removing the skirt, the hose, the panties. Then she lay Catherine down on the sheets and stripped off her own clothes, draping herself over her, kissing her again and tasting the chocolate. She began to explore the glorious body; the full breasts, the slightly rounded stomach, the curve of the hip over the long and beautifully shaped legs. Jan moved to one side and ran a hand up and down, from knee to nose. Catherine's breathing was starting to sound hungry. Jan was hungry, too.

"Please, do something," Catherine said. "I need more."

Jan's lips found a nipple and tugged at it, played with it, lightly bit down. The gasp from Catherine was sharp.

"Yes. That. More."

That voice was like direct pressure between Jan's legs. As she moved all over Catherine, she wondered if she'd come without ever being touched. With each moan from Catherine's mouth she felt a deeper twinge and she became desperate to straddle the slender thigh and ride her. It would just take a moment. But she put her fingers inside Catherine instead and watched her head move from side to side on the pillow, her eyes closed, her hands reaching behind her for the headboard. Jan lowered herself and added her mouth while keeping the fingers moving, and now Catherine's moans were loud and sustained and her body was writhing, rising up from the bed, moving as if possessed. Jan wanted to possess her, she did possess her. She stayed on her as Catherine came, until the spasms subsided and she pulled away from Jan's tongue.

She moved up quickly and straddled Catherine's thigh, moving deeply and rhythmically as she took Catherine's arms and held them over her head, their eyes now locked on each other. Jan never kept her eyes open while making love. Not before now, with Catherine. She saw the feral look in Catherine's eyes as she pushed her thigh upward to increase the pressure and soon Jan came in a long orgasm that ripped sounds out of her body she'd never made before.

They lay welded together, sticky and incapable of moving. They were speechless for a long while.

"I'd say that was more than a little trouble we just got into," Catherine said.

God, yes, Jan thought.

❖

Jan woke at ten Saturday morning, the strong eastern sunlight pouring through the windows. She'd managed at some point during the night to untangle herself from Catherine and roll to the edge of the ship-sized mattress. She was asleep when she'd done so. No conscious part of her wanted distance from Catherine. Her unconscious self was a constant and cruel master.

She moved back over and wrapped herself around Catherine. Her body was warm like a baby's. She tried to stay still to let Catherine sleep, but her hands started to roam. Catherine turned in her arms.

"You're not much for sleeping in, are you?" she murmured.

"Not much. But it is ten o'clock."

"Bloody hell!" Catherine threw off the covers and sprang from the bed. She stood there naked, holding her hands to the sides of her head as if it were about to fall apart. "I'm late for my meetings."

She sounded anguished, at odds with the carefree woman of the night before. Jan watched her sprint to the bathroom. It seemed morning sex was off the table. She followed her and stood at the door.

"You're the new owner, remember? It's okay to be late."

Catherine was checking the temperature of the shower. She glanced at Jan.

"Not the impression I like to give. Listen, I'm sorry for this. Have them charge the valet to my room, will you?" She stepped into the shower.

Jan stared at the figure soaping herself up in the steamy water. She felt sick, dismissed. She got dressed and left the room without saying more. When she got down to the front of the hotel, she paid for her own valet parking.

CHAPTER FIVE

Maddy peered from under her camouflaged cap at the large field dotted with obstacle courses, a rifle range, and stretches of bare ground where dozens of uniformed people were doing exercises, breaking down weapons, and throwing each other around in simulated hand-to-hand combat. It was a cloudless day, the autumn foliage brilliant in the woods surrounding the field.

She stood in a long line of men and women wearing the uniforms issued to them the hour before. Standing in front of the line addressing them was a "sergeant" named Drecker. His camos were clean but well worn, his boots shiny but with many miles on them.

"You sorry suckers have one hell of a day ahead of you. Some of you look worn out from getting up early to drive here. Believe me, that was the best part of your day right there. By the time we finish our last field exercise in the middle of the night, you're going to wish you'd never been born."

Maddy wanted to push her cap up. It was settling on her head and the brim was covering her eyes. They were standing at ease, with hands clasped behind their backs. She must have looked like a fool, but she didn't dare move out of position.

"Unlike a full basic training in the military where a soldier's strength can be built up, we're going to have to work with what you've got, and that ain't much from the looks of things. You'll leave camp tomorrow with a written program of how to continue your conditioning."

All the people Maddy had met at David's kitchen table were here in line with her, except Ed and Warren. They'd already been through multiple training sessions with this outfit and were out making more preparations for the move. Kristi stood next to her, her piercings removed at Drecker's command. Her uniform fit snuggly across her large breasts, and Maddy could see sweat trickling down her face, despite the cool temperature. They'd driven together in the back of David's truck, bundled in blankets and silent the entire way. Occasionally, though, Kristi would give her an encouraging smile and a thumbs-up.

David stood on her other side. She knew he'd been up until very late, long after she'd gone to sleep in her basement bedroom. She'd wake to hear him scraping his chair away from the kitchen table, pacing from one end of the house to the other, scraping the chair back in place. She'd managed to put together enough hours of sleep to make the day bearable. She didn't know how David would manage. She wasn't worried anymore about him not being a man of action. He was a man who didn't know how not to take action.

Before she'd said good night, David put his hand on her forearm. It seemed like something her grandma would do.

"Maddy, I just want you to know how much it's meant that we got to know each other."

Maddy looked at his hand on her arm, wondering if he'd start patting her. She didn't know what to say.

"You're young, probably younger than you're admitting to me, but you've got an amazing mind. I feel like you get what I'm saying, more than any of the others do."

She didn't think that was much of a compliment, but he looked very sincere. She was beginning to believe he genuinely cared for her.

"You and I have a singleness of purpose," he went on, his hand finally sliding off her arms. "We have a simple goal, but we have to be realistic. There are going to be people and circumstances that will keep things complicated."

"What do you mean?"

"I just mean that the reason you and I want to leave all this behind"—his arm swept around the decrepit kitchen as if it were a Four Seasons resort—"is probably not the same reasons others have. And that's okay."

"Is it?" she asked. "I don't want to live in the middle of Idaho with a bunch of people who are running from something. I feel like I'm running toward something."

David smiled as he watched her. "Exactly."

"What are they running from?" She ignored the fact that she was running from something too.

"I didn't say they were. I just said their reasons might be different from ours. We've decided to withhold our creativity from a society that only punishes us for having it. That's not something that most people think that much about. Ed and Warren want to go to Idaho to live like pioneers. Tom is a lost soul who just wants to be part of something. He goes with me everywhere."

"What about Kristi?"

"Well, Kristi is all gruff on the outside, marshmallow on the inside, not an unusual personality profile around here. There are so many people like her that have no job prospects, no special skills, no idea really of what it would be like to have either. Every year she sees her community becoming more hopeless, the people around her more bitter, their resentment poisoning everything. She wants out, but she doesn't really care what she's moving into as long as she believes it's something better. The idea of leaving this place is what's driving her."

"So what does she bring to the table?"

"First of all, malleability. Every community has to have worker bees, and that's what Kristi wants. To be part of something where her labor is valued. She'll be an exceptional worker bee, but that's all she'll ever be. And that's enough for her."

"How do you know that? She didn't come up to you and say, 'Dude, give me all the shit jobs and I'll be happy as a clam.'" Maddy couldn't understand the lack of ambition in that.

"I've known Kristi a long time. Just think about it and it all makes sense."

"Okay. What about Diane? What's her story?"

"Diane? Diane's my girlfriend. I don't want to be entirely self-sufficient."

Maddy didn't like the big grin on his face. She generally found men to be quite pathetic when it came to sex. She went downstairs to bed.

❖

Sergeant Drecker handed off part of the group to a corporal. They were led away to start their scouting exercises while Maddy, Kristi, Tommy, and Diane stayed behind for weapons training. They marched behind Drecker as he took them to a large rifle range.

Drecker addressed them. "This morning we're going to train you on how to safely handle and clean your weapon. You will not be allowed to shoot it until you've mastered these skills."

Kristi was next to her again. While Drecker started handing out rifles, she leaned over to whisper, "How cool is this?"

Maddy saw the gleam in Kristi's eye. "Very cool?"

"Damn right."

Maddy thought about what David told her about Kristi. She was glad Kristi was excited and she was glad they were going through training together. Other than that, she felt like she'd been dropped into an alien nation.

"You two," Drecker barked, pointing at Maddy and Kristi. "Step forward."

Kristi did as she was told. Maddy followed a moment later.

"First rule of camp is that you do not speak while in formation or in the presence of a superior unless you are spoken to first. Do you understand?"

"Yes, sir," Kristi said.

Drecker stared at Maddy.

"Yes, sir."

"Drop and give me ten."

"Ten what?" Maddy said. She heard Diane stifle a laugh behind her.

"Ten push-ups," Drecker said. "Didn't they teach you how to do a push-up in your fancy schools?"

Kristi had already dropped to the ground and was grinding out her first push-up. Maddy was wondering how Decker knew she went to "fancy schools."

"Wait a second," she said. "Shouldn't we be told the rules before we're punished for breaking them?"

Drecker moved to within an inch of Maddy's face. She stepped back and he followed her.

"That just earned you another ten, private. Now drop."

Maddy looked behind her. Tommy looked back at her nervously while the others avoided her eyes. She sighed and got down on the ground, doing her twenty push-ups in the time it took Kristi to finish her ten. Kristi lay face down, her body heaving as she caught her breath.

"Now get back in line so we can get some work done."

Maddy had read as much as she could about the militias. She knew they operated under a military chain of command. But who had made her a private? She was just here to learn to shoot, which she wanted to do. She wasn't here to join a militia. The last chain of command she ever wanted to be part of was the one she'd just fled: father/mother/Maddy.

Once everyone had a rifle, they got on their knees and learned how to disassemble and load them. Their first cartridges were blanks. Two hours later, Maddy was shooting with real bullets, blasting the heads off of targets that looked like someone's version of an Arab terrorist. She tried to ignore the implications of that as she shot round after round. When she paused to reload, she looked over at Kristi. They beamed at each other and bumped fists.

The afternoon was packed with instruction on how to operate covertly in the woods. Since it was hunting season in Michigan, they were issued bright orange hats and vests.

"You'll be in full uniform for tonight's maneuvers," Drecker said.

Maddy and Kristin were teamed up to learn about stealth movement and sensory awareness in the woods, which Maddy took to mean walking quietly with her headphones off. When Drecker started talking about identifying booby traps, she paid more attention. They were operating under a different definition of survival training. This wasn't about building animal traps and picking berries. It was all about outsmarting people who were trying to kill them. They learned to build an Apache limp wire trip set. Maddy had a quick fantasy of her father being strung up by one as he walked in from the garage after another night out carousing. Other than that, she couldn't imagine a scenario where she'd need one.

During a break mid-afternoon, Maddy sat with Kristi and Tommy at the edge of the field. Diane had run off to find David, who'd disappeared during target practice. Tommy looked confused, as if he'd signed up for calculus and found himself in a pottery class. He seemed much more naïve than Maddy about what the training camp would be like. At least she knew these soldiers were preparing for one or more unlikely scenarios: the end of the world as we know it, government breakdown and anarchy, a terrorist attack.

"I don't really need to know how to set traps for humans," Maddy said.

Kristi was sitting against a tree, her rifle across her lap. "Oh, hell yes, you do. What if we're invaded?"

"Invaded?" Tommy said. "Why would anyone invade us?"

"Exactly. One of the reasons we're going there is to be out of everyone's way. We don't bother them and they don't bother us," Maddy said.

"You two are living in a dream world," Kristi said. "There's always someone who wants what's not theirs. We have to know how to protect ourselves."

"It doesn't hurt to be ready, I suppose," Maddy said "And the training's a blast. I can't wait for maneuvers tonight."

Kristi was smiling again. "Right? We are going to kick some ass."

Tommy was sitting on the ground with his legs crossed, his head bent over his lap.

"Hey, Tommy boy. Are you going to puke or something?" Kristi prodded him with her rifle.

He raised his head and smiled grimly. "I hate this."

Drecker called them back into action before they could say anything to Tommy, and Maddy soon forgot it.

That night, under a full moon, Maddy edged toward a clearing in the woods. Ahead of her was another of the course instructors, a sergeant named Cooper. Behind her were Kristi, Tommy, and the other members of their squad. Cooper signaled for them to drop. Maddy had never spent so much time on the ground as she had that day. She was aching from carrying a heavy pack, and the last reserve of her energy had evaporated some time ago. It was nearly midnight and she'd been up since five that morning.

Cooper started a series of rapid hand gestures. He kept pointing at her with two fingers and then pointing to their right, very fast, over and over so it didn't make sense to her. Kristi urged her up by the arm and led her off toward the right, looking at Cooper for more direction. He waved them further on, until they were out of sight of the others. They turned toward the clearing, which was lit up by the moon like a softball field during a night game.

"What are we supposed to do?" Maddy whispered.

"Hell if I know," Kristi said. She looked as weary as Maddy felt. They weren't having much fun anymore.

"I'm going to pee," Maddy said.

"Can't you wait? We might have to move any second."

Maddy peered up at Kristi from under her helmet and handed over her rifle. "Can't wait."

She walked a few yards deeper in the woods and squatted behind a big oak. She'd emptied half her bladder when she heard someone approach. She looked up to see M-16s pointed at her by two guys from the opposing team. A third came toward them pushing Kristi forward with the point of his gun. She had her hands above her head. One of the soldiers hauled Maddy to her feet and pointed to her pants pooling around her ankles. She pulled them up while everyone stared at her.

Their rifles were pointed at them, but Maddy knew that the bullets were blanks. She couldn't see any point in pretending she could be shot or taken on a forced march to a POW camp, so she yelled at the top of her lungs.

"Over here!"

Her voice was still ringing when one of the soldiers hit her in the side of her helmet with the butt of his rifle. She dropped into the puddle of her own urine. Kristi barreled toward him with her shoulders lowered, going for the tackle, but another soldier stuck his foot out and tripped her. She fell next to Maddy. The soldiers ran back into the woods when they heard Cooper and two others from their squad running toward them. Maddy lay still as Cooper ordered three team members to pursue. She wasn't badly hurt, but she was stunned. There's no preparing for a rifle butt to the head. Even with a helmet on, it hurt like hell. She saw Cooper's face over hers.

"You okay, soldier?"

She struggled to get up and Cooper gave her a hand.

"I'll live. I don't think they're supposed to hit us though, are they?"

He smiled. He didn't seem like a bad guy, none of them really did. But one of them had hit her. It was hard to tell out here what was right and wrong, who was good and bad. All she knew was she was done for the day.

❖

Jan ran hard along the lakefront path. On Saturday mornings it was crowded with office workers running, biking, and skating away whatever troubles the week had brought them. The week had delivered a couple of whoppers to Jan. A teenager who didn't want to be found and a woman who couldn't be caught. Jan had no doubt that Catherine's brusque behavior that morning was her way of saying the night before had been a mistake. That Jan was a mistake. Jan thought the night before told her only one thing, that she'd never been with a woman like Catherine and she wanted more. Maybe that was two things. She wanted more than she could have, at any rate, and everything about it felt brand new.

She turned around at Monroe Harbor and headed back north. It was another glorious fall day and the lake sparkled under the blue sky. Across Lake Shore Drive, the Chicago skyline spread along the lakefront. Powerful, beautiful, and in some ways more mesmerizing than the lake itself. When Jan arrived in Chicago at age twenty, she had no feeling about the city other than it was where her new girlfriend wanted to live. Now, almost twenty years later, she couldn't imagine living anywhere else.

She and Josie had come to the city when Josie's brother Dan said he could get her a job at an advertising agency. Josie was twenty-two and had an art degree. Jan had managed to get her GED in LA and hoped to go to college, but she had no money or any real notion of how that was going to happen. By the time Josie had put enough money together for them to move out of Dan's crappy apartment in Uptown, she had fallen in love with an account executive at the agency and moved into her Gold Coast high-rise. Jan was homeless. Again. She took a room at the downtown Y and started selling speed and cocaine for one of Dan's friends. She had applications in for a dozen jobs, but very little money in her pocket. One hour of peddling drugs on the streets near the Board of Trade gave her a week's rent. The rest went to her college fund and a steady diet of hot dogs and ramen noodles.

She operated in the haze of surviving from one day to the next, which she was quite used to. The future was an opaque window. She could keep moving toward the light, but she had no idea what was behind the glass. When she'd saved enough to enroll in one of the city colleges, she took a part-time job as a security guard at TSI and gave up anything to do with drugs. She'd seen enough to know where a life of that would lead her.

She continued running north, past the chess players at Fullerton, the driving range at Diversey, the harbor at Belmont that was now empty of boats. She turned her thoughts to finding Maddy Harrington. It seemed there was no choice but to go to Michigan and try to produce some leads, but she would need her files to plot a course of action. That meant going into the office and possibly seeing Catherine. She picked up her pace.

❖

Jan picked up a file from Vivian's chair. She'd left a report on Maddy for LJ to sign prior to the first billing going out. She didn't need to see the report, but it provided cover. It was Catherine she wanted to see. She could hear her voice in the conference room, but all she could tell was that it was growing more angry by the moment. The blinds had been drawn and she couldn't see into the room.

When Catherine opened the door suddenly and looked out, Jan dropped the file as if she'd been caught doing something naughty.

"What are you doing here?" Catherine asked. She didn't sound very friendly and Jan's heart sank.

"Just grabbing a report from the Harrington file. I work most Saturdays. Sorry if I bothered you."

Jan picked up the file and turned to leave.

"You didn't bother me. I was just startled to see you."

"Okay." She started to walk away.

"Wait." Catherine came closer to her, reaching out a hand. "Will you come in for a moment?"

Jan hesitated and then let herself be led into the conference room. Catherine closed the door.

"I'm sorry the morning was so rushed," Catherine said. She stood in front of Jan, shorter by an inch or more despite her high heels. She took Jan's hands in her own. "The day's not gotten any better."

Jan looked down at their hands. Maybe she'd misunderstood?

"Are you all right? It sounded like you were arguing with someone in here."

"Did it?" Catherine stepped away and picked up a thermos from the table. "Coffee?"

"Sure." She watched her pour. Catherine handed her a cup and sat at the head of the table, pointing to the chair next to her for Jan.

"If you're worried about last night, you don't need to be," Jan said. "I understand it was a one-time thing."

Jan said a quick foxhole prayer that it hadn't been a one-time thing.

"Is that what you think I'm worried about? Apparently, everyone here thinks I have a cold heart."

"What are you talking about? You've only been here one day. How many TSI women have you had sex with?"

Catherine laughed, a sound that produced all kinds of rumblings in Jan. Cello, bow, thrum.

"Clearly, we're on a dangerous course of miscommunication. Believe me, I've not had sex with any other TSI women. I can't stop thinking about the sex I had with you."

Catherine drank her coffee and studied Jan's face.

"I only meant that the managers I met with this morning all seemed to think I was sent here to eviscerate them and their staffs."

"Who were they?"

"Let's see. Davis from Security Operations."

"Paranoid. Forget him."

"And Monroe from IT."

"He's a moron. Practically all the troubles we have here are technology related. He's right to be worried," Jan said.

"Zimmerman from Accounting."

"He should be worried too. It's unlikely your central office won't be handling most of the financial functions, right?"

Catherine stared at her. "That's true. But I'd never take lightly the elimination of someone's job. It's a horrible thing to have to do."

"Is the job situation what you were freaking out about this morning?" she asked.

"I'm sorry. I was a little rude this morning. I was mad at myself for being late to talk with these gentlemen. They were already against me before we even started, and then I made them cool their heels. But that's no excuse for being rude to you."

Jan sat back in her chair, relieved. "No need to apologize. I thought maybe you were regretting last night."

"Regret? I almost wish I did. But I haven't stopped thinking about it for a moment."

"Me neither."

They looked at each other. Jan could see the tiredness around Catherine's eyes, but she seemed much happier than a few minutes earlier. Catherine stood in front of Jan's chair and leaned down for a kiss. By the time the kiss ended, she was in Jan's lap. Jan was still in her running clothes and smelled musky, but so did Catherine.

"How long will you be in Chicago?" Jan asked. She pulled Catherine in for a kiss before she could answer. Somehow the buttons of her blouse opened halfway down.

"What was the question?" Catherine said when she came up for air.

"I wondered how long you're here before we have to say goodbye."

Catherine frowned. "I don't want to think about that."

"A few days, a week?"

"Hmm. I think I can stretch it out to a couple of weeks."

Jan kissed her again. They kissed for a long time. They were still kissing when the door to the conference room opened and Vivian stuck her head in.

"Working overtime?" she said.

Catherine and Jan flew apart. Catherine grabbed the front of her unbuttoned shirt as she tumbled out of the chair, just getting her feet under her in time to avoid a fall. Vivian laughed and closed the door behind her.

Jan drove home from the office, forcing her thoughts once again to how to find Maddy Harrington. Catherine had been mortified by Vivian walking in on them kissing, though Jan tried to reassure her that no one could be less judgmental than Vivian, at least in regard to sex. Vivian was most assuredly pro-sex. But Catherine had become all business by the time she'd straightened her blouse, so Jan took her leave. The important question had been answered for her. Catherine still wanted her. Everything else could be sorted out.

Jan's phone rang and she picked up when she saw it was Peet.

"What's up?"

"Shopping with the girls. Thought I'd call while Kevin helps them pick out dresses."

Jan laughed. "Good idea. I've seen you in a dress you picked out yourself."

"Yeah, well, I'm good with a power saw. We all have our strengths."

"Are you still worried about your job? Because I really think we're going to be fine," Jan said.

"No, I'm more worried about Maddy Harrington. Too much time is going by. Do you have anything new?"

Jan immediately felt guilty. If her mind weren't wrapped around Catherine she would have been putting every bit of time and thought into finding Maddy.

"Not really. Do you?" She sounded a little peevish.

Peet sighed. "Calm down there, sister. I only asked because you said you were going to go through those websites last night. I'm not accusing you of being a slacker. What's going on?"

Jan debated whether to tell Peet about Catherine, but dismissed the thought. She knew Peet would try to talk her out of seeing any more of her new boss and she didn't want to make any promises she couldn't keep. "Sorry. I didn't sleep well last night. We just don't have a lot to go on other than Maddy's fascination with the right-wing groups scattered all over the Internet."

"Any particular ones?" Peet asked.

"I think we need to start in Michigan. It's close by and she spent quite a bit of time looking over a few of the militia sites up there."

"What's your plan?"

Jan didn't have a plan. Just drive to Michigan and start poking around, she supposed, which really didn't constitute a plan. A wing and a prayer was more like it. And she felt reluctant to leave right away. It was Saturday afternoon. Maybe she could see Catherine later, maybe even spend Sunday showing her around Chicago, a simple thing that made it sound like she and Catherine could be a normal couple, with dinners and outings and all the small things people do to get to know each other. She'd read about this in books and seen it in movies; she didn't have any relationship experience that included courting and becoming a couple. The fact that she was already thinking of them as a couple was astonishing to her. And the fact that Catherine lived in London didn't bother her. She could do London.

"Jan?" Peet said.

"Right. Well, the plan is that we drive up to Michigan and talk to some of the people running these training camps and militia groups and hope that they've seen or heard about Maddy. I don't know where else to start. When do you want to go?"

"Crap. I was hoping we wouldn't have to leave town. Have you talked to the Harringtons?"

"No, that's your job. They like you better," Jan said.

"You could try a little harder, you know."

"Not with the Harringtons I can't. It's best I not talk to them at all."

Jan pulled into her parking garage. She heard Peet telling Kevin she'd be done in a minute.

"Okay, I'll call the Harringtons. If they approve the trip, I suppose we should go tonight. Do you at least have a starting point for us, an actual place for us to drive to?"

"Yep. Somewhere south of Detroit. But I think we should leave in the morning. Early."

"You'll get no argument from me. I'll let you know what the Harringtons say."

They rang off and Jan went into her apartment. Normally, she'd already be in Detroit no matter what the client said, but the pull of Catherine was strong. She felt guilty, but the desire to see Catherine that night easily trumped her guilt.

When Jan wasn't working on a Saturday, which was rare, she spent the time cleaning her apartment. There was very little to do. She didn't have many things, so not much got strewn about. She usually ate out, so the kitchen never needed real cleaning. She had a person come in once a week to do the bathrooms and floors. But still she always found something to fuss with, some shoes that needed polishing, a drawer that could be reorganized, a window that could be washed. The few women she'd brought home to her place usually teased her about its minimalism and sterile cleanliness, but Jan had never gotten over the satisfaction of having a place she could actually scrub clean. The cabin in the woods she'd been raised in could never have been called clean. Being simply habitable was a stretch.

But today, instead of cleaning, Jan sat down with her laptop and started Googling. Catherine Engstrom was an unusual enough name that she should be able to see right off whether there was anything on the Internet about her. And in 0.485 seconds she could see there was a lot. Not much of it was concerned with her work at Chartered Global Security. A website called London Arts Beat showed a photo of Catherine and a beautiful woman posing at the entrance to a building. The caption read: *Celebrated painter Ellen Sanderson hosted a reception at the opening of her new show at the Grimes-Brimley Gallery in Chelsea last evening. Accompanying her was her partner, Catherine Engstrom.*

Jan saw that the date of the opening was exactly a month ago. She closed the laptop, went to her freezer, and pulled out a bottle of vodka. Almost as soon as she poured some down her throat she had to lean over the sink and throw it back up.

Packages and paper were strewn throughout David's house, making it look like the aftermath of a savage Christmas party for camping and gun enthusiasts. Boxes of ammunition were stacked next to rifles and shotguns. Down coats were piled high like snowdrifts on the furniture while winter weight army boots lined one wall as if waiting for a platoon to muster. When Maddy, Kristi, and Tommy came through the door in the middle of the night, they tripped over power tools and landed on cookware. David flipped on the living room light as he came in behind them.

"Careful there! We can't afford to break anything."

"Well, can you afford to break people?" Kristi asked. "'Cause I'm about broke, I gotta tell you."

David laughed. "You're unbreakable, Kristi. Strong as an ox. You're just tired is all."

"She's not the only one," Tommy said. He made his way into the kitchen and sat at the rickety table. Maddy sat beside him. She was worn out and her head hurt from taking the rifle butt to her helmet. She was still pissed off about it. No one at the training camp seemed to take the incident seriously.

"I can't believe we have to go back to that place tomorrow," Tommy said. He looked as miserable as he had all day. "There's not one thing I learned there that seems useful to me."

Maddy had to agree. Unless they were planning on hunting in the dark in Idaho, the entire six-hour exercise that evening had been a painful waste of time. Learning how to lob hand grenades didn't seem useful for hunting elk and deer. Knowing counter ambush techniques, fighting positions, and wetlands ambush practice seemed absurd. But everyone involved in the training took it damn seriously.

"Tommy, you've always been big on learning for the sake of learning. Just think of it that way," David said. "I can't get these guys to give us a tailor-made weekend of training. Can't afford to, anyway. We take what we need and don't worry about the rest."

Kristi sat across from Maddy and took her field cap off. Her hair stuck up in a thousand different directions. "I don't know. It all may come in handy. We don't know what's waiting for us out in Idaho. It's the Wild West, right? Maybe we'll have to defend our land."

Maddy thought about their property's real estate brochure, which went on for paragraphs about how suited the acreage was for living a survivalist lifestyle. There were "defensible ridges" where you could take the high ground and track the movements of others approaching your land. If nothing else, she thought it possible they'd have to defend themselves against extremist groups in the area.

"I think I'll just pass on tomorrow's training," Maddy said. "I've been wounded in battle today."

"That son of a bitch," Kristi said. "I can't wait for tomorrow so I can take him down." She looked fierce. Then she looked back at Maddy and her face softened. "I've got some Vicodin. Do you need some?"

"You've got Vicodin?" Maddy said.

"Sure. Steady source of it." She said this as if she were talking about school supplies. Tommy groaned.

"I don't understand. Are you an addict or something?" Maddy said.

Kristi laughed. "Oh, hell no. I'm not stupid."

"Kristi's resourceful," David said. "That's one of the things she brings to the table for us."

"Thanks, man," Kristi said. She smoothed her hair down. "But like I was saying, if you're head hurts bad, I can give you something for it. Maybe you'll feel different about going tomorrow."

"She's going tomorrow," David said. "We need to be strong here, because we're going to have to be twice as strong in Idaho. Right, Maddy?"

They all looked at her. Maddy wasn't used to doing things she didn't want to do. Her parents seldom made her do anything. But she didn't want to look like the weakest link in a chain of weak links.

"Let me sleep on it. I feel like shit."

"Yeah, let's let her sleep on it," Kristi said. "Where are we all sleeping, anyway?"

Tommy looked alert for the first time in hours.

"Kristi, you sleep downstairs with Maddy. Tommy will bunk with me," David said. "Diane will meet back up with us tomorrow."

"Great," Kristi said. "Come on, Maddy. Let's get you to bed."

Maddy didn't know if she liked the sound of that. Kristi suddenly seemed eager.

"But there's only the one mattress down there. Where's Kristi going to sleep?"

David smiled. "Get used to community living, sweetheart. Kristi and you are going to have to share the mattress tonight."

Kristi got up and came around the table. Maddy felt like she was about to be escorted to the honeymoon suite. "Come on, kid. Let's get you to bed. Your head must be splitting."

David kept smiling as they left the room. Maddy's head was pounding and she was starting to consider the Vicodin. When they got down to the basement, Kristi looked at the shabby corner where Maddy slept.

"Look how nice you made this," she said. "It's not half bad. Which side of the bed do you want?"

That was a strange question. Maddy had never shared a bed with anyone. Why would it make any difference which side she had?

"It doesn't matter."

"You sure? Because I always like the left side. I don't know why. I was once with a girl who insisted on the left side and I knew I had to get rid of her."

There it is, Maddy thought. Kristi's a lesbian. She felt simultaneously thrilled and terrified. She'd never had sex with anyone, but when she imagined it, boys never came to mind. But neither did someone like Kristi.

Maddy made quick work of washing up. She asked Kristi to turn around when she used the toilet. Then she put on a T-shirt and shorts and slipped into the bed while Kristi brushed her teeth.

"I am so psyched about getting out of this town," Kristi said. She was talking as she sat on the toilet. "I don't know what your story is yet, but if it's anything like mine, the idea of a place that isn't all fucked up is like heaven to me. This town is dead. Dead to me."

"Did you ever think of just moving to another town?" Maddy said.

"I tried it. I went to Kalamazoo and then to Lansing. It's the same thing everywhere. No one wants to hire me, or if they do it's for shit jobs. I want to build something for myself."

That wasn't so different from what Maddy wanted. She was going to suggest to Kristi that she could try getting an education and find better work, but then she remembered that she was a high school dropout herself.

Kristi got into bed with the same T-shirt she'd been wearing all day. She smelled earthy, but not in an entirely unpleasant way. Maddy could feel her warmth. Or was it her own warmth? Suddenly there was warmth, and she wasn't sure what was happening.

"So what's your story?" Kristi asked. "Did you just graduate from high school this year and decide to leave everything? What did your parents say?"

Kristi was leaning on one elbow, looking down at Maddy.

"I'm not really close to my parents. I'd say they aren't in the loop on this decision."

"You mean they don't know?"

"Well, they know I'm gone, but they don't know where."

"Huh." Kristi considered this. "Well, as long as you're eighteen they don't have a say, do they?"

"That's the whole point, really. I don't want anyone to have a say in what I do."

Kristi lay down with her arms behind her head. The tip of her elbow was next to Maddy's temple. She felt like rubbing her head against it, but she didn't. They were silent for a few minutes.

"How's your head?"

"It'll be okay. Sleep will help."

"Let me feel where he hit you." Kristi raised herself again and gently touched the side of Maddy's head. Maddy lay frozen, but she didn't protest. "Yeah, there's a little knot. It's not too bad. You want that Vicodin?"

"No. We have to get up in a few hours. I'll be a mess."

"So you're going to go tomorrow?"

"Do you think I have to?"

"Yeah. I think if we're all going to make this trip together, you kind of have to."

"That's what I thought."

More silence.

"So much for no one having a say in what you do," Kristi said.

Maddy laughed, maybe for the first time that day. Or that month. She lay awake listening as Kristi's breathing deepened. She felt far from sleep now, the body next to her so foreign. The more she thought about Kristi lying next to her, the more wide-awake she felt. She rolled quietly out of the bed and headed upstairs for some water, the cement of the basement floor cold on her feet. The house was dark, but as she stood in the kitchen with a glass in her hand she heard noises down the hallway to the bedrooms. She put the glass down and crept toward it. There were three bedrooms, with the doors to the two smaller ones open. The third was at the end of the hall, where a hint of light showed at the bottom of its closed door. As Maddy got closer she heard David's voice.

"Yes, yes. Like that. Good boy, like that."

Then there were some unintelligible words and other noises. Maddy wasn't naïve. She'd watched porn on the Internet like everyone else. Tom and David were having sex, obviously. But if Tommy and David were getting it on, what was the deal with Diane the girlfriend? She turned around and tiptoed back to the kitchen before taking another long drink of water. She wondered what else was going on that she didn't know about.

❖

Jan threw her overnight bag into the backseat of her Jeep and climbed in. She put her laptop bag on the seat next to her. She'd been tempted to leave it behind, afraid she'd find herself obsessively searching the Internet for more bad news about Catherine. After throwing up over the first bit of information about Catherine's long-term and apparently well-known relationship with a London artist, Jan had sat back down to torture herself with more news items and photographs of them together. By the time it had grown dark in her apartment, she'd finally had enough. She called Peet.

"I'm headed up to Michigan."

"I know. I'm going with you, remember?"

Jan could hear Lily in the background. It sounded like Peet was in the car.

"I'm going now. You'll have to meet me up there."

Peet sighed. "What's going on, Jan? Did something new come up?"

"I just can't wait any longer. This will give me a head start in the morning. Did you talk to the Harringtons?"

"They're fine with it. Now that they know she's run away and has some money, they're not as anxious. If you can call what they were anxious. At least they still want us to find her."

"That's big of them," Jan said. She pulled onto Lake Shore Drive and headed toward the Skyway.

"Where are you headed?"

"There's an area south of Detroit that seems to have a number of groups that have these weekend things."

"Well, I can't break away now. I'll have to catch up to you. Check in with me in the morning, okay?"

"Right." Jan threw her phone on the seat. It immediately rang. Jan saw Catherine's name on the screen and when she grabbed it, it felt like a hot coal in her hand. She was speeding down the Drive, just as it sharply curved before Monroe Harbor. Her eyes flicked from phone to road and back again until finally the call went to voice mail. It was the second call from Catherine in the last hour. She'd not allowed herself to listen to the first message, but now she played both.

"Jan, it's Catherine. I'm so mortified that the secretary found us like that. My God, the word will be all through the office by the time I get in on Monday morning. Well, nothing to be done about it. I'm not saying I'd do anything differently. The fact is that you've been on my mind almost constantly since we were together. I'm sorry if that sounds like too much, but I want to be honest with you. Can we see each other tonight? Call me as soon as you can."

And the second message: *"It's Catherine again. Sorry if I seem like a pest. I'm just wondering if you got my message earlier. Would love to see you if I can. Maybe you're busy. I suppose you have a whole life I still know nothing about. I'm being presumptuous. Can't help wanting to see you, though. Call me if you can."*

Jan threw the phone back down. She didn't toss it onto the seat, but threw it into the well of the passenger side, out of reach. She tried to guess what Catherine imagined Jan's life was so busy with that she couldn't call her back. Parties, theater dates, poetry readings, cooking dinner for friends? Those were the kinds of things that probably kept Catherine and her artsy girlfriend busy on the weekends, while Jan patrolled her apartment looking for things to clean. Was Catherine planning on telling Jan about her relationship? Probably not. Jan was a proverbial port in the storm, to be forgotten as soon as Catherine went back to England and her high profile life.

There was more on the Internet about Catherine than just her relationship with the painter. There was the news that Catherine had been an officer at MI6, the British security agency. She'd left the agency four years earlier, a fact revealed in an *Evening Standard* piece on "The Painter and the Spy." The gay and lesbian websites had a lot of fun with that, though Jan didn't imagine it went down well in MI6 headquarters. She wondered why Catherine left. Surely not to join Chartered Global Security. It was a step down, as far as Jan could tell.

Halfway to Detroit, the phone rang again, still out of reach. She pulled into the emergency lane and scooped up the phone. It was Catherine again, and Jan waited for her voice mail.

"Now you'll think I'm a clingy, needy thing who can't stop ringing you. You'll have the constables called on me. But I'm not needy or clingy as a general rule; you can feel safe about that. I am, I'm afraid, rather desperate to talk to you, though, and I'm not quite sure what that's about. I just have a bad feeling. I feel deep down that you would call if there weren't something wrong. Would you put me out of my misery please and give me a ring?"

Jan felt her resolve weakening. She pulled back on to the interstate and tried to empty her mind of everything except Maddy Harrington. She'd find her or find something out about her from someone. She'd follow the lead, which would then take her to another lead, and so on until she found Maddy. She understood how to do that and felt confident. What she didn't know how to do was let Catherine know she'd found out about her girlfriend. She wouldn't admit to Catherine that she'd managed to break her heart after one night together. She threw the phone under the seat.

CHAPTER SIX

Jan checked out of the Super 8 Motel and headed south out of Ypsilanti. She'd plotted a course that would take her through several counties of southeastern Michigan, each of which contained at least a few of the advertised gathering spots for the known militia and survivalist groups. She knew from scouring Maddy's Internet activity that she'd concentrated on the websites of two or three groups in particular, and it would take most of the day to cover the ground necessary to reach their locations.

She felt relieved to be on the road. The long night in the motel had amped up her already agitated state. She spent all her waking time on the Internet, rereading the articles on Catherine as if compiling more evidence of her callousness would make her feel better. She didn't miss the irony of thinking Catherine was callous, a label she'd been pasted with herself by more than one bed partner. And wasn't that what she was to Catherine, a bed partner? Well, so what? That would have been the attitude she'd normally have herself. But there had been too much fire the couple of times she'd been with Catherine to compare it to any past experience, and the idea of not having more of it was causing too much pain. She stood a far better chance of finding Maddy than of finding a solution to her Catherine problem.

After an hour on Highway 23, she veered east and pulled into a gas station in a tiny town along a county road. She picked up some bottled water and paid for her gas in the store. The clerk was a spotty teenager with a cigarette hanging out of his mouth and his camouflage cap pulled low.

"Quiet around here," Jan said.

He squinted at her through the smoke. "Tell me about it."

"I'm trying to find an outfit called the Third Regimental Militia. I think they train around here. You know anything about them?"

"Nope." He handed over her change and turned away to continue stocking condoms on a rack.

"Does that mean you've never heard of them?"

He glanced back at her. "I've heard of them. I just don't know anything about them. Ain't my business."

"You never thought of joining up?" Jan asked.

"Hell, no. Bunch of losers. They're all like my dad's age. It's pathetic."

"So you don't agree with their philosophy?"

"I don't know shit about their philosophy. I just know I won't be caught dead running around the woods playing army. They come in here sometimes after they've been out training. It's so sad."

Jan passed a photo of Maddy across the counter. "You ever see this girl around here?"

The boy studied the photo. "You mean with these Third Regiment guys? You're joking? She's like my age. And a girl."

"That's a no?"

He stubbed out his cigarette and laughed. "It's a no. If you're thinking these guys are some sort of evil gang kidnapping girls and shit, you're way wrong."

"Why do you say that?"

"You know how you can tell people are badasses? These guys aren't that. I think they just like to play with guns."

Jan left him with a card and the photo and got a promise that he'd call if Maddy showed up. She headed back on the county road and followed it through a densely wooded stretch before braking sharply to pull into a small gravel parking lot that served as a trailhead. The lot was full of pickup trucks, and at one end of it a card table was set up with a sign that said "Third Regiment—Sign In." A middle-aged man sat at the table wearing cammies, and he appeared to be the only person around. He watched as Jan parked and walked toward him, his hand reaching for a walkie-talkie sitting on the table.

"Good morning," he said, politely enough. "What can I do for you?"

"Good morning. My name is Jan Roberts and I'm investigating the disappearance of a minor from the Chicago area."

The man looked alarmed. "Why are you here?"

Jan passed another copy of the photo over. "We have reason to believe she was interested in joining up with one of the militia groups in this area. Have you seen her?"

"Goodness, no. She's just a child. We have no minors as members of our group."

Jan looked closely at the man and saw someone who would be happy as a member of the Lions or Elks or Moose or some other community service organization that gave men a reason to hang out together. Maybe they didn't have those places anymore.

"I don't imagine you'd mind if I take a look myself?" Jan said.

"Oh, I couldn't let you just go back there. This is a private organization, after all, and they're back there with real guns. I think you'll just have to take my word for it."

Jan paused. "I think we can find some compromise here. This looks like public land. There's nothing stopping me from heading in there if I chose to. But why don't you pick up your radio and call your, what would you call him, your superior officer? Let him know it's important I talk to him to eliminate your group from suspicion."

The man looked seriously worried, but he picked up the radio. "Base to Leader."

Jan watched as he stared at the crackling radio. When the response came he jumped a little, as if it were the last thing he expected to happen.

"What's up, Hap?"

"We have a lady here I think you need to talk to. She seems to think we have some girl back there with you all."

They spent an inordinate amount of time trying to understand each other, while Jan wondered if she should even waste her time going back there. Her gut told her Maddy hadn't joined up with these folks. Still, when a man trotted out to escort her to the training site, Jan was curious enough.

"I'm John Gage," he said, extending his hand. "How is it we can help you?"

When Jan explained her search for Maddy and why she was looking at local militias, John started walking with her toward the trail.

"You're welcome to come back and see our training site. The last thing we want is to have anyone thinking we're harboring minors. We have enough bad press as it is."

"Do you mean you, the Third Regiment?"

"We're all painted with the same brush down here. Just the word 'militia' makes everyone think we're like Timothy McVeigh, that bastard. Excuse my French."

"So you're not plotting to overthrow the government?"

"No, ma'am."

"How would you describe your outfit?"

"I'd say we're all citizens who are proud of using the word militia in its original sense of the word. A group of regular men who care about their community and want to protect it should there be a breakdown of law and order, or a catastrophe of some sort. We're not here to cause the breakdown or catastrophe."

"Is it all men in your group?" Jan asked.

"There are two women, but you probably won't be able to pick them out covered up in their cammies. They're about as tough as they come. Good girls, though."

They followed a trail for a hundred yards or so to a clearing. There were about two acres of land and a small pond surrounded by the woods and dotted with groups of men doing all kinds of things that Jan couldn't take in all at once. Target practice was on one side of the clearing, people were grappling with each other in the middle, and other groups were exercising and marching here and there. She saw a line of men coming into the clearing from the other side of the pond, rifles at the ready and helmets on their heads. Apparently, they'd just been on some kind of scouting mission.

John led her over to the hand-to-hand combat fighters, where a tall man in a pristine BDU was overseeing the action.

"Colonel, this is that lady from Chicago that Hap called in about. I think you should set her straight that we don't have any teenage girls here."

The colonel looked down at Jan with a frozen expression on his face. It was impossible for Jan to not flash back to another clearing in the woods, another colonel, a cold gaze looking down at her. She disliked the man on sight.

She explained why she was looking for Maddy and handed him the photo. The colonel made no move to take it.

"Never seen her."

"Is it possible that she's here without you knowing it? There're a lot of folks out there, and from here they all look alike."

"Not possible. I know all of my soldiers."

"Okay. It won't bother you, I assume, if I just walk around? It would help me to get a sense of what you all are doing during these training camps."

The colonel's expression remained unchanged. "I'd appreciate it if you'd allow Lieutenant Gage to escort you back to your car. I won't have our training time disrupted."

Jan stared back at the man, weighing her options. There weren't many. She could leave kicking and screaming, or she could leave on her own. She didn't doubt she had to leave, for she recognized the steel in his eyes.

"I hope you realize that I will find this girl, and if we find that she's being harbored by, or worse, held by your outfit here it will be very bad for you."

The colonel didn't react. "Your girl is not here. I have no use for her."

Jan believed him. He was a man who brooked no nonsense, and having a teenage girl in his camp would be a whole lot of nonsense in his eyes. She turned without saying good-bye and marched back through the woods, with Gage trying to keep up beside her. She gave him a card before climbing into her car.

"He's all business during training, but the colonel's really a nice guy. He's the pastor at the Methodist church," Gage said.

"I'm sure he's a sweetheart," Jan said and drove off. She pulled at her collar as if it were choking her. If this fake colonel weren't tall like her father, weren't dressed in uniform like her father, if he didn't glare at her like her father, the interview would be just one of a thousand she'd conducted in her years as an investigator. The kind where her instinct and experience guided her. Instead, it felt like Jan had been the one under scrutiny. She felt uncomfortable to the bone.

She pulled into a roadhouse for coffee and a sandwich and texted Peet with details of her next location and her estimated arrival time. Peet should be well on her way to the area by now and she'd be glad for the company. She wasn't sure she was able to read these militia guys correctly. Peet's presence would calm her down. It always did.

A text came in from Peet: "Place and Time received. You'll be met there." Seemed a pretty odd way to put it, Jan thought.

❖

Maddy's head felt fine as she stood in formation early Sunday morning. The man who had hit her on the helmet the night before stood at attention across from her in one of the four lines formed up to listen to Sergeant Drecker run down the day's activities. He cast a malevolent eye at her, which Kristi returned in kind. Maddy felt an intense longing for her computer and a quiet room.

"Last night's exercises ran you through the basics of night ops. Today, we cover as much as we can fit in that will give you the elements of basic guerilla techniques. Why guerilla warfare? Isn't that what those folks resort to against our army? If you're asking yourself those questions, I need only point you to our founders, folks, a guerilla army without peer. We're not here to play like we're in the US Army. We're here to prepare ourselves to protect against an army. We are a militia. We arm ourselves and we use what is at hand.

"Today, we'll use the varied terrain on our land to practice ambush techniques, escape and evasion, firing and reloading under high stress conditions, hand signals, use of spotting scopes, and radio communications. We will end the day with a hostage silhouette shoot off. Those of you with your own weapons, prepare to present them for inspection. Those using our weapons, report to Corporal Gast."

The lines broke formation and Maddy and Kristi moved to a van where a young man was handing out Romanian SKS rifles and checking them off on a clipboard. The gun felt as heavy and awkward to Maddy as it had the day before, but she moved to a table and disassembled it with ease. Kristi was still putting things back together as Maddy loaded her clip of blanks and moved away to give others more room to work. She looked out on the large open field around her and saw squads forming up with their sergeants. Tommy wasn't in their squad today, but she could see him nearby, standing miserably with his SKS cradled in his arms like a baby. He seemed more out of place than Maddy, and Maddy still felt like she'd been dropped into an alien world.

She'd seen no sign of David that morning when they got up and headed out of the house. Ed and Warren drove them in their truck, with Tommy, Kristi, and Maddy in the back, wrapped in blankets again. Maybe David was sleeping in, finally relaxed after the servicing by Tommy. Maddy found the dynamics around her impossible to fathom. It made her look to Kristi as a beacon of straightforwardness. Kristi's simplicity was her strength, as far as Maddy was concerned.

With the squad formed up, Sergeant Cooper took over as their leader and ran them through a one-hour course in moving as a group in silence, using hand signals only. Before she knew it, Maddy became absorbed in the game of it, finally learning and effectively using the signals as well as accurately reading those given by others. Cooper put her in charge of a patrol through the woods running a circle around the training grounds, spreading her team out and sending members forward this way and that. At one point, as she turned to her rear to signal those behind her, she saw Kristi with a big grin on her face, flipping her the finger. Maddy laughed and covered her mouth. She felt she might be having more fun than she ever remembered having.

Kristi and Maddy sat with other squad members at lunch, everyone breaking open MREs and complaining about them.

"If an army runs on its food," Kristi said, "we're in deep trouble."

Maddy ate and chatted and bitched and complained, and she noticed that she was saying just about the same thing as everyone else in the group. This was virtually a first, for in any group she found herself in at home she always felt she was on an entirely different frequency.

"I wonder where Tommy is," Maddy asked Kristi. They were leaning against a tree, separated now from the others.

"I have no idea. But Ed and Warren are over there," she said, pointing to a group huddling together about fifty yards away.

Maddy watched the group—Ed, Warren, Sergeant Drecker, and a man she hadn't seen before.

"Who's that guy with them?" Maddy asked.

"I think the dude's name is Jacovich. He's an officer or something. He comes to David's house sometimes."

Maddy saw David strolling up to the group, wearing the same crappy clothes he'd worn when he picked her up in Chicago. He shook hands with the officer and the group fell back into deep conversation.

"I wonder if Jacovich is going with us to Idaho?"

Kristi peered over at them and shook her head. "I don't think so. I think he's like the top dog around here. He wouldn't leave being a commander to go to Idaho."

"Why not? We're going to Idaho. Maybe he wants to be in on that life too. David did say that some guys from this regiment, or whatever it is, are going out there with us."

Kristi shrugged. "You're asking the wrong person, Maddy. I'm a grunt, remember? But I do know that when he's come in on some of our meetings he's said things like, 'When you're out there,' so I don't think he's going."

Sergeant Cooper yelled for them, and Maddy's squad formed up to head back in the woods and learn how to use their scopes and radios. As they trotted by David's group she saw that their heads were still together and the conversation was heated. She couldn't imagine what they were talking about, but was surprised to find she wasn't much interested. Scopes and radios were a lot more interesting.

❖

Jan pulled onto another of the county roads that had linked her from one camp to the next. The roads were pocked and gutted, ailing from the harsh Michigan winters and the empty county treasuries. Small towns interrupted her drive, often appearing suddenly after a long stretch of thick woods. They were tiny villages, usually with a bar and a convenience store and some auto repair shops. The bigger towns were distinguished by the presence of a Walmart, the Mecca that drew people in like a medieval market day.

Her next destination was a camp that seemed to hold the most frequent and extensive training weekends of any that Maddy visited on her Web searches. None of the websites sent up red flags as being more radical than the other in its politics. But this one, the Fifth Regiment, Michigan Militia, seemed the most organized, developed, and, by dint of size alone, influential. There were jam-packed training sessions almost every weekend, and many had waiting lists for entry. The regimental commander was listed as Major William Jacovich, USMC, Retired, so their leadership was trained military.

She'd phoned Peet twice to report on her progress and let her know when she'd be arriving at the third camp, where they were to meet up. All she'd gotten back were text messages from Peet saying "okay," which was unusually terse for Peet.

Jan was nearing the Ohio border when she finally reached the camp. Wooden signs nailed to trees guided her from the narrow county road onto a rutted dirt one. It was barely wide enough for her Jeep, and with thick woods on either side, there would be no way to move aside for an oncoming car. It was a bright afternoon, but the path to the camp felt dark and gloomy, shaded by the canopy of towering oaks and broad evergreens. More hand painted wooden signs led her through, announcing the distance left to the camp as if urging her to not lose heart and throw her car in reverse. A large pond appeared on her left and the road curved around it, finally bringing her into a parking lot. It looked like she'd pulled into an RV camp. Spread out beyond the parking lot full of pickup trucks were a dozen or so campers, each pulled into its own little camp site. By the pond was an area with picnic tables and rusty old grills. A wobbly looking dock stretched out onto the pond.

She got out of her car and stretched, reaching down to touch her toes and rolling back up until her eyes peered straight forward, toward the RVs. Just as she focused, a woman emerged from between two of the campers and Jan nearly lost her breath. It was Catherine. She blinked and looked again, and she was still there, as if she'd dropped from the skies. As Jan stood paralyzed, Catherine continued to move forward from the campers, turning her head in Jan's direction and breaking into a smile. She waved and started to jog toward her.

It took about ten seconds for Catherine to reach Jan, plenty of time for a complete roller coaster ride inside Jan's brain. Elation—Catherine had come all this way to see her. Terror—something had happened to Peet. Lust—Catherine's breasts were bouncing as she ran. Anger—how could Peet let Catherine blindside her like this? Desire—Catherine looked like no other woman she'd ever known. Relief—Catherine was here, and everything would be okay. Fear—Catherine lied and she was going to break her heart.

Jan was standing completely still when Catherine reached her.

"Hello," Catherine said cheerfully. "Fancy meeting you here and all that."

She reached for Jan's hand, and Jan shoved her hands in her pockets.

"What the hell is going on?" Jan said. Her heart was crashing against her chest.

Catherine was dressed in jeans and a black sweater with a gray silk scarf around her neck, and exquisite, dangling silver earrings.

She looked like the last person in the world you would see in this scruffy RV park. She was gorgeous, but out of place, both in the park and in Jan's life.

"First things first, Jan. Please don't be angry with Peet. I told her I was coming here in her place, ordered her to cooperate with me really. She's very worried that you'll be angry with her."

"She should be."

Catherine stood in front of Jan, looking up at her. Jan leaned against the Jeep and crossed her arms.

"I took advantage of my position, obviously, to come here in her place. It's not Peet's fault. But that's not what I want to talk to you about," Catherine said.

"I'm not here to talk about anything. I'm here to try to find Maddy Harrington."

"Yes, of course. So am I. We can sort this all out later. It's just that I was a bit terrified that you were upset with me for some reason. You didn't return my calls."

Jan didn't respond.

"I called and called, and the more time that went by that you didn't return my calls, the more I thought I'd imagined the whole thing between us," Catherine said. "It drove me crazy."

"So you ordered my partner to stand down and drove up here to confront me in the middle of an investigation?" Jan said. "That's unbelievable." She pushed herself past Catherine and started walking through the parking lot.

"I'm here now. And we have work to do. You can tell me how mad you are at me when we have dinner later."

Jan kept walking.

"I can help, you know. I am an experienced agent, after all. Perhaps you didn't know that."

Jan was about to say that she knew all about Catherine's field agent days, but she only knew that from looking her up on the Internet. She wasn't quite prepared to reveal all that she'd found. She kept walking through the parking lot and out onto the RV campground. She saw a trailhead sign posted nearby: Fifth Regiment Training. As she headed toward it with Catherine in tow, she saw a uniformed man approach the trail opening from the woods, with a clipboard in hand. He stopped short when he saw them.

"May I help you?" He was a tall and rangy man with a prominent forehead and a cleft in his chin so deep you could drop a quarter into it. Jan thought he seemed a little nervous, and his hand was hovering over the radio he wore on his belt, as if he were about to draw on her if she said the wrong thing.

"We're looking to talk with someone from your outfit about this girl," Jan said, handing over the photo of Maddy. The man took the photo and gazed at it. He wore corporal stripes on his shirt with the name "Watson" sewn to the pocket. He handed back the photo.

"What about her?" he said.

"Sounds like you may know her," Catherine said.

"No, I don't know her," Watson said. "Why are you asking me about her is what I want to know."

"We have reason to believe she's up here taking part in your training camp. We need to talk to her," Jan said. "Why don't we just head back there and take a look?"

Watson looked alarmed. "No, that's not going to happen. The major would never allow it."

Catherine and Jan looked at each other. Jan took the photo the corporal was trying to return to her, as if holding it any longer was going to get him in trouble.

"Maybe I'm not understanding something," Jan said. "You've got a bunch of folks back there who have paid money to run around in the woods with you guys for the weekend and you won't let me back there to find one of them because...why? Is there something going on there you don't want people to see?"

"If you would stay right here, ladies."

Watson stepped away a few yards and turned his back before speaking into his radio. He returned to them with more confidence.

"Someone will be here shortly to answer your questions."

"Thank you, Corporal," Catherine said. "You've been most helpful."

Watson took up a post a few yards down the trail as it started to narrow into the woods. Jan considered barging by him and running toward the training camp, but knew he was just the first in a line of defense. She could feel this camp's difference from the other two she'd visited. There was an air of caution and paranoia, which meant answers wouldn't come easily from any member of the Fifth. It also meant they'd climbed right into the top spot of likely places Maddy would be found.

"Do you think our girl is here?" Catherine whispered to her. "It seems a bloody odd spot for a young girl to run away to."

Jan paused. She didn't know if she wanted to start talking about the case with Catherine. She was mad at her. But she was also thrilled. No one had ever done anything like this for her.

"I'm going to hold my thoughts until we talk to whoever they're sending out here. I'm not convinced that so-called corporal hasn't seen Maddy before, though."

They stood awkwardly for another ten minutes before a burly man in a sergeant's uniform came running up from the trail. His face was red and his forehead wrinkled in a frown as he spotted Jan and Catherine. He wore a sidearm on his belt and had an assault rifle slung across his shoulder. He didn't look like he was playing soldiers. He was a soldier.

"You ladies have a problem here?" he asked. There would be no preliminaries with this fellow.

Jan looked at his shirt tag. "Sergeant Drecker? My name is Jan Roberts. I'm investigating the disappearance of someone and we have reason to believe she may be training with you this weekend. We'd like to take a look to see if she's here."

Jan handed the photo over and watched carefully as he peered at it. Drecker was still breathing heavily from his run, but there was no change in his stony face as he handed it back to Jan.

"I have no idea why you're looking here, lady, but I've never seen that girl."

"That girl is a minor, Sergeant. She has parents who are worried sick about her. You can understand that we would feel more comfortable having a look ourselves."

Drecker made quite a show of hocking up some spit and sending it flying to the right of where Jan stood. Catherine had an amused look on her face.

"Not going to happen. This is private property, and unless you have some kind of warrant, I'm not letting you back there. You're going to have to take my word that your girl isn't here."

"Is it a warrant you want?" asked Jan. "I think I can arrange for that, but of course it will mean that I'm accompanied by the local sheriff. That might be interesting for you. I mean, I'm just looking for a girl. But law enforcement? They might be interested in all kinds of things you guys have back there."

Drecker stepped in closer and leaned toward Jan. "Believe me, lady. We are not worried about what the local sheriff might find. If you can get the judge to get you a warrant on a Sunday, by all means come on back and I'll give you the tour. Until then, I'll ask you to leave our property."

The corporal was standing right behind Drecker, ready to act if necessary. Jan sighed and slipped one of her cards into Drecker's shirt pocket. "I can see you're going to force us to do this the hard way. We'll be back." Jan and Catherine turned to leave.

Drecker turned back toward the trail, breaking into a double-time trot. The corporal took up a post at the trailhead.

Catherine followed Jan to her Jeep.

"I don't know what sort of reactions you got at the other camps you visited," Catherine said, "but it feels to me like they know who she is."

"Yep." Jan unlocked her car and started to climb in.

"Wait! What are you doing?"

"I'm getting in my car. Get in if you want."

Catherine settled herself in the passenger seat and looked around the inside of the car. It was spotless.

"Pretty spic-and-span for an investigator's car," she said.

Jan didn't reply. She picked up her phone and hit the speed dial for Peet. The call went to voice mail. "Peet, it's me. I'm sitting up here in Michigan with Catherine in my car. Interested to hear from you how the fuck that happened. Call me."

"I thought I just explained to you how this happened," Catherine said.

"Excuse me if I don't take your word for much right now."

Catherine looked dismayed. "I know we need to talk. I'm not sure what happened, but between the time I last saw you in the conference room, which was so lovely, and now, something has become very tangled. But we need to decide what to do here about Maddy. What do you think?"

Jan's knuckles were white on the steering wheel, as if she were maneuvering a Grand Prix course instead of standing still in a parking lot. She took a deep breath.

"Do you feel like a walk in the woods?" she asked.

Catherine smiled. "That would be brilliant. Let's go find our girl."

Chapter Seven

David joined Maddy and Kristi's squad for the afternoon session on hand-to-hand combat. They were covered with mud after a half hour of practicing break and rolls, their cammies still wet from a disaster in the wetlands ambush session earlier in the day. Maddy lay on the ground and thought if she had to stand up one more time, she'd find a way to take a rifle butt to Sergeant Cooper's head.

David lay sprawled next to Maddy, a smile on his face as he looked over at her. "Isn't this great?"

"I'd rather be coding," she said.

"Come on, Maddy. You can't live your whole life in your head. This is good for you. We're going to be a cohesive unit out in Idaho."

She looked at him and shook her head. "If you say so. It seems to me we'd be better off learning how to chop wood and plant seeds than learning about choke holds and pressure points. But call me crazy."

Sergeant Cooper ordered them up for the next round of exercises. Kristi groaned and hauled herself up. "All I know is I could eat an entire elk right now. I already know how to field dress and butcher it, so I've got that covered for us."

She leaned over to give Maddy a hand up. "Come on, you wimp. Let's practice some more of that close quarters stuff. It's fun."

They lined up facing each other, half the people with dummy knives in their hands, the other half crouched to ward off the attack.

Maddy worried a little at the gleam in Kristi's eye as she stood across from her. Tommy was next to her, standing more slumped than crouched. He stared at David across from him and looked like he was just waiting to be impaled.

Kristi was just moving in with her knife when Sergeant Drecker ran up to their group and pulled David out of the line, holding him by the elbow.

"Sergeant Cooper, dismiss your squad."

"What?" Cooper said.

"You heard me, Sergeant. We're bugging out."

Drecker dragged David a few yards away and began to speak to him. Maddy could tell he was furious. Behind them, they could see Major Jacovich approaching. Something was up.

"Okay, form up. Time to break down and clean weapons," Cooper said.

The squad picked up their rifles and lined up behind Cooper, who led them back across the field to the weapons van. As they walked near Drecker and David, Maddy saw David look over at her. He didn't look happy.

"What the fuck is going on?" asked Kristi.

"I have no idea," Maddy said. But she did. She saw Jacovich look over at her too, and his face was murderous. They must have found out she was a runaway. But how? She couldn't imagine her parents tracking her to a militia training camp in Michigan. She may as well be on the moon as far as they were concerned.

All around the camp the various small groups were packing up whatever they were doing and moving toward the mustering point. People sat on the ground to break open their weapons and begin cleaning them, while sergeants moved from group to group and told them to speed it up. She looked over to where she'd last seen David and saw Drecker and David running toward her. Fast. For a second, she thought of running away from them.

"Maddy," David said, as he stopped in front of her. "You have to come with us."

"Now," Drecker said, reaching for her arm to pull her up.

"Whoa, there," Kristi said. "What's going on?" She stood and moved toward Drecker.

"Not now, Kristi. We have to get Maddy out of here," David said.

Drecker and David got on either side of Maddy and started back across the field, each holding an elbow. Kristi trotted behind them.

"I don't know where you dudes think you're taking her, but I'm going with."

They didn't respond. Maddy stayed quiet and tried to figure out the best approach. Then she realized there wasn't one.

"Are you going to tell me what you're doing?" she asked David. "Have I done something wrong?"

"Do you mean other than lie to us, Maddy?"

She stopped walking. "Lie to you? What do you mean?"

"Keep walking," Drecker barked.

"Someone's come looking for you," David said. "Said you're a minor. I asked you that specifically, Maddy. You lied to me. To us."

Maddy's heart sank. They were kicking her out. Or maybe they were taking her into the woods to shoot her. She wasn't entirely sure which would be worse. As messed up as her little group seemed, she was surprised to feel panic at the idea of not being a part of them.

"I don't understand," she said. "Who came looking for me?"

"Shut up," said Drecker.

They reached the edge of the woods farthest from the entrance to the training field and started down a slim trail. Drecker led, with Maddy behind him, then David and Kristi. They moved at a clip, and whenever Maddy tried to ask questions, Drecker told her to shut up. She turned to David several times, but his face was frozen and he stared down at the trail in front of him. After a half hour's hike, they came out on a small access road that cut through the woods along a row of electrical towers. A pickup truck waited for them there with Corporal Watson behind the wheel.

"The two of you, get in the back," Drecker ordered. Maddy and Kristi scrambled into the truck bed and he threw a tarp over them. "Don't move until I tell you to." Drecker and David climbed into the cab with Watson and they drove off.

Maddy was laying flat on her back with the cold and heavy tarp draping her face and the handle of a sledgehammer wedged under her hip. Kristi was lying on her stomach beside her, her chin propped on her hands like they were having a chat at a slumber party. She didn't look very happy, though.

"What the fuck, Maddy?"

"What?"

"Is it true you're a minor? I knew it. There was something weird about you just showing up like that."

"I didn't just show up," Maddy said. "I've been helping David plan this whole thing all along."

"Well, he didn't know you were a kid. This is fucked up. We could have police swarming all over the place now."

Maddy stayed still. She didn't like Kristi being unhappy with her. And David had looked ready to throw her into the pond. She could hear voices arguing in the cab of the truck. She didn't know if they were driving her to a police station or to someplace where they could handle the situation on their own, whatever that might mean.

"Where do you think they're taking us?" Maddy asked.

"Hell if I know. I hope it's somewhere close and they have a toilet. I have to pee something fierce."

Maddy rummaged in her pants pocket and pulled out a Snickers bar. They shared it while bouncing around under the tarp. When the truck hit a bump in the road, Kristi ended up with the candy bar smashed into her forehead. They got a very serious case of the giggles over that and Kristi moaned that she was about to pee in her pants. By the time they pulled off a main road and started bouncing again up a dirt path, they'd nearly forgotten what had started the journey in the first place.

The truck finally stopped and Drecker pulled the tarp off them and ordered them out. They were in a small clearing in the woods. Watson was walking toward a tiny cabin while David stood with Drecker.

"What is this place?" asked Maddy.

"This is where we're going to hide you until we can figure out what to do," David said. "I don't know if you realize the position you've put us in, Maddy."

"Well, I don't even understand what all is happening. Who came looking for me? I can't believe it was my parents."

"Worse. It was a private investigator," Drecker said. "That means she's paid to find you and she probably won't go away just cause we ask her to. You two aren't at a pay grade privileged enough to know just how much this can fuck us up, so no more questions."

Drecker marched up to the cabin after Watson. Kristi ducked into the woods to pee. Maddy looked up at David and saw a mix of anger and fear on his face.

"I'm sorry, David. I didn't mean to get you in trouble."

"Drecker and Jacovich are really pissed off." He looked down at Maddy and she saw that he was more afraid of them than mad at her.

"I don't understand what they have to do with it anyway," she said. "What do they care whether I'm a minor or not?"

"They care because they want to see us set up in Idaho. They don't want their organization to draw heat for harboring a minor, especially a girl."

"How much do they have to do with Idaho?"

David looked behind him at the cabin and then over where Kristi was emerging from behind a tree, zipping her pants. "Did you honestly think that your twenty thousand dollars and the six of us were going to be able to set up a homestead in Idaho?" he whispered.

Drecker yelled at them from the porch of the cabin to come up. The cabin was so small that he looked odd standing there, as if he were in front of a deluxe doghouse. Watson came out of the cabin and stood next to him and they watched with hooded eyes as David, Kristi, and Maddy walked up.

"You two girls are going to stay here until we come back to get you. There's water and MREs inside, outhouse in back. Don't try to leave. If you hike out, we'll find you and then I will turn you in to the authorities." He was glaring at Maddy.

"Wait a second. You're going to leave us here without a car?" Kristi said. "I've got places I gotta be."

"Yeah? What places?" Drecker asked.

Kristi shrugged. "Places. Not here, anyway."

"You can come back with us, Kristi," David said. "It's Maddy we're keeping out of sight."

Maddy looked at Kristi and tried to keep her face still. She felt panicked at the idea of being left alone.

"Forget it," Kristi said. She put her arm around Maddy. "I'm not leaving her alone here. Are you crazy?"

Drecker moved off the porch. "We'll be back within twenty-four hours. Be ready to move."

The three men went back to the truck without another word and drove off. Once they were gone, the silence almost overwhelmed Maddy. She felt like she was in a fairy tale, left in the middle of a forest, with who knows what sort of creatures hiding behind trees. She spun in a slow circle, but other than the tiny road out of the clearing, there was nothing but thick woods all around. Winnetka seemed very far away.

"This is totally crazy," Kristi said. She stomped up the step to the cabin and banged in through the door. "Let's see what we've got here."

Inside was an eight by eight foot room with a fireplace, two cots, a wobbly table, and one chair. Two crude windows had been cut in the wood siding, but the room was very dark. A rusty lantern stood on the table, with a bottle of kerosene next to it. Kristi opened a metal footlocker between the cots and found some blankets and camp pillows and she set about making up the cots. Maddy stood by the door and watched her.

"Ed and Warren kept telling me you were going to be trouble, and I didn't believe them," Kristi said.

Maddy felt the same way she always did when she learned anyone had been talking about her. A hot flash of something—indignation, shame, fear—shot through her and made her face heat up.

"I don't know what the big deal is," she said. "It's not like I'm twelve. I know what I'm doing."

Kristi turned to her with her hands on her hips. Maddy guessed she was trying to look stern, but she wasn't quite able to pull it off.

"Listen, men freak out when an underage girl is found with them. They can get into big trouble, even if you think you're all grown up and know what you're doing. And these guys are rabid when it comes to anyone knowing what they're up to."

Maddy sat on the chair while Kristi stretched out on one of the cots and put her hands behind her head, staring at the ceiling.

"How old are you, anyway?" Kristi said.

"I'll be seventeen next week."

"Seventeen going on forty. I totally believed you when you said you were eighteen."

"I'm sorry I lied to you."

"Why'd you run away?"

Maddy paused. She knew it would be hard to explain leaving Winnetka and her new car and her hands-off parents. But the idea of going back there made the little cabin seem like heaven. Its stark furnishings felt warmer to her than the sterile environment at home.

"Have you ever run away?" Maddy asked.

Kristi snorted. "Is the Pope Catholic? I was out my window every other week, it seemed."

"Why did you want to leave home?"

Kristi was quiet for a moment. "You know how it is. Dad comes home drunk, looks for something to hit. After Mom left, his favorite target was gone, so he started picking on me."

"Where'd your mom go?" Maddy asked.

"I don't know. I woke up one day when I was twelve and she was gone. I don't blame her though."

Maddy thought that was unlikely. What kind of mom leaves her kid with a drunk, violent father? And what kind of person wouldn't hate her for doing it?

"I hung around as long as I could 'cause I have two little brothers. But as soon as they were big enough to take care of themselves, I left for good. My father never whipped the boys, but anyways, they got big enough to whip him right back."

"So how old were you when you left for good?"

Kristi paused again. "I was sixteen."

"Well, there you go."

Kristi raised herself on one elbow and looked at Maddy. "I'm not going to worry about whether you're too young to be away from home. I know you're not. I'm just worried that David will leave you behind when we head out to Idaho."

"Do you think he'd do that?"

"I don't think he would. But Drecker might talk him into it. I guess we'll have to wait and see."

Kristi got up and found some MREs in the footlocker. "Do you want spaghetti and meatballs or beef stew?"

"Um, beef stew?"

"Good choice." She brought the MREs to the table and showed Maddy how to warm up her stew with the heater in the pack. She set out the crackers and cookies and plastic forks and arranged it all as if they were sitting down to eat at home just like anyone else. "Look at this! They give you toilet paper in these things, and instant coffee, and blueberry cobbler. This ain't too bad."

Their stews burbled in their flameless heat packs while Maddy considered how Kristi seemed to make every obstacle something to be enjoyed. She wanted to be at least a little like that. She'd take some of that joy with her blueberry cobbler, please.

After dinner, Kristi built a fire while Maddy went out in the dark to use the outhouse. She carried the sputtering kerosene lamp with her, but one peek in the outhouse and she headed for the woods to squat there instead. The outhouse wasn't foul smelling, but it was terrifying. She heard scrabbling and scurrying when she opened the door. The woods in the dark were terrifying too. She peed as fast as she could and ran back to the cabin, where the inside looked cheery. Kristi was sitting cross-legged in front of the fireplace, poking at the logs with a stick and whistling. Maddy sat next to her. All they needed was some s'mores.

"Why'd you come with me, Kristi?" Maddy picked up a stick and started poking at the logs too. Their sticks clacked together in the fire.

"I wanted to make sure you'd be okay," Kristi said. "You looked scared."

"I did not."

Kristi looked at her with a smile. "Please. You might have been able to hide your age from me, but there was no mistaking that look on your face. But hell, I'd have been scared too. That Drecker dude is intense."

"So you wanted to what? Protect me?"

Kristi shrugged. "I don't know. Maybe. Maybe I just wanted to be with you."

Poke, poke. The flames danced higher and licked around their sticks. Kristi put hers down to take off her jacket. Then she picked the stick up again and stared very intently at the fire.

"What do you think of that?" Kristi said.

"What?"

"That I wanted to be with you?"

Maddy stilled her stick now in the fire and the end ignited. She shoved it the rest of the way into the flames. "I don't really know what you mean."

"I have to be honest with you. Do you know what the worst thing is about knowing you're sixteen?"

"Almost seventeen."

"It's that I was starting to have feelings for you, and now I know you're just a kid and it makes me feel like an old letch."

This was the kind of news that came as no surprise when she heard it, yet she had completely failed to anticipate it. Kind of like realizing no one was going to ask her to the prom and the dance was that night. But this surprise from Kristi cut the opposite way. It pleased her. She felt startled in a way that made her stomach feel funny. She looked at Kristi, who was still poking at the fire.

"I don't think you're an old letch, Kristi."

"Well, you wouldn't. But people my age or older would. And I'm not one who'd take advantage of a kid. That would be wrong."

They sat for a while longer with the fire. Maddy felt unwilling to say anything to Kristi, afraid the wrong thing would come out of her mouth, because she wasn't sure what the right thing would be. Finally, as they were getting ready to turn in, she touched Kristi on the arm.

"Thanks for being honest with me, especially since I haven't been honest with you."

"That's okay. Did I freak you out?"

"No. But let's talk about this when I'm seventeen, okay?"

A big smile broke out on Kristi's face. "You're on."

❖

"It'll be dark soon," Catherine said. "I'm not sure how much farther we should go."

Jan peered ahead. The dense woods were getting close to impenetrable. They didn't have the benefit of a trail to guide them, nor a known destination. Jan led the way, picking out a route roughly parallel to the trail she'd seen Drecker travel. They hoped it would somehow burp them out onto the area where the training group was gathered. She used the compass on her phone to keep them moving in the same direction, but then they didn't really know if that was the right direction. Jan stopped.

"You may be right. Let's get back to the car and see if we can tail Drecker from the parking lot. I can hardly see a thing anymore."

They turned and headed back toward the car. Catherine moved through the woods as if she lived in Sherwood Forest instead of London, and stayed behind Jan in a clear acknowledgement of who was leading the search. They both turned when a beam of light bounced off the broad tree trunks in front of them.

"Looks like you ladies have taken a wrong turn somewhere."

A broad-shouldered man in cammies stood twenty feet away, a flashlight in his left hand, a nine millimeter in his right, both raised and pointing at them. He walked slowly forward.

"This is private property, ladies. You may have noticed the No Trespassing signs everywhere?"

Jan stood in front of Catherine and shielded her eyes from the beam of light. "It seems we missed seeing those," she said. "But I'd appreciate it if you'd lower your flashlight. And your gun, while you're at it."

The man did neither. "I'm afraid all I'll be doing is escorting you to our commanding officer. He was especially interested to see if there were ladies snooping in our woods. Damn if he wasn't right."

He moved to within three feet of them, holstering his flashlight, but keeping the gun aimed at chest level. Catherine moved to Jan's side as he pulled two plastic handcuffs out of his back pocket, but before he'd even moved his hand past his hip, she had him on the ground, with her knee to the back of his head and his arm twisted up behind him.

"Jesus," said Jan. She picked up the gun that had been knocked from his hand. "Do you need any help there?"

The man started to struggle and Catherine wrenched his arm higher up. He howled.

"Yes, if you could put one of these cuffs on him I'd be ever so grateful."

They both sat on him and wrestled his hands together, cuffing them with the plastic strip. Then they stood and rolled him over. His face was scrunched up with fury.

"You bitches will pay for this. My sergeant will be out here any minute looking for me."

Jan looked down at him and shook her head. "That's going to be awfully embarrassing for you, isn't it? I mean here we are, a couple of ladies, as you put it, and there you are, trussed up like a pig. I wonder what he'll think about that?"

The radio on the man's belt crackled and a voice came through asking him to report in.

"Just turn it off," Jan said. Catherine grabbed the radio and hit the power button. "Now, you're probably right that he'll be coming along soon to find you. My question to you is whether you want to have us wait for him with you, which we're just fine with. Or would you like to help us out and we'll let you go before he sees us? Which will it be?"

"Or we could just knock him out or shoot him or something. That way we can have his sergeant find him and we could ambush them." Catherine leaned down and looked at the man's shirt pocket label. "Does that sound like it would be less embarrassing for you, Private Lawson?"

"He's kind of old for a private, isn't he?" Jan asked Catherine.

"A little. It's probably been hard for him to advance."

"Fuck you!" Lawson said. He tried to spit at them, but the glob landed back on his head.

"That's the spirit!" Jan said. "It's thinking like that that's probably gotten you where you are today, Lawson. But listen, we're running out of time here. All I want is to show you a photo and you tell me whether you've seen the person before."

She grabbed his flashlight and pointed it at the photo of Maddy, holding it in front of his face. He turned his head away.

"Does that mean you haven't seen this girl, Private? Or that you have."

"I ain't seen her."

"May I?" Catherine asked Jan, as she took the flashlight from her. Then she jammed the flashlight up against Lawson's scrotum and pushed. He tried to scramble up on his feet, but Jan held him down.

"I'm afraid you're not being entirely honest with us, Private Lawson. Now, you can tell us what you know, or I can push harder."

His eyes were wild as he stared at Catherine. Jan saw him look up at her for salvation.

"Just tell us. It will go a lot better for you."

Lawson was breathing heavily and looked ready to fall apart. "All I know is that half an hour ago they ordered us to break camp, all of a sudden like, and then sent me and some of the others out in the woods to look for intruders. That's all I know, I swear."

Catherine got up. "What do you think?" she asked Jan.

"I think that's about all he knows." She took a card and put it in Lawson's shirt pocket. "But if you think of anything else, you give me a call. If we find out you knew more and didn't tell us, we'll pay you another visit."

He nodded and lay still, staring up at them. "Don't let them find me like this," he said.

Catherine looked at Jan and she shrugged. Catherine pulled the knife out of Lawson's belt and cut the plastic tie binding his hands.

"Now get out of here," Jan said.

"But what about my gun?"

"We're not giving you the gun back."

"Or the torch," Catherine said.

They turned and marched back the way they came, using the flashlight in the dark woods and keeping quiet. Neither turned back to see what Lawson was doing.

They avoided the parking lot and made their way out to the county road, where they'd stashed the Jeep.

"Let's drive by the lot to see what's there," Jan said.

"Excellent idea," Catherine said.

Jan drove slowly up the road to the parking lot with her lights off, but when they came around the curve by the pond they saw that the cars and the RVs were all gone.

"Blimey," Catherine said.

Jan laughed. "Wow. I didn't know you guys actually said 'blimey.'"

"We do. I can throw a 'crikey' into the conversation if it will get another smile out of you."

Jan stopped smiling. She had to remind herself to resist Catherine, but it was so hard. She kept forgetting.

"I'd say they're a pretty well organized group to get out of here so quickly," she said.

"Except for the look of panic their bugout creates. It can't be a coincidence that we ask about the girl and they are gone within minutes," Catherine said.

"Time to find the sheriff, but I have a feeling we're not going to get much help there."

Jan looked up the contact information on the county's website and placed the call to the sheriff's office. Within five minutes, she'd hung up.

"No joy, I take it?" Catherine said.

"The deputy I spoke to claims there's nothing they can do based on so little information. I'll e-mail the photo to him so they have something on file there. He didn't sound too eager to help out."

"You sound like there's something behind that."

"When I was reading up on the militias and all the citizen patriot groups, I came across an organization of law enforcement officers called Oath Keepers who pledge to not do things like disarm the people or conduct warrantless searches on citizens. When you read their website it's pretty clear they're in support of an anti-government, pro-citizen group philosophy."

"And you're thinking that this sheriff's department might be one of these Oath Keepers?"

"I don't know," Jan said. "Nothing would surprise me. But now we have to figure out a way to track this Drecker guy, and we're not going to get any help at this point from the sheriff."

"Good thing I took a photo of Drecker while we were talking to him," Catherine said. "Maybe we can show it around and get a handle on him."

Jan stared at her and found herself smiling, despite her best efforts to remain stern. "Okay. Now I'm impressed."

"You're impressed that I pushed a button on my phone, but not that I just took down a rather large man pointing a gun at us?"

"That? Child's play. But thanks for getting to him before I did."

Catherine laughed with that throaty tone that drove Jan wild. They sat in the car, both gazing out on the pond. The silence lengthened, but it didn't grow uncomfortable. Finally, Jan started the car and pulled out of the lot.

"Let's head into the town near here and show people the photos. Maybe we'll get lucky," she said.

Five minutes later, they pulled into the Country Corner store in the town nearest the camp. It was more hamlet than town, but with none of the charm that word conjures. The Country Corner was more party store than general store, its dominant display was the largest selection of scratch off lottery tickets Jan had ever seen. There were mini bottles of Thunderbird at the checkout counter, live bait next to a donut rack, and a small magazine display with the newest edition of *Soldier of Fortune* front and center. The young man at the cash register was very much like the clerk at the store she'd visited earlier in the day, only surlier.

Jan pushed the photo of Maddy across the counter. "I'm wondering if you've seen this girl around here?"

He peered down at the photo and looked back up at her. "Why?"

"Because I'm looking for her, that's why. Have you seen her?"

He turned back to the video game in his hands. "Maybe."

"Is this the point where I'm supposed to slip a bill your way to get you to answer my question?" Jan asked.

He looked back at her. "That's an idea."

"Because I've got to say that having to pay for information about a missing girl, a minor let me add, seems kind of, I don't know, insensitive?"

He shrugged. "I'm not a touchy-feely kind of guy."

"Are you the kind of guy that kidnaps teenage girls?"

He gave her a bored looked and went back to his game. Jan was reaching into her pocket just as Catherine put a twenty on the counter and kept her hand on it. "To earn this, we want answers. Have you seen the girl or not?"

He looked at the bill. "I saw her this weekend. Yesterday morning, I think. She was in here early with another chick. Not a chick, really. A dyke."

"Did you hear them say anything? Do you know what they were up to?"

Another shrug. "They bought some stuff and they left. That's all I know." He reached for the bill.

"Hold on." Catherine showed him the photo on her phone. "Have you seen this guy?"

Jan could see his face freeze with the effort of not giving away anything, which gave away everything.

"Nope, never seen him before."

"Are you sure about that? I think he lives around here," Jan said.

"Never seen him."

Catherine released the bill and he scooped it up, turning away from them immediately. Jan left a card on the counter and spoke to his back. "We'll expect to hear from you should your memory clear up on any of this."

Jan and Catherine got back in the car.

"He knows Drecker," Jan said.

"Definitely," Catherine said.

"But short of torture, I'm not sure what we can get from him. I think he's scared of Drecker, or maybe of the whole group of them."

"He may be one of them."

"True. And maybe he didn't know Maddy was heading to the training camp, or he wouldn't have even admitted that he'd seen her. At least we know that Maddy was here. That's something," Jan said.

A hundred yards away was the flashing Vacancy sign of a roadside motel. Next to it was the local tavern. They were both called the Pinehurst Inn.

"Why don't we go pick up my car and then have a drink over there?" Catherine said. "Maybe we'll learn something new. And maybe we can just kip at the inn there."

"Kip?"

"Sleep, I mean. Sorry." Catherine smiled again, and it was killing Jan.

"Sure. I can't think what else we can do now, and I'm starving. I'm hoping they have something more than beer nuts to eat."

They went back to the campground for Catherine's rental and met at the tavern parking lot. The bar had a smattering of people inside, mostly men sitting alone or in pairs at the bar, heads craned up to stare at *Wheel of Fortune* on the television. Jan wondered how many times they guessed the puzzle before the contestant did. Their heads swung around as she and Catherine entered to see who was walking through the door. Some eyes stayed on them as they climbed onto barstools. She imagined there weren't that many strangers coming through the door at the Pinehurst Inn, even in hunting season.

The bartender was a skinny woman who looked to be in a long-term relationship with crystal meth. Her teeth were mostly gone and her eyes were sunken and had deep, dark circles. She was probably thirty, but looked like an unhealthy fifty.

"What d'ya have?" she said, taking a swipe at the bar in front of them with a filthy rag.

"Good evening," Catherine said brightly. "I'd love a beer. What sort do you have?"

The bartender looked at Catherine as if she'd just spoken in Esperanto. Apparently, not many Brits made it down to this part of Michigan.

"Old Style, Bud, Miller. That's it. Oh, yeah, Heineken."

"Two Heinekens," Jan said. "With glasses."

The bartender cracked them open and put them on the bar with the glasses, waiting for her money.

"I was wondering whether you'd seen this girl at all around here," Jan said, handing the photo of Maddy over.

The woman flicked her eyes on the photo and handed it back. "Nope."

"You're sure? Because the fellow at the Country Corner said he'd seen her around."

"She looks a little young to be in a bar. I ain't seen her."

Jan looked at Catherine, who held her phone up to show the photo of Drecker.

"How about this guy?" Jan asked.

The bartender's eyes shifted for a second before she shrugged. "Haven't seen him, either. You two cops or something?"

"No, not cops. We're looking for the girl. She's missing and we want to find her before anything bad happens to her. Are you sure you can't help us with that?"

"Like I said, I haven't seen either of them."

She moved away from them to the far end of the bar, where several of the men leaned toward her and they started whispering to each other.

"Either everyone has reason to fear Drecker or they have reason to protect him from something. No question she knew him," Catherine said.

"Give me your phone. I'm going to ask these gentlemen what they know."

"Do you want me with you?"

"No. I want you to watch them while I'm working the crowd."

Jan stopped at each occupied barstool and chair, showing the photo, moving on to the next with each shake of the head. Five minutes later, she was back on her own barstool.

"One of the men placed a call while you were talking to some of the others," Catherine said. "I wonder if he called Drecker himself."

"Probably. But we're not going to get anything from these guys. They're all reading from the same script."

"Well, we just have to regroup. I've ordered two lovely frozen pizzas, which Annabeth, that's our bartender, is now cooking up in the oven. Let's take them to the inn and check in."

"You want to stay at the Pinehurst?"

"Where else? It'll be fine. Besides, I'm knackered," Catherine said.

"Knackered?"

Catherine laughed again. "Tired, I mean."

Jan knew what knackered meant, but she wanted to hear Catherine's laugh. She felt like a junkie who kept picking up a needle and flipping it around and around in her hands, telling herself she wasn't going to use. It was just a matter of time before she plunged it into her veins.

Annabeth put the hot pizzas and a six-pack of beer into a bag and shoved them over the counter, evidently glad to see the back of them. When they walked the few feet over to the office of the Pinehurst Inn, they were greeted by a woman who looked like a healthier version of Annabeth, maybe fifty years old and looking like fifty years old. Her name was Anna, and Jan understood why Annabeth still had a job in the tavern.

Jan asked for two rooms and she could feel Catherine shift behind her, as if she were about to step forward to say something and then thought better of it. The office was tiny and now filled with the smell of pizza mingling with Anna's cigarette.

"Where you girls from?" Anna asked. She ran Jan's credit card as she talked and seemed to have the sunny side to her daughter's surly. "You don't look much like you're here for hunting. And you can take that as a compliment."

"We came up from Chicago," Jan said. "And we're here looking for a missing teen. Have you seen this girl around here?"

Anna studied the photo. "I haven't, but I'll sure keep my eyes open for her. Is she a runaway?"

"We don't know. A runaway, or kidnapped."

"Oh, dear."

Catherine stepped forward. "We're also looking for this gentleman. Do you know him?"

Anna stared at the phone, trying to get a bead on it through her trifocals. "Hank Drecker? Sure, I know him. He lives just up the road. What's he got to do with this girl?"

"We don't know yet," Jan said. "But there may be some connection. Do you know how we can get hold of him?"

"Hank Drecker can't have anything untoward to do with that girl, if that's what you're thinking. He's got a wife and two kids and I think he's a church deacon or something."

"Well, we'd like to talk to him, anyway. Do you know where up the road he lives?"

Anna looked worried. "I don't. There's a bunch of little houses up about a mile from here. I just know he lives around there because I've heard him talking enough in the bar. Not that he drinks much. He just comes in mostly for their meetings."

"Whose meetings?"

"That army group they all have. You know, they call themselves a militia. But they're not dangerous or anything. And the last thing they'd do is have anything to do with a young girl like that."

"Why do you say that?" Catherine asked.

"Well, they're all very straight-laced, really. God-fearing. They rent the back room at the bar for their meetings, but you don't even hear a peep from them while they're in there. All they drink is iced tea and Cokes."

By the time they'd finished checking in and pulled their cars in front of their rooms, Jan was wondering why Catherine hadn't said anything about booking two rooms instead of one. Didn't she want to sleep with her? Maybe she'd been attacked by her conscience and decided to start acting like she was committed elsewhere. Which she was, Jan reminded herself. She kept swinging wildly back and forth between being furious with Catherine and wanting her desperately. Her head was a very noisy place.

"Are we each going to take a pizza and eat in our separate rooms?" Catherine asked.

"It's an option."

"Good. That implies that there's another option, that we eat together. That's what I opt for."

Jan pulled her bag out of the backseat. "Fine. We'll eat in your room." Jan liked to have an exit available to her at all times.

The room was paneled with knotty pine and decorated with hunting and fishing paintings. The lamps had heavy shades, throwing out a golden light that made the room feel warm and cozy. It felt like a cabin, but not the kind of cabin she grew up in. That was more a stark and desperate feeling, where socks were stuffed into holes in the wall and a crackling fire simply meant you wouldn't freeze to death in the Idaho winter. This room made her want to sit in a chair and read a book.

Catherine sat at the small table in the room and opened two beers and unwrapped the pizza. "What's our next step?" she said.

Jan remained standing. "Why don't you tell me? You're the boss."

Catherine sighed. "You're still angry that I came up here, aren't you?"

"It's not like I've had a long time to get over it," Jan said. She sat down and drank some beer. "It feels like something someone would do who's used to getting her way."

"What do you mean?"

"It's obvious. At least to me. You decided I wasn't answering your calls quickly enough to your liking, so you used your authority to call off my partner and come up here to talk to me. You weren't thinking about what might be best for actually finding this girl, or what I may have thought of the idea."

"Do you feel I'm a hindrance to you in working the case?"

"That's not really the point. Peet was supposed to be here. She's my partner."

Jan ate some pizza as Catherine leaned back in her chair and watched her.

"You're right that I used my position. Absolutely. But only because I could do so and not compromise your case. I know what

I'm doing, though I can't say missing teenagers were my regular beat."

Jan stared at her hard. "No, I don't suppose that was the sort of case you handled at MI6. It must be a hardship to be working on something so mundane."

Catherine looked surprised. "How did you know I was with MI6? I don't think I've mentioned that before."

"That's true."

"So how did you know?"

Jan ate more pizza and stalled. She wasn't sure she was ready to open the can of worms. But if not now, when? "There's quite a bit about it on the Internet," she said.

Catherine was still for a moment. "You looked me up on the Internet? I suppose I should be flattered."

"Flattered?" Jan was incredulous. She stood and walked away from the table with her beer. "More like ashamed or embarrassed, or something."

"Because I worked at MI6?" Catherine looked genuinely confused.

"Haven't you ever Googled yourself, for Christ's sake?"

"I haven't, no. But apparently you've Googled me."

Jan turned on her Mac. She'd saved the Web pages that showed Catherine in photos with Ellen. She handed the laptop over. "You're quite the news item, it seems. You and your girlfriend."

Catherine read through the first article as if she were glancing through a quarterly sales report. Her only visible reaction was the vertical line forming between her brows. She closed the computer and handed it back to Jan.

"At least now I know what you're really mad about."

Jan stared at her. She'd never felt jealousy before, never even cared whether a woman she'd slept with was involved elsewhere. Even when Josie left her years before for another woman, the feeling was more annoyance than pain.

"If I tell you the truth about Ellen, it's going to sound like utter crap. But I haven't any choice."

"There's no point, anyway."

"Yes, there is a point. I don't know what it is we have together, at least not yet. But I do know I don't want to lose it," Catherine said.

Catherine leaned back and ran her hands back through her hair, pulling the mass of it behind her head and letting it fall. She stared at the ceiling. Finally, she looked at Jan.

"The woman in the photo is Ellen, my partner for many years now. We live together in London. There's no other way to put it than we are a married couple and I was a shit to sleep with you. And I won't tell you that it's the first time I've done this sort of thing. You can probably guess that it's not."

Jan tossed the computer on the foot of the bed and took another beer. She remained standing.

"But it is the absolute truth that I've never had the experience I had with you. It's changed everything."

Jan stared as Catherine searched for words.

"Ellen and I haven't been happy for quite some time. I know that's the part that sounds like utter crap, but it's just the way it is. We have not talked about splitting up, but it has been in the back of my mind for months now. I've been putting off the decision. I keep working, traveling, returning home to the same bloody uncomfortable house that I can barely stand to be in anymore."

Jan was determined to not ask leading questions, but her heart was picking up its pace. She was feeling hopeful, she supposed. Catherine leaned forward, resting her elbows on her knees, her hands clasped in front of her.

"One of the reasons I was calling you repeatedly was to tell you about Ellen and to ask you whether you'd agree to spend time with me, to see if you'd like to pursue something. I mean, you don't really know me. I'm not sure you really even like me much. But I know that something happened between us that was so different from anything I've felt with other women. I can't stand the idea of flying back to London without seeing if there really is something there."

Jan sat at the table and fiddled with her beer can. "In other words, if you like what's happening between us you'll dump your girlfriend, but if not, you still have her to go home to."

She spoke in an even tone, as if she weren't ready to explode. There seemed such a narrow path to navigate. One step off of it and she'd be hurt, badly.

"That's not what I mean at all." She reached for Jan's hand, placing her own over the fist Jan reluctantly left on the table. "Please listen to what I'm saying. I'm done with Ellen no matter whether you agree to see me or not. I know that much, and by God, it feels good."

Jan's cell phone rang and she picked it up as quickly as she could, thankful for the interruption.

"This is Anna from the Pinehurst. I'm over at the bar and just heard something that might be about that girl you're looking for."

"I'm on my way," Jan said. She hung up and grabbed her jacket.

"Wait. What's going on?"

"Someone at the bar might know something. You can stay here."

Catherine was up and at her side. "Don't be absurd. I'm coming with you."

"Why?"

"Because I'm your partner."

Jan raised her eyebrow. "Don't get any ideas. You're not my partner."

Catherine smiled and a crack formed in Jan's resolve. Every smile, every laugh out of Catherine's mouth, made the risk of being hurt so much more worth taking. She spun and went out the door, crossing the parking lot with long strides, Catherine keeping pace behind her.

Inside the bar the drinkers were down to a few. It was Sunday night, well into the evening, and the hunched figures were the hardcore regulars. The feel of a barstool below them was more comforting than any living room La-Z-Boy. Annabeth was talking to her mother at the end of the bar. As they approached, Anna discretely pointed at a man sitting by himself at one of the few tables in the tavern. He looked startled when Jan and Catherine sat down at the table with him.

"Excuse us for interrupting you," Jan said, "but we're looking for someone and we'd like to see if you can help us."

"What are you talking about?" the man said. He was middle-aged, tired, his coveralls dirty from whatever it was he worked at during the day. His hand was thick, gripping the bottle of beer in front of him. He was eating one of the tavern pizzas.

"We've been hired to find this girl," Catherine said, as Jan showed him the photo. "She's run away from home."

"And we know she's been training at the militia camp that's near here. Do you know anything about her?" Jan said.

The man turned around and looked at Anna, who just waved cheerily back. He sighed.

"I didn't know that Anna was going to call you in here. I don't want to get involved in nothing." He didn't seem hostile. He could have been saying he didn't want to buy any Girl Scout cookies. He just wasn't interested.

"If you could just tell us what you told Anna," Catherine said. He cocked his head at her, most likely because she talked funny. "She's just a girl, you see. We need to find her."

"I don't know if I do know anything at all about her. When Anna mentioned there were people here looking for a missing girl, I told her what I heard when I was at the gas station a bit ago. A couple fellas from the training camp were there and I overheard them saying they all had to scramble out of there 'cause it turned out there was a runaway in the camp and someone had come looking for her. They thought she was part of the group of young folks who are heading out to Idaho."

Catherine and Jan looked at each other.

The man gave the photo back to Jan. "I didn't see her myself, so I don't know if that's her."

"Do you know the names of any of the people going to Idaho?"

"David Conlon is the only one I know of. I've heard him in the bar here talking about Idaho. They're crazy, if you ask me."

"Why do you say that?" Jan asked.

"Well, what the hell are they going to do out there? There aren't any more jobs in the middle of Idaho than there are here, and they won't have their parents' homes to go to when they run out of money. And Idaho is hard country. A Michigan winter is nothing compared to what they have."

Jan had to agree with that. The winters of her childhood were endless months of freezing cold and unending snow. Every fall was spent shoring up the sorry structures in their camp in the hope they'd be sturdy enough to keep them alive until spring. Men cut wood non-stop, piling split logs into small mountains that never seemed large enough to keep them warm through the season.

"Do you have any idea where they planned to go in Idaho? Did it sound like they have a destination?"

"Conlon was boasting that they had some property they bought, with a house and some stables and who knows what else. I couldn't tell you where it was. Didn't hear him mention it."

"Do you know where we can find David Conlon?"

"He lives somewhere around here, I guess. I've seen him in here enough. I couldn't tell you what town he's in though."

"What about the men you overheard at the gas station?" Catherine asked. "Can you tell us who they were? They might know more about the girl we're looking for."

The man shrugged. "Sorry. I didn't know those fellas."

Catherine looked at Jan, who then turned for a final question.

"Can you give us your name, sir?"

"It's Fred Hansen. But I'd appreciate you not spreading it around that I talked to you. People don't much like it when you talk about them to outsiders."

"I understand. I'll leave my card with you and ask that you call me if you hear anything else about the group going to Idaho or the girl we're trying to find. Her name's Maddy Harrington."

Hansen nodded and turned back to his pizza as Jan and Catherine got up from the table. When they returned to the motel they stopped in front of their two rooms.

"What do we do now?" Catherine said. She stood facing Jan, close enough to put her arms around her neck and pull her down for a kiss, which she looked like she was about to do. Jan pulled back a step.

"I'm going to try to find David Conlon. You can do whatever you want."

She put her key in her door and left Catherine standing outside, her hands on her hips.

❖

Maddy woke to find herself in Kristi's cot, tucked under her arm and buried under their coats and the two thin blankets they'd found in the cabin. She barely remembered waking earlier in the night, freezing, not thinking twice about climbing in with Kristi and her generous body heat. Kristi had simply grunted and moved over a bit, wrapping an arm around Maddy.

Kristi's vibrating cell phone went off. She could hear it skittering along the floor below her. Kristi slept on.

"Hello?" she answered the phone knowing it was probably David.

"We're five minutes away," he said. "Get yourselves ready to roll. We're heading to Idaho."

"Now?"

"Yes. We have to. People are looking for you and we need to get out of here." David didn't sound like his usual easygoing self. She felt Kristi shift behind her.

"Okay. We'll be ready."

"You know, Maddy, there are some who want to leave you behind. And they may be right. You shouldn't have lied to me," David said.

"Why are you taking me then?" She didn't want to go where she wasn't wanted. She'd had a lifetime of that, she felt. But she wanted to go to Idaho, more than ever before.

"I don't know. It might be stupid of me. But you and I talked so much about this together that it doesn't feel right to leave you. Let's hope I don't regret this."

"You won't. I promise."

Now Kristi was sitting up. "What's happening?"

"Can't you talk to your parents and call them off the search? I thought you said they don't care much what you do," David said.

"They don't. This is just for show. So they can tell people they did what they could. They're not going to hunt me to the ends of the earth."

"They did send this investigator to Michigan."

"Don't worry, David. The investigator will lose the scent, we'll be out of the Midwest, and that will be the end of it."

"We're heading up the road to the cabin. Meet us out front."

Maddy disconnected and handed the phone to Kristi, who looked dazed.

"Come on. We're heading out to Idaho. David's almost here."

"What? What about my stuff? Am I supposed to go to Idaho with literally the clothes on my back?"

Maddy shrugged. "I don't know. Maybe he plans for us to swing by your place. Where do you live, anyway?"

"It's not far. My brother's garage. I've got to get my stuff. It'll take me ten minutes."

They heard a truck roll up out front and scrambled into their coats and out the door. The fire was dead; whoever came to this hole next would have to fold the thin scraps they called blankets. David was driving his pickup and they climbed into the front with him.

"What the hell, dude?" Kristi said. "We aren't going without me getting my stuff, are we?"

Maddy was starting to become fascinated with Kristi's stuff. When she ran away from home, the only thing she cared about bringing were her computer and a few changes of clothes. She wondered what Kristi valued.

"Don't worry, Kris. We'll swing by your brother's, then on to meet the rest of our caravan at Ed's. We're heading out from there. Maddy, I threw your things in your bag. It's all in the hold."

A few miles down the county road and another Michigan hamlet appeared, with trailer courts leading the way into the town and then popping up again on the other side. They drove beyond the last of these and then down a gravel road where actual houses were scattered about. David turned off his lights and pulled into the dirt driveway of one of them, a one-story ramshackle structure, badly in need of paint. It was a few hours before dawn, but the moonlight showed off everything most people would just as soon keep hidden—the peeling paint, the cockeyed screen door, the falling gutters, and missing roof shingles.

"Wait here. I'll be right back," Kristi said, but Maddy slipped out with her.

"I'm coming too," she whispered. "I'll help you carry."

Kristi gave her a sort of helpless look and shrugged. She led her up the driveway to the back of the property, shrouded in trees and much darker than up front. The garage wasn't what Maddy expected. Instead of a two-story structure with a cute studio apartment on top, it was simply a garage. No toilet, no kitchen. There was a mattress on the floor. The setup was so dismal that Maddy could instantly see why Kristi thought David's basement was upscale.

Kristi's dresser was a duffle bag gaping open by the mattress. She started to throw some scattered clothes into the bag and then bent to unplug a handheld gaming device. She wrapped the cord around it and tucked it safely into her jacket pocket. There was a kit bag and a well-thumbed romance novel that went into the bag also, and that was it. She zipped it up.

"I really didn't need any help carrying," she said.

Jan spent several minutes on the Internet before locating an address for a house owned by a Frank Conlon. Google Maps pinpointed the house at about a mile away from the Pinehurst Inn. Catherine remained quiet as Jan worked. She finished off a beer and checked e-mails on her phone. Jan glanced at her repeatedly, worried Catherine would keep at her about their personal mess, worried also that she wouldn't.

"I've got something," Jan said, pulling on her jacket. She clipped her Glock back onto her belt.

"Should I be armed?" Catherine asked.

"What do you think, Secret Agent Woman?"

"Hilarious. But I'm afraid I'm without my weapon. It appears you'll have to protect me."

Jan handed her a revolver to be on the safe side.

"Take my backup."

Catherine handled the gun with ease and slid it into the back of her jeans. "Right. Are we going in Western style, guns a-blazin' and all that? Or have you considered calling the authorities?"

Jan locked the room door behind them and then opened her car door for Catherine. "I considered it, but I want to see what's out there first."

The Jeep bounced along a rutted dirt road, its gravel cover long since spit off to the side. Jan followed a blue dot on her phone's GPS until she came upon a row of dilapidated ranch houses. The address Jan found on the county assessor's site was the last in the row. There were no streetlights, but the blue glow of TV screens shone from every front window but the last one. Jan pulled up across the street and stared at the dark house. A party was rocking the house next door, the heavy bass thundering out into the street and cars lining the driveway and crowding onto the lawn.

"It doesn't appear Mr. Conlon or anyone else is at home," Catherine said.

"Let's go find out."

Jan didn't bother knocking on the door. The house was dark inside, the blinds and drapes left wide open. They circled the house, staying low. The noise from the party made Jan nervous, leaving her unable to tell if anyone was approaching.

"What I need to know," she said, "is whether Conlon's just out for the night or they've taken off for Idaho."

They were standing in the backyard, where the scrubby lawn ran right up to the wall of the house. There wasn't a sliding glass door leading to a patio. It wasn't that kind of house. The mud from the yard had coated the basement windows, but one of them was cranked open.

"If you had a mind to break into the house, it looks like they've saved you some trouble," Catherine said.

"I have the mind, but I don't have the body. Will you fit, do you think?"

Catherine handed the revolver to Jan and quickly angled her body feet first through the window. The only thing that seemed to have a hard time making it through were her breasts, which flattened disturbingly against the dirty glass as she slipped through. Jan ran around to the front to meet her at the door, ready to shoot it open if she heard anything.

Catherine flung the door open with a bright smile.

"Lovely digs, and we have the place all to ourselves."

"Let's clear it, just in case."

She handed the gun back to Catherine and they worked their way through the house room by room. Jan wasn't a law enforcement officer, but she knew how to clear a room. Still, she felt a little cowed by Catherine, who stepped into a room and swept it with her gun in a way that dared anyone to pop up and try to shoot her. There was just something about the way she did it that was sexy as hell. Jan was in serious trouble with this woman. If Catherine were to stop right in the middle of the sweep and blow her nose, Jan would probably think there was something enchanting about the way she did it. It had become as bad as that.

There was no one in the house, but plenty of evidence they hadn't been gone long. The dryer was still warm in the basement, the shower stall still wet in the bathroom. But other than the crappy furniture and knickknacks, the food in the kitchen, and the overflowing trashcans, there wasn't anything left in the house. The closets and bathroom had been cleaned out. They got to work on the trash.

Jan went through the basement while Catherine started upstairs. A plastic bag from a grocery store held some garbage near a mattress on the floor. There were a couple of Tampax wrappers, an empty can of Red Bull, used Kleenex, and a receipt for a cash purchase at the Kroger. A brush had been left behind at the sink, and there was used soap in the shower. The hair in the brush looked like it could have been Maddy's. The rest of the basement was even less promising. An ancient workbench held tools that hadn't see any work in a long time, a laundry room with rickety old machines, and a utility room with an ancient furnace and a rusty hot water heater. No secret rooms or hidden caches of weapons.

She bumped into Catherine at the top of the stairs from the basement.

"I was just coming to get you," she said. "I think I've found something."

Catherine was holding a plastic garbage bag that she placed on the dining room table. She handed over a receipt she'd dug out of the bag.

"I found this in one of the bedrooms. It looks like they've recently loaded up on outdoor equipment and clothing," she said.

Jan used her flashlight and looked at the long receipt from Walmart. The purchase had been charged to David Conlon two days earlier. Jan smiled.

"Fantastic. Maybe he'll charge his way across the country."

"Yes, he may just be dumb enough to do that. But in case he's not, there's something else here that might help," Catherine said.

She pulled out a sheaf of documents, copies of real estate listing sheets for property in Idaho.

"This is great," Jan said. "Did you see anything else up here worth looking at?"

"Not unless you want to see the lovely collection of used condoms I discovered."

"I'll pass. Let's take this bag with us and head out."

The music was still blaring through the walls from the house next door. Jan poked her head out, looking for partiers who may have stumbled from the house. There was no one out there. Jan closed the door behind them and they trotted to the Jeep.

"I know this isn't relevant, really, but I'm glad to be out of there," Catherine said. "I found it depressing, somehow."

"Yeah, there's something a little depressing about everything around here."

"What do you think that is? I don't know anything about Michigan."

Jan shrugged. "There are a lot of things about Michigan that are great. But obviously things are tough in this part of the state. I think it's a hard life here."

"Which may be why these young people are getting out."

"Right. But I can tell you, Idaho is not the answer. Things are even tougher out there," Jan said.

Catherine looked at her. "Is that based on personal knowledge? I don't know anything about you, I realize. Maybe you're from that area?"

Jan turned the Jeep around and drove back toward the motel. She was afraid to tell Catherine anything other than the manufactured biography of herself. Orphaned, raised in foster homes, put herself through school and the like. But for the first time, she was equally afraid of telling a lie.

"I've heard about the job situation out west," she said. "It's not necessarily any easier to make money out there. But I think they're going there to start their own homestead, not to find a factory job."

Catherine looked pensive. When they got back to the motel they took the bag into Jan's room and started to go through the trash.

"I'll contact the Winnetka police in the morning," Jan said. "They can trace the credit card number and hopefully give us an idea where they are."

"Can you tell me where you are?"

Jan was separating real trash from potentially interesting trash. She stopped smoothing out a sheet of paper. "What do you mean?"

"I mean, what are your thoughts about what we were talking about earlier? About my decision to leave Ellen?"

"Do you honestly think that's what I'm thinking about? I'm a little more concerned about tracking down this girl." She started smoothing papers again.

"Are you being honest?" Catherine asked. She was sitting in the chair opposite Jan, perfectly relaxed. Her hair had been pulled back into a ponytail, making her look younger. She watched Jan, but her look wasn't challenging. "I know that if you're anything like me, you can think about work and at least one other thing at the same time. Right now, for me, that other thing is you."

Jan sighed. She kept flipping though papers. She couldn't focus on what was on them, nor could she think of what to say to Catherine. She'd completely lost track of why she was supposed to resist her. If there was no more Ellen, was there any reason to shut her out? Catherine slid her hand across the table until it rested on Jan's, holding it still.

All Jan could focus on now was what her body told her to do. Her mind was a mess. She stood and reached for Catherine, pulling her up and kissing her, feeling something work its way loose as Catherine's arms snaked around her neck and pulled her closer. They kissed for a very long time, breaking just long enough for Jan to lock the door, turn off the lights, and guide Catherine down onto the bed. They were well into their lovemaking before Jan realized they were in her room and she'd not left herself her usual exit. She didn't even want one.

Chapter Eight

By mid-day Monday, the two-vehicle caravan to Idaho had made its way well into Iowa, progress that seemed agonizingly slow to Maddy. She rode in the lead car with David, Diane, and Kristi, a camper van with a pop-up top, a couple of sleeping benches, and frilly curtains on the rear windows. Kristi was sprawled on one of the benches, sound asleep with her mouth open and her cap tilted over her eyes. David was driving, with Diane asleep in the seat beside him. Maddy sat on the other sleeping bench, hidden from David by a tie-dyed curtain pulled halfway shut. The curtains and the tie-dye and the fact that the van was painted a mauve color irritated the hell out of her. As if that were the thing to be irritated about in her situation. David was listening to an audio recording of *Atlas Shrugged*, a gift from Maddy when she arrived in Michigan. Ayn Rand was what brought them together. Maddy had thought that it was enough, but now even Ayn Rand irritated her.

Beneath her bench were two banker boxes. David put them there after she and Kristi climbed into the van the night before. Most of the other cargo they were bringing to Idaho was being hauled in the pickup truck behind them. Tommy was traveling in the cab with Ed and Warren, a situation that couldn't have made Tommy very happy. She was still trying to figure out how these people held together, or why. How did a boy like Tommy run in the same group as guys like Ed and Warren? She knew that David was the glue, but she was only beginning to realize how strong the bond was. She had always been on the outside looking in at groups, never a member.

Except for her family, but how they stayed together was the biggest mystery of all. The Harringtons had less in common with each other than this band of runaways.

Maddy's feet kept hitting the boxes below her as she fidgeted. She glanced toward the front of the van and saw that Diane was still asleep. She got on her knees and slid one of the boxes out. She opened it to find it tightly packed with file folders, all of them unlabeled. This seemed insane. Maddy was a believer in tagging, labeling, hierarchical file structures, and logical organization, all of it on her computer. Just having this much paper seemed stupid. This was why God had invented the scanner and the PDF format.

She began riffling through the files. There were school records, family legal documents, and a great number of magazine and Internet articles on familiar topics: survivalism, anti-government tax actions, patriot and militia groups. There was a whole file on Ayn Rand and Objectivism. At the rear of the box was a file with names and contact information for members of an Idaho militia group. There was also login information for the group's intranet. Both the user name and password were long and complicated, too much for even Maddy to memorize. She pulled out her phone and wrote it down.

Maddy heard a loud yawn and looked to the front of the van to see Diane stretching her arms like a cat and rolling her head from side to side. She quickly put the last file back and shoved the box back in place. She lay down and pretended to sleep, listening to David and Diane laugh and Kristi mumble something as she dreamed. She felt anxious. What if David was getting himself involved with one of those hardcore militia groups? Didn't that make them all involved? She didn't know if she was more worried about what that might mean for them or whether David was leaving her out of something, leaving her outside looking in. What if this new family was as disappointing as the old?

❖

Jan got back to the office in Chicago by late Monday afternoon. It had been impossible to leave Catherine as she lay asleep in her bed, impossible to nudge her awake when she could watch her instead. And when she did wake, it was impossible to resist when Catherine pulled her close and wrapped her legs around her. It was nearly noon when they got in their separate cars for the drive back.

Jan found Peet at her desk, finishing up a call.

"It's about time you rolled in," Peet said. Her forehead was pinched and her lips stretched thin, and Jan thought it made her nearly unrecognizable. She threw her bag onto her desk and took a seat, taking her time before turning to face Peet.

"You're pissed off?" she asked.

"What do you think?"

"I don't know what to tell you, exactly. We made some good progress up there. I think we have a few things to go on to find Maddy."

"That's not what I'm talking about. Don't dick around with me."

"Peet, I'm sorry that our new boss threw her weight around and came up to Michigan instead of you. It's not like Michigan is a prize travel assignment, you know. I don't even know why she did it."

Peet remained silent. It was the kind of silence that said a lot.

"And it turns out she knows what she's doing. Did you know she's a former MI6 agent?"

"How did that come up?" Peet asked. "Pillow talk?"

Now it was Jan's turn to stare. She wondered if Peet had psychic powers. Or maybe Vivian had already spread the story about the conference room kiss.

"What are you talking about?"

"There's only one reason the new owner of this company would risk pissing off their new employees by elbowing her way onto a routine assignment. She's either after you or you're already an item. Though even for you that seems like remarkably fast work."

Jan glared at Peet before she stood and went into the break room. She wanted a cigarette, and she hadn't had one in ten years. She felt transparent. Both Peet and Catherine seemed to be able to tell her what she was thinking and doing before she quite realized it herself. Certainly before she was ready to share with them what they already found so obvious.

She started a new pot of coffee and was staring at it as Peet came in the room.

"Jan, you've got to level with me here. I'm not interested in being mad at you, but I won't be played by you and the new boss. Just tell me what's going on."

"No one's playing you." Jan poured her coffee before the pot finished brewing, juggling her mug and pot and spilling all over. Peet kept her arms crossed over her substantial chest, the furrow marks still in place on her forehead. She finished wiping up the spill and doctoring her coffee before she turned to Peet.

"Maybe there is something between Catherine and me. Is that a problem?"

Peet's expression dissolved into a smile. "Really? I was just guessing, to tell you the truth. Tell me everything."

"You mean that doesn't upset you?"

"I don't like being lied to. That upsets me. But you sleeping with the boss? Probably not a smart move, but I'm sure you've made worse."

"Gee, thanks."

Peet sat at the table and motioned for Jan to sit. Jan sat with great reluctance. But she owed Peet. More than that, she needed Peet.

"How did this start?" Peet asked.

Jan shifted in her chair. "I'm not going to kiss and tell."

"So you've kissed? What else?"

Jan laughed. "I'm taking the fifth."

Peet looked serious again. "Honestly, this isn't a good thing, you know. Are you in love with her? She lives in London, for God's sake. What do you even know about her?"

She wasn't about to tell Peet that in London, Catherine had a lover who still thought everything was fine. Jan knew Peet well enough to know she'd not approve of Catherine sleeping with Jan when she was already in a relationship. In truth, it wasn't high on Jan's list of things she liked about Catherine.

"Peet, please. Let me figure this all out on my own, okay? I'm a big girl."

Peet snorted.

"And I'm sorry that she treated you badly on the Michigan thing. Let's just say she felt some urgency to find me and that's the best thing she could come up with."

"Did you get any work done up there? Or were you just dealing with Catherine's sense of urgency?"

"We worked plenty, and she knows what she's doing. She took a guy down in the woods like he was a scarecrow."

Jan filled Peet in on what they'd discovered during their trip. They returned to their desks and Jan pulled out a folder with the papers rescued from David Conlon's trash.

"We need to finish going through these to see if there's anything we missed last night. I sped through them, but I did pick up some listing sheets for property in Idaho. One of these may be the place they're headed to."

"Why don't we call an agent out there and see what's closed recently?"

"I'll do that. I need you to contact the Harringtons and let them know what's happening. We're going to need to go to Idaho."

"Who is 'we'? Would that be you and me, or you and Catherine?"

Jan paused. "How much does it matter to you?"

"As long as I know I have a job here, I'm willing to do what the boss says. I just want to be dealt with straight up."

"Understood. We'll leave it to her then."

Peet looked pensive. "But don't trust her completely with everything, Jan. Like your heart, for instance. You've only known her a couple days."

Vivian sashayed up to their desks and handed them each a piece of paper.

"What's this?" Peet asked.

"As part of the new regime's assumption of power," Vivian said, "we're all required to undergo a new background check. You have to fill that out and get it back to me by tomorrow."

Jan stared at the questionnaire in front of her. "What the fuck? Why don't they just look at all our files?"

"I have a background check from not that long ago," Peet said. "Why do they need new ones?"

"Listen, in case you two don't realize it yet, Global Chartered Security is a top-drawer firm. It's not like our provincial, pea brain of a company can be trusted to have checked out our people properly."

"What a pain in the ass," Peet said. She picked up a pen as she looked the form over.

"What happens if we don't do it?" Jan asked.

"That they were very clear on. I just heard it from Engstrom herself. If you don't comply with the background check, or the background check turns up something hinky, you're out. She says it's about their insurance coverage."

Vivian looked at Jan and patted her cheek. "Don't be so worried. They probably won't turn up that drug ring you run on your off time. Have fun, girls."

She sashayed away.

This was bad news. By the time Jan started as a security guard at Titan when she was twenty years old, she'd gathered enough documents and references supporting her identity as Jan Roberts that she could easily pass the scrutiny of Titan's background check on her. But that was almost twenty years ago. And GCS would certainly have a more rigorous routine check, powered by the Internet and their own vast resources. They would discover that as far as Jan Roberts goes, there was no there there.

Peet was calmly filling out her form. She didn't have anything to worry about. She was a straight-laced wife and mother, albeit a big, dykey one. She was a former homicide detective with ribbons on her dress uniform. She was generous of spirit because she had plenty to give. Jan felt mean and desperate; the tenuous hold she had on bringing Catherine into her life, bringing something in that could glue her together and make her a vessel and not so much of a sieve; that would all slide away as soon as she filled out the damn form and the drill started spinning down into her past. She felt like a house of cards with someone's finger about to give a little push.

She got up and moved to the other side of the office. Maybe if she just saw Catherine's face she'd know what to do, though her choices were limited. She could submit the form and endure an agonizing wait. Would they be able to tell that the birth certificate she had for "Jan Roberts" was one she bought from some guy in LA? It was in her file, slipped in by Junior Begala after the most cursory of glances, she was sure. Would they bother to check anything prior to age sixteen? Would they see a red flag when she couldn't list a single relative, an emergency contact, anyone at all who could confirm she was who she said she was? She didn't really know how vulnerable she was to exposure. It had all worked for so long without mishap.

She'd long ago checked the national databases to see if there was anything there related to a girl named Grace Anderson, her given name, one that she now barely remembered. There was no investigation into the shooting of her father that she could find, and she would have been surprised if there had been. If her father had been killed by her shot, the others in the camp might have buried him, but she doubted they would have sought justice. And if he were wounded, he wouldn't have wanted the police contacted—either to report that his daughter was missing or that she'd shot him.

Her other option was to tell Catherine all about it. It was a thought so large and unexpected it was like a boulder dropping right in front of her. Or a bridge? Maybe it was an unexpected bridge, one that would take her somewhere she'd never been—into someone's confidence. No other person had inspired the thought in her. Catherine did.

Jan saw Vivian back at her desk, near the conference room that Catherine had appropriated as her office. The room was empty.

"Have you seen Catherine?"

Vivian slowly turned from her computer and looked up at Jan.

"Hoping for another make out session, are we?"

Jan decided to pretend she didn't know what Vivian was talking about. She couldn't take the teasing just now.

"I need to talk to her about something."

"Uh huh. Well, you're in luck. She left about half an hour ago to go back to her hotel. Perhaps you'd care to join her there?"

"Did she say if she'd be back?"

Vivian smiled in that way that said a person both pitied and wanted to comfort you, which wasn't in the least comforting. "Is she not keeping you up-to-date on her whereabouts, sugar? That's rough. I'd be careful with her if I were you."

"Why do you say that?" Jan took the bait. She wanted to know.

"She runs at a different speed than you, I think. Maybe not in your wheelhouse."

Jan didn't feel insulted. She thought it was probably true. "Just tell me what you know about when she'll be back."

"She didn't say. She just blasted out of here and told me to reach her on her cell with anything important. I can tell you where she's staying if you'd like."

"That's okay. I already know."

"Good girl," Vivian said as she turned to her computer. "Just be careful. And don't forget that form I dropped off."

Jan left her car with the Ritz valet and took the two elevators up to Catherine's room. The contrast with the Pinehurst Inn wasn't lost on her, nor the realization that the Pinehurst fit her much better than the Ritz, and the opposite was true for Catherine.

She knocked on the door to Catherine's room.

"Who is it?" Catherine's voice came through the thick wood door.

"It's Jan."

"I'm afraid this isn't a good time. May I call you?"

Jan's heart started to sink. Something wasn't right. She heard another muffled voice in the room, and before she could decide whether to stay or flee, the door was thrown open. Standing before her in a white Ritz bathrobe was Ellen. Jan recognized her from the photos she'd studied online, but she was more beautiful in person. Catherine stood behind her, taking Ellen's arm and tugging her away from the door.

"Is this the new woman?" Ellen asked. She didn't seem angry as much as contemptuous. Jan stood frozen in place as Catherine stepped closer to her. "Ellen, please. This is someone from my office. Jan, I'm very sorry. I'll have to get back to you later."

"Don't be silly, sweetheart. Let's let Jan in and you two can take care of your business matter." She pulled Jan in by the arm. She felt she was being pulled into a drama she wanted no part of. She lifted her arm away from Ellen and stepped back.

"Oh, sorry," Ellen said. "I haven't properly introduced myself, since Catherine is apparently not going to do the honors. I'm Ellen, Catherine's wife. Maybe you didn't know she was married?"

Jan turned and left, striding down the long hallway as fast as she could without breaking into a trot, but not fast enough to escape the sound of Ellen's laughter. A mad sort of laughter, as if catching Catherine with another woman was a form of triumph rather than a source of sadness or anger. Then she heard the door slam shut.

It was only October, but already the white holiday lights were hung up and down Michigan Avenue, sparkling now as Jan drove through the rush hour traffic. The days were short. But not as short, Jan thought, as the time she seemed to be allowed to be happy. Half a day here, perhaps an overnight there. It was stripped away almost as soon as she realized how good she felt. She was being dunked in and out of happiness. She was pissed off.

Jan realized she might be a little unrealistic about how long it took to end a long-term relationship, a marriage, given her complete lack of experience at either having one or getting out of one. But the way Catherine seemed to be nearly cowering in the room behind Ellen made Jan lose heart. She felt betrayed and utterly confused. When her phone rang she checked to make sure it wasn't Catherine before taking the call.

"It's Natalie Towne," the voice said. It took a moment for Jan to remember the high school teacher. The very helpful, quite good-looking high school teacher. "I'm sorry if I'm catching you at a bad time."

"Not a bad time at all. What can I do for you?"

"I don't know if you're at liberty to say, but I was hoping you could tell me if you've found Maddy. We haven't heard a word at the school."

Jan drove down the ramp that took her onto Lake Shore Drive and sped north with the traffic.

"It's nice that you called. And I wish I could tell you that we have found Maddy, but we haven't."

"I'm so sorry to hear that. Her parents must be frantic."

Jan bit her tongue. It never paid to disparage her clients, but it was sometimes very tempting.

"I think we have some leads to go on. We're heading out to Idaho tomorrow morning to try to track her down."

"Idaho?"

"It turns out the term paper she wrote for your class was practically a road map. We just missed her in Michigan and have reason to believe she and others are heading to Idaho."

Natalie was quiet for a moment. "That's astounding. I mean, I didn't think she was really going to do anything about this living free from society thing she wrote about. She's only sixteen."

Jan was nearing Belmont, where she'd turn off to go to her place. Or to a bar.

"This may seem out of the blue," Natalie said, "but could you meet for a drink by any chance?"

"Where are you now?"

"I'm at home. I live in Lakeview. You live in the city, don't you?"

"Yeah, in Lakeview."

"Can you meet me at The Closet?" Natalie said.

The Closet was one of the oldest gay bars in the city. This put a whole new light on meeting Natalie for a drink.

"I can be there in a few minutes."

Jan hung up and got off the Drive at Belmont and then north on Broadway, back into the heart of Boystown. All roads lead to Boystown, it seemed. And everyone was gay. She hadn't really picked up a vibe from Natalie, had only thought she was pretty when she first met her, and a welcome distraction when she called a few minutes before. And now she was poised to be a pretty big distraction, which was just what she needed. She resolved to put Catherine out of her mind and concentrated on finding parking within hiking distance of The Closet.

The bar was half full when Jan entered. She settled onto a barstool at the end farthest from the door, away from a noisy group of young lesbians who were acting like it was two in the morning rather than six in the evening. Jan never acted like it was two in the morning, even when it was, even when she'd been their age. She was sober even when she was drunk, serious even when she joked. She thought she must be a complete drag to be around.

She saw Natalie enter and look around the bar for Jan. When Natalie spotted her she began to make her way back, stopped a couple times along the way by people—men and women—who wanted to say hello to her. She was not a drag to be around, it seemed. And she looked great—layers of clothes in fall colors, the kind of assemblage of disparate pieces that some women put together so brilliantly, and seemingly effortlessly. They knew how to tie scarves twelve different ways, all of which looked like they'd been flung carelessly around the neck and fallen into an arrangement that perfectly complimented the look and feel of what they wore. It was all well beyond Jan how any of this was possible. Catherine was the same way.

"I'm so glad you could meet me," Natalie said. She climbed onto the stool next to Jan, deposited her bag at her feet, and shrugged out of her jacket. "I didn't think you'd say yes."

"Why is that?" Jan asked.

The bartender came by and Natalie insisted on buying Jan a drink. She ordered beer. Natalie ordered Scotch. "Long day," she said. She looked at Jan. "I guess I thought you might be all business and not willing to strike up anything beyond that."

"Is that why you called? To see if I was all business?"

"Mostly it was because I wanted to find out about Maddy. I called her parents, but they never got back to me."

"You had a much better idea of what's been going on with Maddy than her parents probably ever have. It looks like she's hooked up with some folks in Michigan who are either in or at least involved with militia groups there."

"As I said, I find that remarkable and really scary. I've been looking into these groups more since we last talked. They can be extremely radical."

"None of it makes much sense to me," Jan said. "I have a hard time buying that it was the politics of these groups that lured her in."

Natalie shrugged. "If you think it through, it's not that illogical. Say Maddy gets an intensely romantic vision of what it would be like to live away from the society she knows and feels trapped in. She's read some Ayn Rand, maybe even Thoreau or Emerson. Her head is filled with the notion that if you have control over your environment, you can control your happiness. Even solitude in the right environment will produce a rich life. None of this is unusual for kids her age."

"Right. And running away from home isn't unusual either."

"But it can have disastrous consequences, especially for a girl. But Maddy, thanks to the Internet, finds someone, or a group of people, that she must have connected with in a way that made her fantasy about a new life seem like a possibility. At her age, she's not very capable of seeing all the pitfalls or dangers of whatever plan they came up with. Everything seems not only completely possible, but righteous as well."

Jan drank her beer and tried to remember any feeling of righteousness when she ran away from home at sixteen. Desperation, maybe. Paralyzing fear, certainly. Still, she understood Maddy's desire to leave and wondered if returning her to her home was doing the girl any favors.

"We're leaving tomorrow for Idaho to find her," Jan said. "But it's a big state."

"Do you know the area?" Natalie looked relaxed. She was being conversational.

"I've been there."

Natalie waited for more, but there was none. Jan finished her beer.

"Let me get you another," Natalie said.

"No, thanks. I should go." Jan started to get up from her stool and Natalie placed her hand on Jan's arm.

"Please. One more. We only got to the business part."

Natalie was looking intently in her eyes. Jan didn't think she was mistaking what Natalie intended. She felt her phone vibrate in her pocket and wondered if it was Catherine calling. Catherine, who was in her hotel room with her half-dressed lover.

"Okay. But these are on me. And let's make it a Scotch this time. I've had a long day too."

Natalie smiled and took her hand off Jan's arm, but kept it close by.

"How long will you be in Idaho?" she asked.

"I have no idea. Why?"

"I have tickets for a concert next weekend and thought you might enjoy it. If you're around, of course."

"What's the concert?" Jan was buying time. Did she want to go on a date? The phone in her pocket vibrated again. She thought of Catherine, of their night together and how that felt, how incredible it felt. She reached in her pocket and pulled the phone out.

"Excuse me, I have to take this," she said, standing up and moving a few feet away to the jukebox. She picked up the call but didn't say hello.

"Will you ever forgive me?" Catherine asked. "What a horrible thing to subject you to. I'm so sorry."

"I don't think I'm in a position to be granting forgiveness," Jan said. "I'm the other woman, remember?"

"This is so vastly more complicated than we can address on the phone. Please just promise me that you won't do anything, go anywhere, until we talk."

"I'm going to Idaho in the morning."

"And I'll be on the plane with you. I have to run, love. Don't give up on me."

Catherine rang off. Jan looked from the phone to the bar and knew what she had to do. She drank down her Scotch and told Natalie she wasn't much for concerts, and then excused herself. She was a fool for Catherine, but she'd never been a fool for anyone before. Even the uncertainty about where they were headed felt better than anything she'd ever experienced. She had to see it through.

Chapter Nine

After thirty-six hours of driving, with stops to eat, buy gas, change two flat tires, and re-build one carburetor, David Conlon led his small band of travelers up a long, winding dirt road to their new Idaho home. They were up in the narrow part of the state where it looks like someone squeezed out the borders from a tube of toothpaste with Washington on one side and Montana on the other.

David was grinning madly. "Home sweet home," he said, though it was the first time he was seeing the property. The entire purchase had been done remotely. The keys were in an envelope in the roadside mailbox, with a note from the realtor saying she hoped the keys worked, but no one had used them in years. Maddy began to see why as they drove a full two miles before reaching the ranch clearing. She and Kristi stared wide-eyed out the window as their new home came into view.

The first thing Maddy noticed were the two plank-sided cabins set at cockeyed angles, pointing toward each other. They were weather-stained and rickety looking, but she expected worse. The photos on the Internet made them look smaller than they actually were. But the house they would live in was harder to spot. It was built underground, its entrance a small door nearly hidden in the side of a mound of weed-covered earth. It made a hobbit's home look like high-rise living.

David pulled up between the two cabins and hopped out. Maddy and Kristi emerged from the back of the van. Diane was just waking up from another nap. Ed, Warren, and Tommy pulled up a few minutes later in the pickup. Maddy stretched and thought she'd never been so glad to be anywhere in her life. As the rest of the group found the entrance to the underground house and went in, she wandered around the cleared homestead. It sat on a ridge high enough to see miles in all directions, with blankets of forest interrupted by creeks, some pasture and farm land, and in the distance, the county road. This was the "defensible ridge" the real estate brochure had described, presumably to entice those who saw great value in holding the high ground in case of invasion.

The two cabins were nearly identical, with one bedroom fitted with bunks, a large living space, and huge wood-burning stove. Behind the cabins was a large fenced garden area, and beyond that was a metal storage building, a barn, and a workshop. That led to an open field that stretched for some distance before being swallowed up by the forest. She imagined that's where they'd keep the cows and goats they'd been talking about. And they'd plant vegetables in the garden and have chickens. That should be everything they need.

Maddy walked over to the underground house. This was her one problem with David choosing this property over some of the others she'd seen online. Why live underground when you have this kind of scenery at your doorstep? As she opened the door she heard everyone talking excitedly. She walked down the steep stairs and came into a large room. Kristi was standing at one end of the room, near a large hearth built with flagstone into the wall. She rushed over and took Maddy by the arm.

"Where've you been?" she said. "You won't believe this place."

It was surprisingly large and pleasant. Overhead lights and a half dozen floor lamps made the room almost overly bright. The walls smelled of fresh paint and were interrupted by timber beam supports reaching up to the high ceiling. If it weren't for the complete absence of windows, Maddy thought it looked like the loft her aunt had in the West Loop in Chicago. A full kitchen was off of one end of the room, adjacent to a long farmhouse dining table with eight chairs. She had a quick vision of dinners every night with her new group of friends. They'd laugh and tease each other and occasionally throw bits of food and then argue about whose turn it was to do dishes. She turned to Kristi.

"It's great."

"Come back here. I want to show you our room."

A hallway led off the main room and cut a narrow path, with four small bedrooms branching off it. Kristi took her into the first one on the right.

"I put dibs on this one for us," Kristi said. Maddy thought it looked about the size of a prison cell, complete with bunk bed. She thought she could smell the earth on the other side of the wall and tried not to feel claustrophobic. "We'll fix it up; you'll see. It will be cool. Do you want the top bunk or the bottom?"

"I don't care. Why don't you pick?"

"Top," she said promptly. And then she winked.

They headed further back in the house. Ed and Warren came out of one of the rooms and walked behind them as they reached the end of the hall. There a door opened onto a huge storage room. She saw David, Tommy, and Diane standing in the middle of the room, looking around. The room had shelves built all around the perimeter of the room, stuffed with supplies that the previous owner left behind. Maddy saw rows of canned goods, boxes of MREs and other freeze-dried foods, gas masks, propane and kerosene containers. On the floor sat two small generators. In the middle of the room was a folding buffet table with metal chairs tucked in all around it.

"Holy crap," Warren said. "I guess we won't starve if the hunting doesn't pan out."

"We're counting on you two to keep us away from the canned beef stew," David said. "The hunting will be plenty good here." He turned to look at everyone in the room. "Can you believe this? It's better than I even imagined."

Diane gave him a hug, but everyone else stood there looking a little shell-shocked. Suddenly, it seemed they really were in Idaho, in a brand new home.

Maddy went to unload her things and make up her little underground room.

❖

Jan was running well ahead of time for her flight to Spokane. She'd traveled so little in her life that she took quite seriously the airline's suggestion that she get to the airport two hours ahead of her flight. She made it through security and found it was still ninety minutes before departure.

O'Hare Airport was a small country in itself and she was locked into the city that was Terminal 3. She found her gate, crowded with passengers for a flight just starting to board. She backtracked to a nearly empty gate and took a seat by the window. It was just starting to rain. She checked the weather app on her phone for the third time that morning. A storm was heading toward them. The race was on to see whether it reached Chicago before flight time. Her phone lit up with a call. It was Peet.

"Are you at the office?" Jan asked. "Do you know if Catherine has left yet?"

She'd had no word from Catherine since the call at the bar the evening before, other than a text telling her she'd meet Jan at the plane. Catherine had not been at the office before Jan left for the airport, but Vivian reported that Catherine had breezed in with a suitcase and was busy on the phone in her conference room.

"I was over there a few minutes ago," Peet said. "Catherine was still there."

"She's not going to make it here on time."

"Sure she will. Listen, I just got a call back, finally, from Detective Hock in Winnetka."

"And?"

"He followed up with the Michigan police after I told him what you found up there."

"And they said there's nothing they can do, right?"

"Actually, there isn't anything they can do. They checked Conlon's house and asked around and agreed that he's left town, but as far as they're concerned there's nothing wrong with that and there's no evidence he has a minor with him."

"I'm surprised they did as much as that."

"Hock also said there's been no response on the BOLO he put out nationwide for Conlon's car. He's probably not driving his own car anyway."

"Okay. We'll be heading to the first property as soon as we land."

"I've also taken the precaution of telling the Idaho police that you'll be in the state looking for a missing teen, just in case something happens," Peet said. "It might help if they have some kind of heads-up about you."

"Have you found out any more about who the buyers are on some of those properties we identified?"

Jan and Peet had spent time on the phone the previous day with Penny Harper, a real estate agent in northern Idaho who agreed to help them out. Her base was Coeur d'Alene, but the amount of land she helped people buy and sell spread out for hundreds of miles from that city.

"She's on it, but the information takes time to track down. The recent sales aren't recorded with the county yet, so she's contacting the agents who handled the properties we identified. There's no telling whether they'll get back to her or tell her who the buyers were."

"I'll be wandering around Idaho forever if that's the case."

"You won't be alone at least," Peet said. She sounded like she was teasing. "And a girl's gotta sleep, and stuff."

"Don't start on that," Jan said. The funny thing was, she wanted to talk about Catherine. She didn't understand why Catherine hadn't called her again after the short conversation last night. She didn't understand why she wasn't furious about having to play second fiddle. But she didn't know how to talk about this stuff. She only knew how to pretend that everything was okay.

Peet laughed. "You're so much fun to tease, Jan. I'll call as soon as I hear anything else from Penny."

By the time the boarding agent had called the last group of passengers for her flight, Jan was pacing back and forth at the gate. The storm had held off, but Vivian reported that Catherine had left the office just half an hour ago. What was the matter with her? Did she think they'd hold the flight for her? Maybe Catherine was one of those people who thought everyone could work around her needs and her schedule, to the extent they thought about it at all. She turned to see Catherine walking toward her, wheeling a case behind her and looking more relaxed than she should, in Jan's opinion.

"They've called everyone on," Jan said. "We should get in there."

"Of course." Catherine smiled. "I'm surprised you're not already on the plane."

The plane closed up not long after they were seated. They were in a two across section, far back in coach. Jan put Catherine's bag in the overhead bin after squeezing other people's coats and shopping bags out of the way. When she settled in her aisle seat she saw Catherine looking intently at her.

"We have so much to talk about."

"You get right to things, don't you?" Jan wedged her laptop bag under the seat in front of her and buckled in. "Don't you think we should talk about work first?"

"Certainly. Here's how I see it. We're going to Idaho. If you have a plan, I'm fine with it. If you'd like me to consult on a plan, I'm fine with that too."

"Peet and I worked up a plan."

"That's fine then."

They were quiet for a bit while the flight attendants squawked over the PA system and they got underway.

"How upset are you about what happened at the hotel?"

"I don't know if upset is the word I'd use," Jan said.

"It was ugly and I'm so sorry you had to go through that."

"Had you just told your girlfriend about me? Is that why she acted that way?"

Catherine sat with her back to the window, angled toward Jan. She looked like she'd lost some of her calm and most of her confidence. "Part of what I wanted to say to you today is that I'm not going to lie about anything. I hadn't told Ellen about you before you came to the hotel. She simply leapt to the conclusion that I had an out of town lover. I don't know how she could have possibly got wind of that, but we did have a nasty argument on the phone the other day. Any time I make noises about the relationship being at an end, she accuses me of having a lover."

"Was that such a leap? You've had other lovers since you've been together."

Catherine kept her eye contact. "I did take a lover once and Ellen found out about it. All I can say is that it's not like it's a regular habit. It was still wrong to do, but I'm not a player, Jan."

Jan had interviewed many witnesses over the years and she thought she was a pretty good judge of when someone was lying and when they were being sincere. She thought Catherine was being candid with her, but knew also that she wanted to believe that. Catherine had been a spy, after all, one who'd fooled harder cases than herself.

"When Ellen first found out that I'd slept with someone else, it seemed like the final blow to a relationship that was cracked straight through. Instead of breaking us apart, we stayed together, but rather more in the way that prisoners are kept together in a cell than anything approaching a loving relationship. I felt too guilty to leave her and she felt too angry to let me go."

"It sounds awful." Jan found this totally believable, having had a glimpse of Ellen's venom.

"Still, none of that has anything to do with you, and I am so sorry you've been dragged into it."

"But didn't you drag me into it when you decided to sleep with me?"

Catherine looked pained. "I dragged you into it when I realized that I felt something for you. Felt a lot for you, almost right away. Then I knew it could be a mess."

Jan did not like sitting on a high horse. She was extremely vulnerable up there, having no claim to any higher moral ground than Catherine. How many women had she slept with herself whom she didn't really feel anything for or know anything about?

"So you knew you felt something for me before we slept together that first night?"

"Let's just say that at that point I knew I was really, really attracted to you. By the end of the night, I knew it could be something more."

The drinks cart rattled down the aisle and stopped in front of them. Catherine ordered a Bloody Mary, Jan a Coke. When it moved on, Catherine continued.

"I know that you're probably more than a little wary of me, and I don't blame you. But Ellen and I are over. We talked well into the night and it seems, at least for right now, that she's accepted that. It will take awhile for everything to get sorted out."

She looked at Jan for some kind of response.

"I don't really know what to say."

"The only thing I need to know from you is whether I'm crazy to think there may be something between us. Am I imagining that?"

The self-assured woman who strode through the airport minutes before now looked like a very uncertain girl, and Jan realized that the vulnerability wasn't all on her side. She wanted to wrap Catherine in her arms and reassure her. Instead, she reached for Catherine's hand.

"No, you didn't imagine it."

They sat quietly side-by-side, hands together, and then their arms pressing against each other, trying to push into each other's space as much as possible. Jan felt the charge racing through her body, now familiar from each time she'd been in Catherine's presence.

"Do you feel it right now?" Catherine said.

"Yes."

They stayed that way, their bodies humming like an electrical plant, until the flight attendant stopped by with her open garbage bag and they tossed their drinks into it. Catherine collected herself.

"While we're on the plane, and I can't run away from you or any of this, I want to tell you everything," she said. "I want to tell you my worst bits so you can decide if you want to stay and see where this goes."

Jan doubted Catherine was going to tell her anything that could trump shooting your own father. But she was curious.

"You don't have to tell me anything. I'm not interested in your past," Jan said. But she was lying. She was interested in everything about her.

"You will be when I tell you this, because there are certain things I think I have to be honest about if I have a chance of really having you in my life, really knowing me for exactly who I am. What I'm not interested in is anything less than that."

She looked at Jan, as if for permission to continue. It was Hobson's choice for her. If she said she didn't want to know, then it was as if she were saying she really didn't want to be truly close to Catherine. If she listened to whatever confession she was about to make, withholding her own secret was the worst kind of lying, and she didn't want to start out that way with her. She nodded at Catherine to continue.

"You remember I told you I worked for years at MI6, the British security force."

"Kind of like our CIA."

"Kind of. The Brits have a very long history of spying; we're quite keen on it. My father was an intelligence officer before going into medicine, and I'd wanted to join up from a very early age. And somehow, I made it happen.

"For ten years, everything was fantastic. I had great assignments, great working partnerships. It wasn't all high-wire excitement. A lot is boring analytical work, interrupted by moments of terror. But I was well suited for it.

"Then the war in Iraq happened. MI6 and our military intelligence were very active there, both in tracking and sorting intelligence and in the specific mission of finding Saddam Hussein. I can't tell you all that much about our operations, but it's just the one day, the one moment you need to know about."

Jan couldn't imagine where she was going with this. But she could see Catherine had taken on an almost robotic quality as she recited her facts.

"My partner, Adam, and I had been working to identify individuals who may have known where Saddam was. We got as far as finding some blokes who might know the men who knew where he was. It's all a matter of inches, really, and this was one of the first solid leads we had.

"Adam and I went out late at night to track this guy, and we caught up with him on the outskirts of Basrah. He was alone, coming out of a house, and even though there was a curfew on, he didn't seem the least concerned about breaking it. We circled around him and managed to slip him into an alley without much fuss. Adam was putting restraints on him as we were going to take him in for interrogation. I covered, but I didn't do a good job of it. Suddenly, three men were on top of us, screaming at the top of their lungs. Adam and I fought like the devil, but this is the only salient thing about it. One of our attackers took hold of my arm, my gun hand. I don't remember clearly—I think he had me in a choke hold. I just remember struggling as he wrapped his hand around mine and pulled the trigger. And Adam went down.

"I would have gone down next, of course. And there were bad moments afterward when I thought it would have been better if I had. But a British patrol came round, drawn by the noise, and our attackers and the target scrambled. So I was safe, and Adam was dead."

Jan took Catherine's hand back into her own.

"It must have been terrifying," she said. Really, what do you say when someone tells you a story like that? She had no reference point. She was trying to imagine herself in the same situation and couldn't even get a picture in her head. How would she feel if Peet had been shot under the same circumstances?

"I suppose, but we're well trained to handle situations more chaotic than that. I failed, and my partner died. I left MI6 shortly after that."

"But you loved it, or at least that's what I heard you say."

"You can love something and then it can go incredibly sour. In a heartbeat. There was an investigation afterward, a friendly fire sort of thing. They didn't find anything they could charge me with, or even suspend me over. But it didn't matter. I was finished. You can't shoot your own partner and ever expect to work in the field again."

"Is that when you joined Global Security?"

"Yes. Ellen had been after me for a long time to take a private position. She was thrilled."

"But you were not."

Catherine looked sad, her loss fresh again. "I hate it, to be honest. And that's what I want to be—completely honest. The first interesting thing that's happened to me in six years with this company is coming to Chicago and meeting you, but that's not really job related, is it?"

"I hope not."

"Does this change your mind about anything?" Catherine looked at her nervously. "You're the first person I've told that story to. Ellen thinks I left the agency to please her."

"I'm glad you shared it."

Catherine snuggled closer to Jan and leaned against her shoulder. Jan tried to open her mouth to say she had something to share also, but it remained clamped shut. She hated herself for it.

The night fell quickly on their first day on the ranch. Maddy sat around a fire ring that had been built behind the cabins, near the vegetable gardens. She nursed some kindling underneath a couple of split logs she'd found behind one of the cabins, feeling anxious for the flames to grow and cast off some of the impenetrable darkness all around her. She found the quiet and the darkness spooky, so unlike her suburban landscape that her imagination started to run wild, mostly along the lines of a horror film, something her brother may have watched.

She saw a flashlight coming from the buildings and heard Kristi whistling. She whistled a lot, which was mostly annoying, but right now the most welcome sound Maddy could think of. Flames started to lick around the logs and take hold just as Kristi reached the fire ring. Tommy walked silently behind her.

"Look, you're a regular Girl Scout," Kristi said. She turned off the flashlight and sat on one of the large flat rocks circling the fire.

Maddy shrugged. "I got sent to camp every summer," she said. "When you finally get old enough, just about the time you swear you'll kill yourself if you get sent to summer camp again, they start teaching you some useful things. Like how to start a fire."

"Anything else that's useful to us out here?" Tommy asked.

Maddy thought about it for a minute. "Maybe. I can get back in a canoe or kayak if I fall out, and shoot a bow and arrow pretty well. I think if a deer stands absolutely still exactly twenty-five feet away from me and wears a bull's-eye, I can put some food on the table."

"None of us have any business being out here, from what I can tell," Tommy said. "I don't even know what we're supposed to be doing with ourselves. All I've done since we got here today is wander around and stare at things."

"Hell, Tommy. It's just the first day. We'll get things sorted out. I know one thing we'll be doing and that's splitting a shit load of logs. Every damn building here is heated with wood, and it's already cold out," Kristi said.

They all stared at the fire, their winter coats on. Maddy kept poking away with a stick. She hadn't seen David since dinner when he disappeared down in the storage room and shut the door behind him. He'd been holed up in there most of the day since their arrival.

"What was David like in high school?" Maddy asked.

"He was exactly like he is today," Kristi said. "Smarter than what's good for him and always in charge. We got up to a bunch of shit back then, didn't we, Tommy?"

"Yeah. David came up with a lot of ideas, and he wanted to try everything, even if he knew it was stupid."

"How about if you thought his ideas were stupid? Would you go along with David?" Maddy asked.

Kristi was quiet for a moment. Tommy just looked at the fire. "I guess I didn't ever think his ideas were stupid."

"Me neither," Tommy said.

"I just hope someone knows what they're doing. We are totally on our own here," Maddy said.

"But that's what you wanted, isn't it?" Kristi said.

"Well, yeah. But I don't want to die out here, either."

Maddy shifted around on her rock, poking at the fire. She felt nervous, a little afraid of the dark and the woods. It made her cranky. Kristi moved over and put her arm around her.

"Don't worry, Maddy. I won't let anything happen to you. It's going to be great. We have this beautiful place all to ourselves. We'll figure out what to do."

Maddy saw another flashlight pierce the darkness. She wanted to call out to see who it was, but she didn't want to seem scared in front of the others. Diane came up to the fire ring and turned her flashlight off.

"Hey, what's up?" she said. She was cheery, as she usually was. She had taken charge in the kitchen and gotten a meal put together from goods in the storeroom, then dove right in to do the dishes after they were done eating. She was on task. Maddy envied her.

"Not much," Tommy said. "Just killing time. What's going on back there?"

"We've got some visitors."

"What?" said Maddy. How could they have visitors? "Who are they?"

"Friends of David's. Or really, friends of Drecker and those guys. There's four or five of them and they all went into the storeroom with David."

Maddy thought of the pages she'd seen in David's box of files with information and photos of some Idaho militia members. She supposed that's who was in the storeroom with him.

"Did they act like they were having a secret meeting or something?" Maddy asked.

"They didn't ask me to join them. I don't know if it was secret. Do you have a problem with something?" Diane sounded a little suspicious.

"It's probably the guys Drecker wanted to connect with here once we got the ranch. That's one of the reasons they bought it," Tommy said.

Now Maddy's head was spinning. "Wait a second. What do you mean 'they bought it'? I thought we bought the ranch."

Tommy looked a little confused. Kristi looked like she felt a little guilty. Diane looked contemptuous.

"You thought that we, the six of us, bought this property?"

"Well, yeah. I thought that's what David said. It's why I gave him the twenty thousand."

"Oh, honey. You are young, aren't you? That money you gave us is what we needed for a down payment. Drecker and a few others took out the loan for the property. We're just the full-time staff here."

Kristi put her arm back around Maddy's shoulder, but she shrugged it off and stood up.

"I am nobody's full-time staff," she said. She headed back to the house, fishing her flashlight out of her pocket as she stumbled over the rocks scattered all around the area.

She heard Diane say, "Let her go," and she thought Kristi probably was trying to come after her. The hell with her and all the rest of them. They had left her out, tricked her, made her look foolish. She was going to let David know what she thought about that.

The entrance to the underground house was perfectly dark. The whole clearing that held the ranch's buildings was dark, but some cloud cover had parted and the moon was starting to rise. She saw a huge pickup truck parked behind Ed's old one. She opened the door to the underground house and headed down the stairs, relieved to see the artificial light streaming up from below. The quiet matched the quiet outside; there was no one in the main room of the house, no one in the kitchen. As she moved down the hall toward the storeroom, she strained to hear anything at all, but it was still dead quiet.

She took a deep breath and opened the door to the storeroom. David sat at the table with four men and they turned their heads toward her as she entered the room. Ed and Warren were in chairs set against a wall. The men were all big. They made David look like a boy sitting next to them. His limbs were so slender and his hair was long and very deliberately messy. The other men had military haircuts and wore camouflage. David did not look in charge.

He leaped up from the table and came to the door, taking Maddy by the elbow and steering her out, then closing it behind him.

"What the hell is going on?" Maddy said.

He kept hold of her elbow and took her down the hall to the main room.

"Maddy, you can't just barge in like that. We were having a meeting."

"But who are those guys?"

He looked confused, as if he couldn't figure out why she was asking the question. "What do you mean, who are they? They're the guys we'll be working with out here, with the co-owners."

"What co-owners? I thought this place was just ours." She felt a little frantic. "I don't understand this."

David was steering her to the stairs. "I can't explain it to you now, Maddy. You'll just have to wait. I have to get back in there." He flashed her his smile, which looked fake to her now, like the car salesman's did when she first walked into the CarMax. "Go on back out. We'll talk later."

"But it's cold out there."

"I'm afraid you're just going to have to get used to that. Go on."

He pushed her gently up the first stair and she glared at him before stomping up the steps. She didn't know what to do with herself. Going back to the fire seemed impossible. She hardly felt a part of them anymore. She waited for a few minutes and then crept back down the stairs into the house and into her bedroom. She had a right to be in the bedroom. Her $20,000 should have bought her that at least.

She dug under the bunk bed for her bag and dragged it out. She had brought a few electronic gadgets with her to Idaho, but she hadn't really expected to use her secret spy recording pen. She'd bought it online the year before to bug her parents' bedroom. She wanted to see if they were as horrible in private as they were in front of her and Justin. Were they always that mean to each other? Did they ever talk about her when they were alone? The experiment lasted a week or so, when Maddy finally got bored listening in. It turned out that they were just as horrible to each other as she saw them be every day, and they never talked about anything but themselves. And they didn't have sex, which was a relief.

But now the pen might help her find out what was in store for her at the ranch. She didn't trust these other men, the ones in

Michigan or the ones sitting with David in the storeroom. She didn't think they were intent on building something small and special and uniquely their own, a place for them to grow in ways that weren't defined by others. She guessed, based on her reading, that they were intent on bringing down something large, and she didn't want to be a part of that. She didn't know if Kristi and the others knew about any of this and had been deliberately holding information back from her. She didn't know why she'd even come out here. But now that she was here, she'd find out what was going on and get out if she had to.

All she had to do was place the pen somewhere in the storeroom; it was powerful enough to pick up voices from almost any point in the room, and there were plenty of places to hide it in there. Then she just needed some private time to listen to what was recorded, which might be the trickier part. She stuffed the pen into her pocket as she heard the door to the storeroom open and the men walk down the hall past her room. A few minutes later, she heard someone walk back down the hall and the door to the storeroom closed again. She went into the main room a short while later and she could hear Diane and Tommy banging around in the kitchen. It wasn't going to be easy to get the bug planted.

Two hours later, when the house had been stone silent for a long time, an hour after she heard David and Ed and Warren come out of the storeroom and go into their rooms, Maddy got quietly off her bed and opened the bedroom door. Kristi snored softly on the top bunk. She tiptoed the few feet down the hallway and shined her flashlight onto the door of the storeroom. A padlock had been placed on the hasp outside the door. No, this wasn't going to be easy at all. But now Maddy knew she really had to find out what they were up to.

❖

The forty-minute drive from Spokane to Coeur d'Alene was passed in silence. Jan drove the rental car and Catherine stared out the passenger window. Jan could feel her turning her head to look at her. She did it every few minutes, and when Jan didn't look back at her, she turned her face back to the window. One time she sighed. The closeness Jan had felt in the plane seemed to have receded beyond reach, and for no apparent reason, or so Catherine must have felt.

For Jan, the reason stretched out before her as soon as they crossed into Idaho, her first time in the state since her escape at sixteen. Once she started plotting on a map the location of the several properties they were going to check out, there was no escaping the inevitable. She was going to be in the area of her father's camp. She had no idea where exactly that camp was—her escape had been blind, from one unknown location into an unknown world. All she knew was she had somehow made her way to Coeur d'Alene, and from there to the west coast. All the properties they were visiting were about as far away from Coeur d'Alene as she guessed she'd travelled that night and into the following day, after she'd shot her father.

The night was so dark there wasn't a thing visible outside of the beam of her headlights. But the feeling of familiarity settled on her like a cloak. Some part of her lizard brain was activated by the smell of Idaho, the ions in the air, undoubtedly something she didn't understand but unmistakably felt. She'd nearly forgotten that Catherine was beside her when she was startled by her voice.

"I'm quite convinced that you are reevaluating everything and have decided I'm entirely too much trouble to bother with. Am I right?"

"What?" Jan looked over and saw Catherine with her arms crossed, looking partly angry, partly frightened.

"You should know that I don't deal well with silences. If you're upset, if you're angry, just come out with it."

"I don't know what you're talking about."

They were entering town and a Holiday Inn appeared on their right. She parked in front of the motel entrance and shot out of the car with Catherine right behind her. There was no line to check in, no one else in the lobby. The young woman at the front desk greeted them brightly. She seemed more a girl, really. She had pigtails. "Good evening, ladies. Will that be one room or two for you gals?"

Jan felt Catherine's hand wrap around her forearm, keeping her from talking. "We'll take one room, please."

"Oh my God, are you English? I love English accents! Say something."

Catherine looked at her blankly. Jan passed her credit card over and said, "If you wouldn't mind? We're anxious to get to our room."

She felt Catherine's hand squeeze her arm again. The clerk briskly ran the credit card and turned over the key cards, all the while telling them how lucky they were to be in Idaho during such a beautiful time of year. They got out as quickly as they could.

The room had two queen beds. Jan threw her bag on one of them and threw herself on the bed after it. Catherine kicked off her shoes and without a word or a bit of hesitation, draped herself over Jan, hip to hip, nose to nose. "I don't like silence, except for when I like silence," she said, lowering her lips to Jan's and kissing her softly. "I don't know how to figure out what you're feeling, except this way."

Jan held her close. She wanted to hug her right into her being, hoping Catherine knew that was what she was trying to say as she pulled her in tightly. Were there words for that? Jan didn't know them if there were. Not adequate ones. She moved Catherine to her side and held her gently by the side of the face. She kissed her for a long time. Every second of it felt right, while so much of her life had always felt wrong.

They made love ferociously, consuming each other in large gulps. Jan was silent even when she was nearly shattered by her orgasm, while Catherine gave full throat to her pleasure. The other guests at the Holiday Inn would not be confused about what was happening in room 203.

"I'm not very good with words," Jan said.

"But you're an excellent communicator in other ways," Catherine said. She looked up and smiled at Jan.

"I meant everything I just did. If that makes any sense."

"Just hold me. That's all I need you to do."

Jan drew her close and wrapped her arms tightly around Catherine's slender frame. She could feel her breasts against her own. She could feel.

Catherine lay tucked under Jan's arm, quiet as she caught her breath. Jan wondered how long she'd have to wait before she could make Catherine come again. She'd never seen anything as sexy as the look on her face as she cried out. It wasn't just sexy, though. It was powerful, a connection she'd never felt before. This was not sex as she'd ever experienced it. This was vulnerability and trust.

"I have something I have to tell you," Jan said. She held Catherine tight, wanting her close while she told her. Vulnerability and trust were not just about sex. She needed to give Catherine more than just her body.

"I'm listening," she said. Her voice was neutral. She must have known it was something big. She stayed as still as a rabbit.

Jan told her everything and it took a long time to tell. What her life was like in the camp, how she escaped it, how she'd lived all these years not knowing whether her father was dead or injured, not caring much either way. She told her about her made-up identity and her life between the escape and settling down with her job at TSI. Catherine was quiet for a bit after Jan stopped talking.

"Is it all right if I say something now?" she asked.

"Yes." Jan was so unfamiliar with everything she'd been feeling since meeting Catherine that the relief she felt from her confession didn't seem that remarkable. It was just another new feeling.

"I think that being back in Idaho must be hugely disturbing to you. I wish I'd known, only so Peet and I, or Peet and someone else could have come out here instead."

Jan loosened her arms and pulled away from Catherine. She sat up and looked down at her.

"I'd think the thing that's hugely disturbing would be the story itself. Doesn't it, I don't know, make you think I'm sick, or disturbed, or awful in some way?"

Catherine put a pillow behind her back and relaxed comfortably against the headboard. "Look, if you want reassurance that I don't think any less of you, you should know this. I hope you did kill the son of a bitch."

"Huh."

She pulled Jan into her arms. "Let's enjoy getting all these horrible secrets out and into safekeeping with each other."

Jan lay with her head on Catherine's shoulder, trying to assess the fallout from telling her story. There didn't appear to be any. Catherine moved her fingers softly up and down Jan's arm and kissed her on the top of the head.

"You've never told anyone this, have you?" Catherine said.

"No one."

"It means everything that you've given that to me. I'm afraid I haven't given you many reasons to trust me."

Jan paused. "And yet, strangely, I do."

Catherine gently lifted Jan's face so they could see each other. "I hope that's because you know how much I love you. How much I've fallen in love with you."

Jan blinked. "I'm not sure if I know what being in love is, but it must be this. I've never felt this before—this constant, completely unsettling thinking about you. The butterflies I feel every time you're near, the instant arousal as soon as I see you. Does that mean I'm in love?"

Catherine smiled. "Some would find it convincing evidence."

"Then I love you. And I've never told anyone that before either."

They lay quietly for a long time before Jan was stirred by another thought.

"I'm worried about the background check Chartered insists on doing on all of us. Is that going to show that there really isn't a Jan Roberts?"

"Don't worry about that. I can sort it easily."

"And you'd do that?"

"Like I said, I will keep your secret safe. I'll keep you safe, if you'll let me."

Jan soon fell into the best sleep of her life.

CHAPTER TEN

Maddy was awake shortly after dawn. She would normally choose to sleep in. She was a teenager, as she often had pointed out to her parents, and teenagers were programmed to stay up late and sleep late. Noon was the crack of dawn, really. But she reasoned that everything was going to be different here in Idaho, and she needed to take advantage of every bit of daylight here.

It sounded as if she was the first one awake. Kristi was sound asleep as Maddy put her pen recorder into her pocket and slipped out the door. The underground house was dark. No one was up; no lights were on. No dawn's early light coming through the windows. She shined her flashlight on the door of the storeroom, but it was still padlocked. She went to the kitchen and made coffee and brought two mugs back with her to her room. Kristi stirred in the upper bunk.

"Get up," Maddy whispered. "I brought you coffee."

Kristi's face appeared at the side of the bed, looking down at Maddy in total confusion. "I don't even know where I am right now. Am I still drunk or something?"

"You're not drunk. Here." She passed a mug up to Kristi and then sat along the wall opposite the beds. They both drank.

"Is it coming back to you now? That we're in Idaho?"

Kristi grinned. "Yeah. I'm not quite sure what to make of it, though."

"I know. It's pretty weird."

"It feels like the middle of the night. What time is it?"

"Six thirty? It's not that early."

They were quiet for a bit. Maddy wondered what the hell they were supposed to be doing with themselves.

"Why don't we go for a hike?" she said. "Get the lay of the land."

"Just the two of us?" Kristi sounded hopeful.

"Absolutely."

They got dressed and grabbed some protein bars from the kitchen and quietly climbed up the stairs and out into the world. Maddy felt like a mole emerging from her tunnel. The daylight, as muted as it was, felt blinding. Kristi crammed her cap ever further down on her head and peered out from under it.

"Where should we go?"

"Let's head north, away from the road. I think our land spreads out some that way."

The clearing for the working area of the ranch was about a hundred yards end to end, with the underground house located smack in the middle. They walked north, past the barn and the vegetable gardens, a corral, and then into thick, dark woods. It was disorienting. Maddy pulled a compass out of her pocket and got her bearings.

"Geez, you are a Girl Scout," Kristi said.

"I got kicked out of Girl Scouts. But I took orienteering at the stupid summer camp. This is the same compass I got back then."

"Cool. You can keep us from getting lost."

There was no path to follow, unlike the only forest Maddy was acquainted with—the suburban Chicago kind where trails intersected each other all over the place, like the interstate system heading into the city. There was no way to get lost or even to feel like you were in the forest. Here the feeling was completely different. The weak sunlight tried to poke through the treetops. Their forward progress consisted of stumbling and lurching through the ground cover and fallen branches. She realized they were making a terrible racket and stopped for a moment.

"What?" Kristi said.

"Quiet. I want to hear what the forest sounds like."

They stood quietly for a few moments before Maddy started picking up the sound of the birds scattering about from tree to tree, the squirrels racing up tree trunks, the crack of a falling branch.

"I wonder if we'll see any animals," Maddy said.

"As long as it's not a bear."

"I hadn't thought of that. We could run into a bear. But probably not, right? I just want to see something."

"A moose would be good," Kristi said.

"Let's be really quiet. Like the Indians. I mean, Native Americans."

They went into a sort of stealth crouch and tried to tread lightly as they moved forward.

"It's kind of like what we did in training," Kristi whispered. Then she stepped in a giant pile of scat and swore loudly.

"Maybe there are moose here," Maddy said. She didn't know moose scat from bear scat. It could be bear, she thought.

Maddy had no idea how far they had travelled, but after an hour heading straight north they took a break and sat with their backs to an enormous tree trunk. Its top seemed impossibly high above them, but she could see a sharp blue sky between the trees, filtering light to the forest floor around them. Maddy took her jacket off, twisting her body as she tried to free her arms. She froze when she looked behind them and turned quickly back, scrunching down against the tree trunk.

"Get down!" she said, pulling Kristi by the arm. She put her finger to her mouth and then pointed behind her. Kristi twisted herself around so she could see where Maddy pointed and then quickly turned back and scrunched down beside her.

A man had appeared about thirty yards away, walking toward them. He was wearing a camouflage uniform and carried a gun on his shoulder, walking lazily and kicking at the fallen leaves. He started whistling. He seemed completely unaware of their presence. Maddy slowly twisted around to have another look and was relieved to see he had turned and was slowly heading away from them. Then he stopped, looked at his watch, and stood at parade rest. If he turned 180 degrees, he'd be able to see their legs sticking out in front of the tree, their blue jeans and white sneakers like a neon sign. Maddy tried to tuck herself in against the tree as tightly as she could. Kristi did too, but with less success.

They heard the crashing sound of boots on the ground, or at least it sounded like a cannon to Maddy. Her heart leapt to her throat thinking the man had spotted them and was marching over. But then she remembered that they weren't doing anything wrong. Didn't they own this land? What was this guy doing in their woods? But maybe they were trespassing. She really had no idea. The noise stopped. When they heard voices, both Maddy and Kristi twisted around to look.

Now there were three men standing there, all of them armed. The first man, who looked fairly young, a middle-aged guy who'd just arrived, and a really old, grizzled guy who clearly seemed to be in charge. The first guy was standing at attention. He stepped forward and switched positions with the middle-aged guy. She couldn't hear what they were saying, but soon the old guy and the first guy marched off, to the east. They watched as the new guard used his radio. They could hear it hiss. Then all was quiet again.

Kristi gave Maddy a look that said, "What are we going to do?" and Maddy signaled for a little more time. They lay quietly for ten minutes or so, and then heard the guard begin moving north. When he was out of sight, they slipped away and moved as quickly as they could back the way they came.

"What the hell was that?" Kristi said. She was ahead of Maddy, moving at a blistering pace. She looked behind her shoulder to see if Maddy was keeping up.

"I don't know. Looks like militia guys, I guess. I know I didn't want them finding us if we were on their land."

"How the hell do you even tell out here? I thought it was our land."

They made it back to the ranch and Maddy took a deep breath when they entered the clearing. Since arriving on the land the day before she'd felt nothing but constricted and afraid—by the windowless walls of the underground house, the impenetrable darkness of the nights, the dangerous looking men in her new home and, it now seemed, the threatening forest.

She saw the group of men as soon as they passed the barn. David was standing by the entrance to the house with the same men as the night before, with the addition of Sergeant Drecker and Major Jacovich from the Michigan militia.

"Shit," Kristi said. "I was kind of hoping we wouldn't see much of those guys."

"I didn't know we were going to see them at all. Come on, let's go to the barn."

They ducked back to the barn and squeezed through the partially open door. There were so many holes in the roof that the interior was well lit. There was one window at the far end of the building, boarded over, and one high above, smeared with grime. The barn was empty, except for a few rusted bits of equipment. Maddy hadn't the faintest idea what they were meant to be used for. She headed to the stairs up to the hayloft.

"What are you doing?" Kristi asked. She followed Maddy up the stairs.

"I just want to watch them for a bit. This window should look out over the other buildings."

They crawled along the hayloft to the grimy window and peered out. Maddy could see the group moving toward one of the cabins. They were taking a tour, as if they were at Monticello or something, with David acting as docent. They made their way through the two cabins, examined the solar power station, and started heading toward the barn. Maddy grabbed Kristin and pulled her as far back into the hayloft as they could go. She didn't think they were visible from below. She hoped they weren't.

"Now what are you doing?" Kristi asked. She was laughing, as if Maddy were planning to start kissing her in the hayloft.

"Quiet. I don't want them to know we're here."

"Why? I don't get why you're so against these guys."

"I'm not against them. I just don't trust them. I want to hear what they say."

The door to the barn was pushed further open. It screeched as it scraped against the cracked cement flooring. They heard David's voice as they entered.

"This will have to be cleaned up some, but it should be fine. I hope to have horses in here one day."

"What about the armory?" one of the men asked.

"You can't have the armory in the damn barn. It's not secure." Maddy thought this might be Jacovich. He sounded mean.

"I think David's on the right track." She recognized Drecker's voice. "We have the regular ranch life open for anyone to see who comes on the land, and the rest we'll have well hidden."

"What I was thinking of for the armory is that we do something like the house. We just build it underground, but not visible at all to anyone not looking for it."

It was David speaking and Maddy's heart sank as she realized he'd been thinking about armories, and God knows what else, as part of his plan for their ranch.

"That's going to take a lot of labor," another man said.

"We've got plenty of that," Jacovich said. "We're here to build a place that will last, that will serve our cause for a long time to come. We can spend the time seeing it's done right."

They poked around the barn for a little while longer, talking about the right time of year to purchase livestock and how much it costs to feed them. Then they headed out of the barn and pulled the door closed.

"Well, fuck me," Kristi said.

Maddy stared into space, holding her spy pen in her hand. She didn't think she'd need to plant it in the storeroom. She'd just gotten more information than she wanted to have.

Jan was anxious for an early start in the morning, She'd mapped out the first three ranches that seemed likely candidates. All had sold in the past month and were among the listing sheets found in David Conlon's house. But there were a couple hundred miles between the first and the third ranch, and just checking these would take all day. Catherine, however, was on a conference call to London that seemed endless. Jan pointed to her watch. Catherine held up a finger.

Jan took their bags out to the car and had finished loading them when Catherine emerged from the motel room.

"Sorry, sorry. They need lots of hand holding back home, and I didn't want to make them suspicious that I'm not in the Chicago office."

Jan was folding herself into the car and unfolded herself to stare at Catherine. "They don't know you're in Idaho?"

"No, they don't. It's just simpler this way."

"You mean they wouldn't approve of you joining the hunt for a teenager your first week in Chicago."

"Or any week, I suppose. But that's what I hate about this job. I'm not meant to be a desk person. Not at all."

Catherine got into the car and threw her purse in the back. "And anyway, there's nothing I need to do in Chicago over the next couple of days that I can't do by phone or computer. It'll be fine."

Jan pulled out of the motel and headed north. "Your chief job right now is navigator." She pointed to some sheets of paper lying on the console between them. "There are the directions to the first ranch."

"Yes, ma'am. Maybe we'll get lucky and she'll be at the first place."

Jan looked over at her. Catherine was dressed in jeans and a sweatshirt, but it was the kind of sweatshirt that probably cost a couple hundred bucks. You wouldn't wear it to the gym. She looked relaxed and happy, as if she didn't have a care in the world.

"If she's at the first place, or even the third place, it will be almost too good to be true. But still, the whole thing will be a lot easier than trying to find Saddam Hussein," Jan said.

Catherine laughed, but didn't comment.

"Doesn't this seem a little boring to you? Being in the field with me is a lot different than with MI6."

"The last thing I am is bored." Catherine leaned over and kissed Jan on the cheek, moving her hand down to her thigh, which immediately tensed. "I have you here with me and this lovely country we're driving through. And we're going to find a missing girl, who's every bit as important as Saddam Hussein, don't you think?"

Catherine's phone rang and she took another call from the office, where Vivian was running point for her. Jan drove. After an hour or so they found the dirt road that led to the first property, and Jan bumped the sedan along for a mile before they saw the ranch house. She pulled up in front of it and slowly got out of the car to look around. The house and the surrounding buildings looked abandoned. If someone recently bought the place, they hadn't yet moved in. Jan walked up to the door of the house to double check, but she was certain no one was around. There weren't any vehicles in sight either.

Catherine had gone to the barn to look it over and Jan watched her as she walked back to the car. Jan's phone rang and she answered it as her eyes stayed locked on Catherine.

"It's Penny Harper," the woman said. "I think I've found the ranch you're looking for."

"You've got something new?" Jan asked.

"I just talked to a broker I hadn't been able to track down until this morning. He had the listing for a ranch that closed last week, but the big thing about it is that he said the buyers were from Michigan."

"Bingo," Jan said.

"Looks like. Where are you now?"

Jan gave her their location and Penny looked up directions to get to the new place. It was fifty miles north of them. She waved Catherine over and got back in the car. "Great job, Penny. I appreciate your help."

"It's a missing kid. I'm glad to do it."

Jan filled Catherine in as she turned the car around and headed back to the main road.

"What do you think we'll find there?" Catherine asked.

"I don't know. Not a welcome wagon, though."

"Do you think Maddy will be fully against us? I would think a young girl like that might start wishing she were back home, now that she's had a bit of adventure."

Jan shrugged. They were speeding up the road, but even with the scenery going by in a blur she could feel something settle on her with an awful familiarity. Déjà vu, she supposed it was. There was nothing in particular that she'd recognized since arriving in Idaho the night before, but the farther they travelled north, the more closely the feeling wrapped around her.

"I can practically hear you thinking," Catherine said. "Your brow is all scrunched up."

"Sorry."

"No, don't be sorry. Talk to me. Remember that you've told me about your past here? That means you don't have to keep all of this bottled up anymore."

"I don't know what to say," Jan said. "And we're working. I just want to concentrate on that."

Catherine sighed and leaned back against her seat. She didn't seem terribly concerned about whatever it was they would find at the next ranch.

It was close to an hour before they found the road that led to the property. Penny had warned her of the long entrance road, otherwise Jan would have thought she'd taken a wrong turn. The trip up the dirt road made her feel vulnerable, as if they were being observed and sights were being drawn on them as they bounced along. The feeling of familiarity was stronger here than at the last ranch.

"Let's take the pistols out. They're in the glove compartment."

Catherine took the Glock and the revolver out and handed the automatic to Jan.

"So you are expecting trouble?"

"I don't want to be surprised by trouble. Let's put it that way."

A final bend in the road brought them in sight of the ranch. Jan quickly took in the buildings scattered about—a couple of wood cabins, and farther back, a sorry looking barn. But what grabbed her immediate attention was the group of men standing in front of one of the cabins. At the sound of their car pulling up, the men turned toward them.

"That's the bloke from the last camp in Michigan, right?" said Catherine.

Jan watched as Drecker led the men toward the car. He wore his camouflage, as did several others. The rest, the younger ones, all wore jeans and sweatshirts.

"That's Drecker, and it looks like the guy next to him is claiming to be a major," Jan said.

She put her gun in her jacket pocket and saw Catherine do the same. They opened the doors to step out of the car, just as Drecker reached its hood. When he saw their faces he pulled his sidearm and leveled it at Jan. Guns flew into the hands of the uniformed men, who quickly spread into a circle around the car.

"Easy now," Jan said. She held her arms up, palms out.

"Sergeant, do you know these women?" The major stood next to Drecker, his hand on top of his weapon. He hadn't bothered to draw it.

"Yes, sir. They were at our Michigan training camp just a few days ago. Now they're nosing around—"

The major raised his hand to cut Drecker off. He moved forward and stood in front of Jan.

"State your business."

Jan looked at the man, but out of the corner of her eye she kept track of Catherine. She didn't like the way three of the men were surrounding her.

"We're here for the same reason as in Michigan. We're looking for a missing girl. A missing underage girl."

"I told you there that we'd never seen the girl you're looking for. That hasn't changed," Drecker said.

Jan kept looking at the major.

"If you'd allow me to reach into my jacket," she said. "I'll pull out a photo of her to show you."

She reached into her left pocket and could see every gun hand brace for shooting. The major raised his hand again, this time to stop her.

"Don't bother with the photo," he said. "I haven't seen a girl here, and neither have my men. Right, men?"

The uniformed men barked out a "Yes, sir!" The ones in sweatshirts were less sure of themselves. Jan supposed they were frightened, but they looked more guilty than anything else. She wondered which one was David Conlon.

Drecker walked over to the sweatshirt group and sent one of them running to the back of the property.

"Now, I'll have to ask you to leave. This is private property, and as of right now, you're trespassing."

Jan looked at Catherine, who shrugged and seemed as if none of it mattered to her one way or the other.

"I suppose it's your prerogative," she said to the major. "But it seems a shame for us to have to bring the sheriff out here."

Drecker motioned with his gun for them to get back in the car.

"You're only making this harder on yourselves," Jan said. "Maddy Harrington has now been transported across state lines and that makes the charge federal." She paused and looked straight at Jacovich, ignoring the guns pointed at her head. "You don't much like anything that's federal, isn't that right, Major?"

Jacovich took his gun out of its holster and kept it pointed at the ground. Jan knew he was mad, but she guessed he couldn't decide who he was most mad at. The young men in the sweatshirts looked frightened now.

"Now, ladies," he said. "I've about run out of patience."

"Let's go," Jan said, turning her back on the guns and looking over at Catherine. She had a bemused look on her face, as if she were watching a group of boys playing in a schoolyard. Jan got in the car, followed by Catherine, and quickly backed up, scattering the armed men behind them. She turned back onto the road and gunned it, punishing the sedan's undercarriage at each bump and rut along the way.

"The direct approach didn't work," Jan said, "so let's go with Plan B."

"I find that Plan B is usually the one that works," Catherine said. "But it doesn't hurt to try Plan A."

"It might have. Now they're on high alert. And they have time to hide Maddy, which is what they sent that one guy off to do."

"Still, we didn't even know if this was the right property. Now we do."

Jan handed Catherine her iPhone. "Use the map function and see if you can pinpoint our location."

"We'll have to go around the back, don't you think?"

"Yep. And I bet there's no way to drive to it."

Jan looked for a place to hide the car.

"Another walk in the woods with you would be lovely," Catherine said. She leaned toward Jan. "Will we have time to tumble around a little?"

"That's not even funny," Jan said.

But they both laughed.

❖

After David led the others out of the barn, Maddy and Kristi climbed down from the hayloft. Kristi walked over to a push broom leaning against the wall and started to sweep.

"I'm going to start cleaning. This place is horrible."

Maddy stared at her. "That's your response? To start cleaning?"

Kristi looked confused. "Response to what?"

"To them talking about underground armories, that's what. I didn't come out here to build a fort."

"What exactly did you come out here for? Aside from wanting to be with me, of course." Kristi was flapping her eyes most ineffectually. Maddy decided not to answer the question because she hardly knew the answer anymore. Instead, she sat in the middle of the barn floor and watched Kristi push clouds of dust in circles around her.

The door screeched open, loud and fast, and Tommy stumbled in.

"You guys have to run. Now!"

He was panting as he grabbed Maddy by the arm and tried to haul her up. Kristi stepped over and pulled his arm away.

"What the hell, Tommy?"

"I'm not kidding Those private investigators are here, the ones looking for you in Michigan. You can't get caught here. David would get into a lot of trouble."

He hustled them out of the barn and pointed north toward the woods. He put his phone into Maddy's hand.

"I don't know if this will get a signal, but I'll try to call when the coast is clear. If the line's dead just stay away until we come get you."

"How are you going to know where we are?" Maddy asked.

Tommy kept pushing them toward the woods and looking behind his shoulder. "I don't know, but we will. Just stay north."

Maddy hesitated. She didn't know if Drecker was sending her away permanently, left to wander aimlessly in the vast woods, or whether she could count on David to come get her.

"Come on," Kristi said. "We have to get moving."

"You shouldn't come with me. I'd rather have you finding out what's going on here." Maddy said the words, but she desperately wanted Kristi to come with her.

Tommy pushed both of them forward. "Get the hell out of here. Now."

They sprinted to the cover of the woods and found their way along the same path as their first trip into the woods. Only there wasn't a path. There was only their slight memory of the route they'd taken. She tried to pinpoint the sun to orient them, but the thick tree cover made that impossible.

Kristi was leading the way, keeping up a brisk pace. "We've been here twenty-four hours and already everything is fucked up."

Maddy felt stung. She was the reason things were a mess, and now Kristi hated her for it. She stopped walking and Kristi turned around.

"I think you should go back," Maddy said. "The more you stay with me, the more screwed up things will be for you."

"Girl, I am not letting you run into these woods alone. Are you crazy? The important thing is we get you out of sight so they don't snatch you away."

"I shouldn't have come. I really didn't think my parents would send people looking for me."

A crashing noise came from behind Kristi, and Maddy gasped as she saw a huge buck loping through the woods. He stopped and observed them for a moment, but it was Maddy and Kristi who resembled the deer caught in the headlights. They froze in place and watched as the deer slowly turned his head away and ambled off.

"That would have been cool if I wasn't scared to death," Kristi said. "I thought it was one of those soldier dudes again."

"If we keep heading north, we're going to be right where we saw that guy. We should go east. I think our property goes pretty far that way."

"They're going to be looking for us north."

"I'm not sure yet that I want them to find us. Like I said, you should go back. It will be better for you."

"No way."

Maddy headed east leading the way this time. She was feeling more sure-footed marching through the forest, but completely at sea as to what she was doing. If the investigators really had shown up, she knew Drecker would kick her out. And if he didn't, did she really want to stay? Her idea of the ranch hadn't included soldiers and armories and old men. But the idea of being grabbed by the investigators and taken back home to Winnetka was horrifying.

They walked on and on, not sure how far to go to be safe. They hadn't brought any water along, but Maddy knew there was a stream that ran through the eastern portion of the property. After another few minutes she could hear it, and soon they saw a creek at the base of a gully with steep sides carved into the earth who knows how long ago. The noise they heard was from a small stretch of rapids where the water hit some rocks and tumbled down a declivity in the stream. Above it, the water ran gently, and as clear as glass. Maddy scrambled down and knelt beside the water, scooping handfuls of water to her mouth. Kristi put her face right to the water and slurped it up.

"Didn't anyone ever teach you the right way to drink from a creek?" Maddy said.

Kristi grinned. "We have never had creeks clean enough to drink from, so no. I just thought the direct approach was fine."

Maddy sat back on her heels. "Let's just go a little farther and then hole up for a while. We can come back here if we need more water, but it feels a little exposed to me."

She took out Tommy's phone, but there was no signal.

"Looks like we're on our own," Kristi said.

"It's either good news or bad news that there's no way they can track us. I haven't decided which it is."

They crossed the creek by hopping on stones and continued east on the other side. Kristi was leading the way when she screamed and dropped like a stone. Maddy could hear or see nothing around them; it was as if Kristi had been smote from above.

Kristi was laying flat on her back, her hand on her right thigh. She groaned.

"What happened?" Maddy said. She took Kristi's other hand, still looking all around, expecting something bad to show up and explain it all.

"There's a fence there. Look. It's low. Hit my leg."

Maddy looked where Kristi pointed and saw three thin wires, almost invisible if you weren't looking for them. But now that she was, she could see them stretching as far as the eye could see in both directions, held up with short stakes pounded in every six feet or so.

"It's electrified," Kristi said. "Fried my leg."

"Fried it?" She couldn't see anything on Kristi's pants leg, no scorch mark or anything. "How bad is it?"

Kristi got up and hobbled around a bit. "It's okay. I can walk it off."

"Why is there an electric fence in the middle of the forest? I'm pretty sure this is still our land."

"Really? This is like the Ponderosa or something. I didn't know we had so much land."

"I think that if we stay on our land, we're more likely to be caught by whoever's following us. Let's keep going."

Maddy found a slender tree she could use to boost herself up and over the electric fence, and Kristi followed close behind her, landing on the other side with a grunt.

"Maybe the fence is actually our fence," Maddy said, "and it's meant to keep people from coming in. That's possible, right?"

"Let's just put some distance between us and the fence. Then we need to rest for a bit. My leg actually hurts."

They hiked another hundred yards or so, keeping their eyes on the forest floor, picking their way forward. Maddy didn't see the three men approaching, but suddenly they were right in front of them, their rifles pointed at their chests. They were wearing camouflage like the man they'd seen the day before.

"Get your hands up," said the man standing in front. He had a name sewn onto his uniform—Martin—and appeared to be in charge. He wore lieutenant's bars on the collar of his shirt.

Maddy and Kristi raised their hands, just like in the movies, which was the only reference they had for what was happening.

"I think there's been some mistake—" Maddy started to say.

"Shut up," Martin said. He motioned with his head to one of the men behind him, keeping his rifle trained on them. The man came forward and pulled restraints from his back pocket. He reached Maddy first and started to pull her arms down and behind her back.

"Now, wait a minute," Kristi said. "If we're on your land, all you have to do is ask us to leave. There's no reason to go crazy on us."

Martin strode forward quickly and hit Kristi in the midsection with his rifle butt. She dropped to the ground and Maddy could hear her struggling for breath.

"You assholes!" Maddy screamed.

"Get a gag on them," he said, and the other man moved up to assist. Within a minute, they had both Kristi and Maddy on the ground, gagged and with their hands tied behind them.

Maddy was lying on her side, face-to-face with Kristi. She worried about Kristi's labored breathing, though she felt strangely calm, as if she were watching events unfold in a video game and she just needed to be smart about her next move. Her own situation didn't feel real, but Kristi's terrified face did.

The men didn't talk after Martin ordered the other two to pick them up and force-march them through the woods. Maddy's arm hurt where her guy gripped it tightly. She felt unbalanced and as floppy as a rag doll. She looked at the man holding on to her; he was about her parents' age, pretty old, and he stank and had a scraggly beard. She could see that the uniform he wore was ancient with patched elbows and knees, frayed collar and cuffs. He wore one of those floppy camouflage hats. If it were white it could have said

"Aruba" on it and been at home on the beach. It didn't look like this man had ever spent a day on a beach. He kept his eyes grimly forward as he dragged Maddy along.

Ahead of her, Kristi was having a harder time, her one arm gripped by her guard and the other hugging her stomach. When she sagged, her man barked at her and tugged ferociously at her arm. Ahead of them was Martin, setting a brisk pace as they moved farther and farther away from the ranch. Even if she weren't gagged, Maddy wouldn't have bothered to scream for help. It was clear there wasn't anyone coming. She guessed these were the Idaho cronies of Drecker's, the ones they were hooking up with out here. She knew that Drecker must have called them or radioed them or sent smoke signals. She wasn't sure how they had it worked out, but he wanted Maddy gone and these guys were going to oblige him.

After a half hour's march, Maddy and Kristi were brought into a large clearing in the middle of the woods. There were no roads leading in or out of it. It was as if some force had planted a cookie cutter from above and simply lifted a large circle of forest up and away. Maddy tried to get her bearings as they were dragged toward the far side of the clearing. They saw a large wood structure in the middle of the clearing, low and wide, with smoke coming out of its chimney. In front of it was a group of women staring at them, their eyes wide in surprise. Several of the women moved to gather the children running around in the area in front of them. They all looked like they were dressed in homespun clothing. Maddy had seen similar clothing at some of the museums her parents dragged her through on their vacations.

There was a row of small shacks lining the northern perimeter of the clearing. She saw several more children playing in front of those. She did not see any men, other than the ones dragging them toward two large cabins on the eastern edge. Maddy felt her first frisson of fear. What if they locked Kristi and her up in a dark cabin, tied up and gagged? When they got to the cabin, she dug her heels in and struggled, uselessly, she knew, but the idea of going into the cabin was sending her into a panic. When her guard yanked at her arm, Maddy tried to drop to the ground, making herself boneless and too heavy to hold. It was a trick she'd used as a child, when her parents tried to drag her someplace she didn't want to go.

"Pick her up," Martin barked. The guard picked Maddy up from behind and under her arms, dragging her into the cabin behind Martin and the others. Then he dropped her on the floor. Her shoulder nearly popped out of the socket as she landed on her back with her arms tied behind her.

"We've captured intruders, sir," Martin said. "Two girls."

Maddy twisted around to see who Martin was talking to. As her eyes adjusted to the dark she could see more detail in the cabin. It was rectangular, all one room, with a bare minimum of furniture in it. A square table and chairs at one end, a cot along the side, and, at the end farthest from her, a fireplace and a straight-backed chair beside it. She could see someone sitting in the chair, leaning back on the two rear legs with his back against the wall. The chair tipped forward and the man stood up.

"Bring them to me," he said.

Maddy was hauled to her feet and the group moved to stand in front of the cold fireplace. She got a good look at the man as he got a good look at them. He also wore a camouflage uniform, a little worse for wear, but his boots were shiny. He looked really old, like her grandfather, but with a fire in his eye that she never had seen in her grandpa. He looked mean, and Maddy knew the situation was only getting worse, that these men weren't going to just send them back to their ranch or home to her parents. She looked at Kristi standing next to her and saw she was staring at her feet with tears in her eyes.

The man looked at Martin with a question in his eyes. He wore a colonel's insignia, shiny on his worn lapel. "Report."

"Colonel, we got a report of the fencing being activated, and when we investigated we found these two trespassing. They were headed straight here, Colonel. They did not appear to be lost."

"Remove their gags. And radio the others to maintain their patrol. There may be more of them out there."

Maddy heard Kristi take a huge breath when her gag was removed, and Maddy worked her jaw to ease the ache hers had caused. Then she spit on the floor of the cabin. The gag had been her guard's dirty bandana.

Martin reached over and slapped Maddy hard across the face, which made her stumble and fall, again against her back, straining her shoulders. This time she screamed. The colonel sat back in his chair as Maddy was picked back up to stand in front of him.

"Now, you'll tell me quickly what you're doing on our land, or you will regret not telling us. Your choice."

Kristi looked at Maddy.

"Look, mister, I'm sorry if we came onto your land. It was an accident. But I don't know why you're making such a big deal about it. We're happy to leave."

The colonel stared at her. "You're not going anywhere just yet. Now, tell me why you're on my land."

"Didn't I just say it was an accident? We didn't know it was your land. We were just taking a walk in the woods. We live on the ranch on the other side of your property."

"There is no ranch on the other side of my property. You're lying."

Now Maddy looked at Kristi, and she could see her own confusion reflected on Kristi's face. She turned back to the colonel.

"I don't know what your problem is, but you can't just hold us here. Let us go and we'll be on our way."

"I'm giving you one more chance to tell me who sent you here. You better take advantage of it."

The colonel looked calm except for his eyes. They were a deep, almost black color, eerie and frightening. Maddy could see he was furious and quite possibly crazy. She knew these people weren't Drecker's Idaho cronies, and she dearly wished they were.

"Okay, I'll tell you everything, but this is all I've got. I was running away from the people who own the ranch nearby and that's why we accidentally came onto your land. We didn't know any better."

The colonel reached over and picked up a poker from the fireplace. Without missing a beat, he swung it at Kristi's knee, catching it full on the side. She screamed and fell, her hands still tied. Maddy moved toward her but one of the men grabbed her arm again and held her close.

"There's no accident involved when you continue into our land after hitting the electric fence. Now, you can tell me the truth, or we can continue along in this manner. Again, it's your choice."

Maddy could find nothing to say. With every word she seemed to make things worse, and for some reason they kept taking it out on Kristi instead of her. The room was perfectly still as the colonel stared at her. Kristi was groaning as she lay on the floor.

"I would tell you what you want to hear if I had any idea what that is," she finally said. "Telling you the truth doesn't seem to be enough."

For a moment, the colonel almost looked impressed. He regarded Maddy for a bit before his eyes hardened again. He looked up at Martin.

"Lieutenant, I think our prisoners need some time in the stocks to think their situation over. See to that."

"Yes, sir."

Martin led them out of the dark cabin and into the clearing. He held them there while the two other men disappeared into the cabin next to the colonel's and came out with a set of stocks, rolling it on a cart to the center of the clearing. It took two of them to lift the wooden contraption off the cart and set it up. Martin pushed them forward toward the stocks. Things were getting worse by the minute.

Chapter Eleven

After ditching the car halfway back to the county road, as far out of sight of the access road as they could manage, Jan and Catherine hiked north along the western edge of the property. They kept their guns in hand. Jan didn't doubt that the uniforms were spreading out in the forest to keep them from getting to the property again. Between the compass and the map on her phone, Jan led them far enough north to be able to circle around to the rear of the ranch. Catherine remained silent as she walked behind her, and Jan was glad to have her at her back.

As they moved east, the barn became visible, and then the rest of the ranch behind it. They knelt while still at the edge of the trees, scanning the area for signs of anyone. No one seemed to be about.

"Let's give it a few minutes here," Jan said. "Maybe we'll be able to see what building they're hiding in."

"We can't do much if they're armed," Catherine said.

"True. But I'm betting at some point they won't be at the ready, and that's when we'll have to make our move. First we have to see how they're set up here."

After a few minutes, the barn door creaked open and a young man walked out, the same one Drecker had sent running an hour before. He stood in front of the barn door, slowly turning a full circle as if he were surveying the scene as well. Then he sat on the ground and leaned against the barn, staring off into space.

"You go right, I'll go left," Jan said. "Let's meet on either side of him and see what he knows."

They slipped away from their cover and split in two directions, coming around the barn on either side of the young man. He shot up as soon as he saw Jan approaching from his right with a gun pointed his way. He turned to run and saw Catherine coming at him from the other side. He put his hands up in front of him.

"For God sake, don't shoot me," he said.

"We don't want to shoot you," Catherine said. "We want information from you."

"What's your name?" Jan asked.

"Tommy."

"Tommy, where's Maddy Harrington? That's all we're here to find out."

He put his hands down and looked at his feet. "I can't tell you that. David would be furious."

Jan and Catherine looked at each other.

"So she is here?" Catherine said.

Tommy didn't respond.

"Tommy, David will be in a lot of trouble if the authorities come in and find he's been harboring a minor. You don't want that to happen, do you?"

"I don't. But he knows what he's doing. He's got it under control."

"I think not," Catherine said. "It doesn't look to me like he's in control at all."

"I'd say it's the guys with the guns who are calling the shots around here, don't you think, Tommy?"

He shrugged.

"We need to get Maddy out of here," Jan said. "You don't want it on your shoulders if something bad happens to her because of these soldier friends of David's, do you? Just let us know where she is and we won't let on that you told us."

"Where are David and Drecker and everyone else?" Catherine asked.

"I sent the others into the woods to look for Maddy and Kristi," Tommy said.

"Which way?"

Tommy pointed to the west and Jan and Catherine moved toward it immediately.

"But you won't find Maddy and Kristi there," he said.

Jan stopped and looked at him. "What do you mean?"

"'Cause I sent them that way," he said, pointing to the north.

"You're a good man, Tommy," Jan said.

"Who's Kristi?" Catherine said.

Tommy paused. "She's Maddy's friend. She'll look out for her."

Catherine and Jan headed north.

As they moved as fast as they could through the woods, the feeling of strangling familiarity washed over Jan again. It was as if they were in an Amazonian forest, the cloying heat and humidity making it hard for her to breathe, rather than a backwoods forest in crisp, dry air. She pulled at the collar of her shirt, felt herself gasping a little for air.

She tried to concentrate on tracking the two girls. Her tracking skills were excellent, even after all these years, for she depended on them when she hunted as a girl and had been taught by the best tracker she could ever imagine, her father. When they entered the woods, she began to pick up the broken twigs and trampled undergrowth that kept them on pace behind Maddy and Kristi. But each step brought her into more intense rebellion, as if her body was trying to keep her from going forward. She stopped for a moment to catch her breath.

"What's the matter?" Catherine said. She put a hand to Jan's face. "Are you ill?"

Jan stepped away, trying to shake off the feeling as well as Catherine's concern.

"I'm fine. Just trying to keep us on their trail. I'm not entirely sure we're still behind them."

She thought they were, but it was impossible to know. She looked around, trying to act as if searching for trail markers was the reason she stopped.

"It's just that you looked a little green for a minute."

"I said I'm fine."

"Wait, is this around where your father's camp is? Is that what's going on with you?"

Jan's eyes fell on a fallen tree just to their east and she went to inspect the ground in front of it. "I think they rested here. See how the leaves are moved around?" She walked a few paces farther east, looking at the ground, before turning back to Catherine. "Let's head this way. I'm pretty sure they changed course"

Jan moved quickly now, drawn by the fresh scent and by something more primal, the same thing that makes a horse pick up its pace when its rider turns toward home. Home, without comfort, without love, without even a bag of oats waiting, still had its pull. Jan hated every step forward, but could not have turned away. Maddy Harrington seemed a secondary part of this journey.

She stopped to check her compass and saw they were heading straight east. The sun was overhead and bright, doing its best to penetrate the treetops. They heard a sound farther east and Catherine pulled Jan down to lay flat on the ground.

"Militia guy about twenty yards on," she whispered.

They lay perfectly still as the sound of a single person picking his way toward them grew louder. Jan slowly drew her gun from her jacket pocket. Catherine already had hers in her hand. When it seemed that there was only a tree or two between them and the man, he turned away. They heard his steps recede to the north. They lay quietly for another few minutes before sitting up.

"Fuck," Jan said.

"Who do you think it was?" Catherine asked.

"It's either someone from the welcoming committee at the ranch, or . . ."

"Or what? You think it's someone from your father's camp, don't you?"

Jan looked Catherine in the eye. "I had a feeling we were somewhere close to it, and now I have more reason to think we are. And I know one way to find out."

Jan headed east again, softly now, with her eyes straight ahead.

"Clue me in here," Catherine said. "I don't like an operation where I don't have the facts."

Jan looked back at her. "There used to be an electrified fence around the whole perimeter of the Colonel's property. Unless he finally gave up on maintaining it, we should be able to see it. I don't know if Maddy would see it though. If she ran into it, it would give her a pretty good shock."

"Does it signal anywhere when it's activated? I mean, would your father know if someone hit the fence?"

"Not when I was here. Maybe he's gotten more sophisticated since then, but I doubt it."

They crossed a creek and crept forward another fifty yards before Jan spotted it, the wires of the fence a greenish color and so thin that they'd be easy to miss. They stood and stared at it.

"This is what you had to get past when you ran away. When you were sixteen?"

"Yes."

"It's unbelievable. It's mad, really."

"I think Maddy's in there. We have to go in," Jan said. She said it urgently, as if she thought Catherine needed convincing.

"Of course we do. Let's find a place to climb and get over the fence."

Within minutes they had climbed up and over the fence, and Jan was back in her own heart of darkness. She knew the way now. It was all as familiar as her hand, as any home would be.

❖

Maddy looked straight ahead as a little girl addressed her solemnly.

"Did you do something bad?" the girl asked.

"No, I didn't."

"Because people only have to stand there like that when they do something bad."

The girl seemed confused, but no more so than Maddy was. A woman came up and shooed the girl away, looking at Maddy and

Kristi with disdain before walking away from them. Maddy could see others from the corner of her eye, but she could barely turn her head to get a look at them. When Kristi and Maddy both angled their heads toward each other they could just see the other's face. Kristi's was white, as if she'd seen a ghost. Maddy felt like hers must be bright red. She'd never been so mad in her life.

Their heads and hands had been stuck into an old-fashioned set of stocks, planted in the center of the camp so they'd be scorned and mocked by the residents, just like in Puritan days. Behind them was the colonel's cabin. To their right was the larger building that seemed to be some kind of community house. The women and children congregated there, making occasional forays to stand in front of the stocks and stare at them. A few little boys threw rocks at them, but one of the mothers put a stop to that. Maddy heard her say they "were not that kind of people," whatever that meant. They were not like any people Maddy had ever heard of.

Straight ahead were the shacks, and she assumed that's where people slept. There didn't seem to be any men about, and if they were, they were in with the colonel deciding their fate.

"What the fuck are we going to do?" Kristi said.

"I don't know. I don't think these are the guys who know Drecker. I don't know what they want from us."

A tall, gangly boy came up to them, holding a long stick. He poked Maddy in the thigh with it.

"Be quiet," he said. "There's no talking when you're in the punishment."

Maddy had a feeling these stocks got dragged out here with some regularity. "What happens to people from the outside who end up in these things?"

He looked surprised that she had asked him a question. "I don't know. We've never had someone from outside here."

"I don't understand. What kind of place is this?"

The boy poked her again. "No questions," he said, poking her once more. He seemed to want to stay and continue poking, but a woman's voice called him and he ran away, dropping the stick as he went.

They stood locked in place for what seemed hours, but may have been minutes. Maddy's feet barely touched the ground, and the strain on her calves was painful. Kristi's knee hurt and she kept shifting her weight around. They both were sweating, though the air was cool. Eventually, they heard boots approaching from behind and the colonel telling the women and children to get into the cookhouse and stay there. Maddy's anger started to dissolve into fear.

"I don't want to fucking die," Kristi said.

Maddy didn't either. She watched as the colonel and two of his men gathered in front of them, and the thought that she was about to die lay over her like a shroud. The colonel looked much older in the brighter light. His wrinkles were cavernously deep, his jaw sunken by too many missing teeth. But still, he held his body straight, and had about him the air of someone who was used to being obeyed. His men were behind him, two steps back on either side. He looked squarely at them and spoke in a clear voice.

"We have conducted a tribunal to determine the charges against you and the sentences to be imposed."

"A tribunal?" Maddy said. "Is that like a kangaroo court?"

The colonel raised his hand as his men stepped toward Maddy. They held back.

"Unless you'd like your gag replaced, you will listen silently as I pass sentence. You'll have your opportunity to speak."

A radio crackled and one of the men stepped a few feet away to respond.

"Colonel, B squad is reporting in. They've spread out and covered the property. They've found nothing. Should I have them come in?"

The colonel looked directly at Maddy and Kristi as he spoke. "They stay out there until I tell them to come in. These two are not acting alone."

"Yes, sir."

The colonel took a step closer to the stocks.

"You've been found guilty of trespassing and are being charged with espionage," he said. His voice was cadenced as if he were reading from a grand jury indictment. "You'll be punished for the first. In regard to the second, we will find out who you're working with. Now, your punishment for trespassing is twenty-four hours in those stocks. You may end this punishment at any time by telling us who sent you here. If you don't offer this information within the twenty-four hours, a second tribunal will be held to determine your guilt on the espionage charge."

Maddy's neck ached from holding her head up to look at the colonel. But she didn't want to hang her head in front of him. She looked over at Kristi and saw she'd given up that battle. Her head was hanging, and Maddy thought she was crying. She turned back to the colonel.

"I'm not sure where you got the idea that you have this kind of authority over me, but I'm a citizen of a country that has laws. And procedures. Call the police if you think I've done something wrong. This is crazy."

The colonel held her gaze as he spoke. "Lieutenant, give her an adjustment."

The lieutenant named Martin marched quickly up to Maddy. She thought she saw the other men wince. Without hesitation, Martin slugged her across the face. Kristi screamed. Maddy's body slumped as she tried to keep from throwing up. She fought hard to come up through the pain that seemed to drown all five of her senses. When she saw the blood dripping from her nose and mouth, pooling in the dirt beneath her, she started crying too.

Jan estimated they had entered the land about midway between the two perimeter guard posts and were now fifty yards or so from the center of the camp. She led the way as quietly as she could. She could barely hear Catherine moving behind her. She turned to her to make sure she was still there, to remind herself that she wasn't alone. Seeing her there felt almost as surreal as being back in these woods. How had this woman come so fully into her life so quickly? And how the hell did she end up back in the place she risked her life to escape?

Just as she started to speak, Catherine put her finger to her lips and pointed to the north, easing slowly to the ground and pulling Jan down with her.

"Man at nine o'clock, armed."

Jan looked over and saw a young man about twenty yards away, sitting with his back to a tree and tossing acorns. There were a lot of trees and undergrowth between them. Jan was surprised that Catherine had spotted him. Jan knew the risk was too great to try to ambush him. He'd hear them before they got close enough to jump him and any gunfire would be heard in the camp. They couldn't move forward for the same reason. They'd have to wait him out and hope he didn't move their way and spot them.

Jan made a hand gesture that she thought indicated they should stay put. Her PI work had never required this kind of teamwork, this kind of stealth maneuvering. She thought of Catherine in the Middle East, outfoxing opponents more daunting than these and it made her feel both more and less confidant. Catherine, no doubt, knew all kinds of hand signals.

A radio crackled in the silence and they saw the man stand up quickly as he grabbed his radio to respond. The message was unintelligible, but as soon as the transmission ended the guard headed east and was soon out of sight.

"I hope that doesn't mean they've found Maddy," Catherine whispered.

"That was my thought. If they've called everyone back into camp, that will give us a clear passage there. Let's wait a few minutes in case any more pass this way."

They lay on their bellies, face-to-face, for another five minutes. Jan kept looking at her watch, and each time she glanced back, Catherine was searching her face.

"What?" Jan said. "Why are you looking at me like that?" She found it annoying.

"I can't believe you're so calm," she said. "What if you actually see your father?"

"I think it's certain I will. We will. I don't think this camp would still be here if the old man was dead."

"Actually, we're not certain the camp is still there, are we?"

"That guard tells me it is. Normal people don't have armed guards patrolling their property in the middle of nowhere. Not even here in Idaho."

"I'm here for you. Just remember that."

Jan looked at her watch again. "We should go."

Now individual trees seemed recognizable to Jan, huge fallen trunks that she remembered running and jumping over as a kid, sometimes hiding in. She spotted a tree that had been a favorite for reading her stolen magazines, its massive low-slung branch perfect for nestling in. It looked exactly the same, as if time had indeed stopped here.

They saw one more guard, a man so heavy footed that they heard him stomping through the woods in plenty of time to make themselves invisible. When he was out of sight they covered the final thirty yards and came up behind the camp's armory.

"This is an armory?" Catherine whispered.

Jan pointed to the cabin next to it. "That's the Colonel's cabin."

They stepped around the armory, keeping low, trying to get a look at the clearing. Jan was the first to see the stocks in the middle of the large circle. She recognized Maddy locked into one side of it with another girl in the other side. Three men stood facing them and Jan knew instantly that the man in front was her father. Not stooped with age, though he was in his eighties. Not dead, either. She felt Catherine's hand wrap around her forearm, reassuring her, questioning her.

Jan scanned the rest of the clearing. She could see that the door to the cookhouse was closed and she guessed the Colonel had sent the women and children inside, the way he always did when he was going to do something nasty to someone. Jan had been in the cookhouse plenty of times when she heard someone scream outside. Never for long, never too agonizingly. Just loud and anguished enough to make the little kids cry and the women pull them to their skirts. Then they'd all be let out again and everyone acted like nothing had happened. Jan didn't believe that the two strangers in the stocks were going to be met with the same leniency from the Colonel. She had to get them out of there.

Catherine slipped away from Jan and went to the door of the armory just as one of the men behind the Colonel strode up to Maddy and punched her square in the face. As Kristi screamed, Jan ran straight into the clearing, put her shoulder down and tackled the man who had hit Maddy. They sprawled onto the hard dirt. As Jan scrambled to her feet she saw the rifles aimed at her, ready to shoot.

The man on the ground was up on his feet and grabbed Jan from behind, locking her in a half nelson, pointing her head at the Colonel, who raised his hand to keep his men from shooting. He slowly walked toward Jan and stopped a couple of paces in front of her to study her face.

"Release her," he said to Martin.

Martin let go of her and backed a couple paces behind her. Jan looked at the two girls and saw that Maddy was bleeding onto the ground. Kristi looked okay, but scared to death. Then she slowly looked back at the Colonel.

He was staring at her and she knew he saw who she was. His face was still as marble, but she could see it in his eyes, the way they wandered around her face, disbelieving even as he registered the truth.

"Long time no see," Jan said. Martin came around from behind her and looked at her closely.

"Jesus, it's Grace. It's your daughter, Colonel."

"I know who it is. Resume your position."

Jan looked at the man and recognized Trevor Martin, her erstwhile suitor and all-around brown nose. She looked back at the Colonel without acknowledging him.

"Colonel, I can see that not much has changed around here, except that you look about a hundred years older. Where've all your men gone? Have they run away like I did?"

The Colonel spat on the ground at her feet. His reaction was the last one she expected. It hurt, as if she had some kind of expectation that her father was going to welcome her with open arms, the long-lost daughter who shot him on her way out of his life. She hated him. At the moment, she hated herself for caring that he despised her in turn.

"I knew these girls weren't here on their own, but I admit the thought didn't even occur to me that it was you trying to invade our land."

"I see the paranoia is about the same as ever. Your notion of other people's interest in you and your land has always been grandiose. I think that's the right word for it."

"You should have killed me when you had a chance, daughter. Because you are about to regret that you didn't."

Jan looked at the two girls again. Maddy kept her head hanging, still dripping blood. Kristi stared at them.

She turned back to the Colonel. "I'm asking you, for your own sake, to let these girls go. I'll stay and you can deal with me as you will. But there are people looking for these girls, and those people will be on your land before you know it. They'll be a lot more prepared than I am to overwhelm your tiny army. If you let the girls go, they won't have any reason to track them here."

The Colonel turned to the men behind him and motioned for them to lower their rifles. They stood at the ready. A little boy burst from the cookhouse and raced across the clearing. A young woman ran out after him.

"Martin, get those two back in there and tell them to control those kids. If I see one more of them there's going to be hell to pay."

Martin ran off and herded the two back to the cookhouse. Everyone remained quiet except the boy, who complained the whole way. Martin returned to stand behind Jan, his rifle at his side.

"You'll stay here whether the girls are let go or not, and I'd just as soon keep them around. They're serving their sentence, and I believe we have now gotten a little more information regarding the espionage charge against them."

"Espionage charge?" Jan could feel herself losing it, losing the battle to speak rationally to an irrational man. "You are fucking crazy. Do you know that?" She looked at the men behind the Colonel. "Do you know he's crazy? Or you, Trevor? I knew he was mean. That's why I ran away. That's why I didn't give a shit when I shot him. I didn't care whether I killed him or not, and until today I didn't know which way it had gone. And you know what? I'm sorry that my aim was a little off."

She looked straight at the Colonel, took a step toward him. "You're a mean, crazy, hateful son of a bitch."

Jan spat at his feet. The Colonel looked at her with coal black eyes.

"Lieutenant, take her into custody."

Martin moved forward, but before he'd taken a full step, Jan had her pistol out of her pocket and aimed at the Colonel's head.

"Stand back, or the Colonel's a dead man," Jan said. She looked at the men behind the Colonel. They looked startled, their guns still at their sides. "If any of you make a move, I'm putting a bullet in his head, and I won't miss this time."

Jan could hear the rush of her own breathing, but beyond that was silence. Trevor seemed to be motionless behind her; the other two men also stood still. The Colonel, however, seemed annoyed and not the least bit concerned.

"Girl, you are making a fatal mistake. There are three guns to your one. The second you shoot me, you're dead. Is that what you want?"

"I'd prefer that to being tied up in this hellhole again."

He looked at her for a moment and then turned his head to Martin.

"Shoot her," he said

Jan heard Martin raise his rifle as she locked her hands in place to fire. A shot cracked out of the woods from the direction of the armory, and Martin went down. The other two soldiers swung their rifles toward the armory and opened fire and they quickly went down with two more shots from the woods. Jan kept her pistol trained on the Colonel and looked to see if the soldiers were moving. The Colonel drew his own pistol as she looked away.

"Don't do it, Colonel. There are two guns to your one. Now it's you who'll be making a fatal mistake."

"Don't you think I know that?" he said as he cocked his old revolver.

Another shot rang out from the woods and the Colonel fell to the ground, giving Jan a clear view of the bullet hole in the back of his head. Jan swept the area with her gun in both hands as Catherine raced into the clearing and pulled the rifles away from the two soldiers on the ground.

"They're alive," she said, moving over to Martin to take his weapon as well. "He's cold."

Jan heard Maddy crying behind her and looked to see them both staring wild-eyed at them. She moved quickly toward them.

"We've got to get out of here quickly," she said. "The other men will be on their way."

She and Catherine tried to open the stocks and found it shackled shut. Catherine reached into first the Colonel's and then Martin's pants pockets to find the key.

"Jesus Christ, Jesus Christ, Jesus Christ," Kristi was saying. She seemed catatonic.

Catherine came up with the key and as she unlocked the stocks, Jan went to the cook tent and called in through the closed door.

"Do not come out," she said as forcefully as she could. "Your children are not safe. Wait until your men return and let you out. Do you understand?"

She heard some children crying in there and then a woman's voice saying they understood. It would have to do. She raced back to the stocks and helped Catherine with Maddy and Kristi, each holding them up by an arm. Maddy was especially wobbly.

"Where to?" Catherine said.

"There's only one way. Let's head east. There should be a car about half a mile that way. They used to leave the key in the front seat. I don't know if they still do that."

"They probably do. The armory was unlocked. Nice selection of rifles in there," Catherine said. "Anyway, if the key's not there, I can start the car. It's not a problem."

"Nice shooting, by the way. I guess I owe you one."

"Believe me, I'll be happy to collect. Perhaps a bit later though?"

They hustled back into the woods. Jan didn't look back at her father.

CHAPTER TWELVE

V ivian brought a thermos of coffee into the conference room and poured them each a cup. This was almost unheard of behavior for her, but even Vivian had been a little in awe of Jan and Catherine since their return the day before from Idaho. They were cautious, solicitous. Everyone acted like they were strangers. Jan hated it. She watched as Vivian slipped out the door and closed it behind her.

"It's a bit like they think we'll pull a gun on them," Catherine said.

"No one's had to so much as draw a weapon in all the years I've been here. I suppose they're a little freaked out."

"Not the ex-police, surely."

"No, not them. Though Peet was shocked. It's not like the police are in that many shootouts themselves."

Catherine scrolled through e-mails on her laptop and stopped to read one. Jan watched as her normally relaxed expression turned to alarm.

"What is it?" Jan asked.

"The home office. They're ordering me back to London."

Jan sat up straight. "But why? You still have at least a week here."

"Apparently, they're not happy that I've killed two people during a field assignment when I was supposed to be here in the office." She shrugged.

"Fuck." Jan sprang from her chair and began pacing. "Is there anything you can do?"

"I don't think so. They already have someone on their way here to replace me."

Catherine was leaning back in her chair, her face relaxed again, but her eyes looking far away. She didn't seem to notice Jan's agitation.

There was a quick knock on the door before LJ came in, looking unusually somber.

"Jan, would you give us a moment?" he said.

Jan met Catherine's eyes and waited for her to nod before walking out of the room. She moved quickly past Vivian, anxious to get back to her desk without talking to anyone. Peet was hanging up her phone as Jan sat down and started to close down her computer. She felt on the verge of panic.

"What are you doing?" Peet said.

"Getting the hell out of here."

Peet watched for a moment as Jan stuffed her things into her bag. "That was Mrs. Harrington on the phone. She said they have Maddy in therapy, but that she seems to be okay. Except for the broken jaw that is."

"Yeah, she seemed okay when I talked to her. She's a tough kid."

"I talked to her too. She's got a thing for you. She kept asking about you, wanting to know all about you. I should have just said that no one knows all about you. It's a state secret or something."

"Funny." Yet now there was someone who knew everything about her. Jan never believed that would or could happen.

"Maddy thinks you're a hero. She wants to thank you in person."

"It's Catherine she should be thanking. But she'll have to do it quickly. The London office is sending her home."

"What? When?"

"Immediately. That's all I know. LJ is in with her now."

Peet sighed and stared at Jan some more. "When you're on the job, you have to go see a shrink after you're involved in a shooting. Maybe you should do the same."

Jan glared at her. "I didn't shoot anyone."

"It's really the same as. I think so, anyway. You're having a tsunami of stress right now."

"I'm fine"

"This thing with Catherine only adds to it. That's all I'm saying."

"I'm fine. And that's all I'm saying." As far as the events in Idaho, Jan did feel fine. If she felt anything about it at all, it was relief. But she was suspicious of how muted her reaction was. The last thing she wanted was a shrink poking away at her.

All of that paled compared to what losing Catherine would do to her. She knew that once Catherine left, whatever feelings she had for Jan in Chicago would evaporate quickly in London. The distance would kill the very tenuous beginning of whatever it was they had. She'd been counting on their remaining time together to try to figure out where they were going and how they were going to get there. Catherine seemed unfazed by her orders to return to London.

"Too bad the Idaho prosecutor didn't press charges against Catherine," Peet said. "Then she wouldn't have been able to leave." Peet was like a fucking mind reader.

Jan's phone rang.

"It's me," Catherine said.

"I know."

"Can you come back to me?"

Jan hesitated.

"Jan, I need you. Please."

Jan marched back across the office and saw that the blinds in the conference room were drawn. She looked at Vivian.

"She's in there. Alone," Vivian said.

Jan knocked and found Catherine pouring more coffee.

"Another cup?"

Jan nodded. She tried for some of the nonchalance Catherine seemed to always have at her fingertips. She felt in danger of crying as Catherine came around the table with the thermos and poured into Jan's cup, standing inches from her.

"What was that about with LJ?" Jan said. Her voice sounded harsh, as if she were accusing them of having an affair.

"He was very excited to tell me that he's been put in charge until my replacement arrives. I was just going to pack up my things and head to the hotel."

Catherine seemed very cheery, a dispiriting contrast to her own misery. Didn't she care that they had to part?

"I won't keep you then," Jan said. She tried to keep her tone neutral, but she could hear the sadness in her voice. It didn't sound very attractive. It sounded needy. How had she gone from someone who pushed people away to one who wanted to attach this woman to her hip? She felt clueless about how to find the middle ground most people seemed to operate in. She was exhausted by her own extremes. Instead of walking out the door as she'd planned, she sat down and motioned for Catherine to sit next to her. Catherine reached for Jan's hand.

"Talk to me," Catherine said.

Jan looked up and sideways and then down, finally resting her eyes on Catherine's "I'm scared."

"Of what?"

"I'm scared that you're leaving and I'm scared I'm telling you that it scares me. I'm fucked up."

Catherine laughed and leaned over to kiss her. "No, you're beautiful. And the bravest person I know."

Jan was horrified as a tear started in her eye. Her throat felt under attack as it tried to control an upswell of emotion. She was about to cry and she fought desperately to beat it back. Catherine rubbed her thumb along the top of her hand.

"It would be horrible to leave now with so much left unsaid between us." Catherine got up and moved to Jan's lap, holding her head to her breast. "I won't let that happen."

"But you don't have a choice."

"I quit. That's my choice."

Jan moved her head away and looked up at Catherine in shock. "You quit?"

"I just sent the e-mail and I feel absolutely fantastic. Should have done it long ago."

"You shouldn't have done that for me."

"Darling, I did it for me. If there's one thing I've sworn to change in my post-Ellen years, it's to live my own life, not someone else's. Not even yours."

"I don't know what to think," Jan said.

Catherine leaned down to kiss her, a slow, gentle, inviting kiss. When their lips parted, she whispered in Jan's ear. "Come to my hotel. We'll think it through together."

"If I come to your hotel, I don't think we'll be doing much thinking."

"Exactly. We have time to figure this out. Let's just see."

As they kissed again, Vivian opened the door and stuck her head in. "Christ. Will you two please get a room?"

"We were just about to," Jan said.

About the Author

Anne Laughlin's first novel for Bold Strokes Books, *Veritas*, won the 2010 Goldie award in the mystery category. Her short stories have appeared in numerous LGBT anthologies, including *Best Lesbian Romance* (Cleis Press), *Best Lesbian Love Stories* (Alyson Books), *Women of the Mean Streets: Lesbian Noir*, and the Erotic Interludes series (Bold Strokes Books).

In 2008 Anne was named an Emerging Writer Fellow by the Lambda Literary Foundation. She has been accepted into several writing residencies, including Ragdale and Vermont Studio Center.

Anne lives in Chicago.

Books Available from Bold Strokes Books

Night Hunt by L.L. Raand. When dormant powers ignite, the wolf Were pack is thrown into violent upheaval, and Sylvan's pregnant mate is at the center of the turmoil. A Midnight Hunters novel. (978-1-60282-647-2)

Demons are Forever by Kim Baldwin and Xenia Alexiou. Elite Operative Landis "Chase" Coolidge enlists the help of high-class call girl Heather Snyder to track down a kidnapped colleague embroiled in a global black market organ-harvesting ring. (978-1-60282-648-9)

Runaway by Anne Laughlin. When Jan Roberts is hired to find a teenager who has run away to live with a group of anti-government survivalists, she's forced to return to the life she escaped when she was a teenager herself. (978-1-60282-649-6)

Street Dreams by Tama Wise. Tyson Rua has more than his fair share of problems growing up in New Zealand—he's gay, he's falling in love, and he's run afoul of the local hip-hop crew leader just as he's trying to make it as a graffiti artist. (978-1-60282-650-2)

Women of the Dark Streets: Lesbian Paranormal edited by Radclyffe and Stacia Seaman. Erotic tales of the supernatural—a world of vampires, werewolves, witches, ghosts, and demons—by the authors of Bold Strokes Books. (978-1-60282-651-9)

Tyger, Tyger, Burning Bright by Justine Saracen. Love does not conquer all, but when all of Europe is on fire, it's better than going to hell alone. (978-1-60282-652-6)

Words to Die By by William Holden. Sixteen answers to the question: What causes a mind to curdle? (978-1-60282-653-3)

Haunting Whispers by VK Powell. Detective Rae Butler faces two challenges: a serial attacker who targets attractive women, and Audrey Everhart, a compelling woman who knows too much about the case and offers too little—professionally and personally. (978-1-60282-593-2)

Wholehearted by Ronica Black. When therapist Madison Clark and attorney Grace Hollings are forced together to help Grace's troubled nephew at Madison's healing ranch, worlds and hearts collide. (978-1-60282-594-9)

Fugitives of Love by Lisa Girolami. Artist Sinclair Grady has an unspeakable secret, but the only chance she has for love with gallery owner Brenna Wright is to reveal the secret and face the potentially devastating consequences. (978-1-60282-595-6)

Derrick Steele: Private Dick The Case of the Hollywood Hustler by Zavo. Derrick Steele, a hard-drinking, lusty private detective, is being framed for the murder of a hustler in downtown Los Angeles. When his best friend Daniel McAllister joins the investigation, their growing attraction might prove to be more explosive than the case. (978-1-60282-596-3)

Nice Butt: Gay Anal Eroticism by Shane Allison. From toys to teasing, spanking to sporting, some of the best gay erotic scribes celebrate the hottest and most creative in new erotica. (978-1-60282-635-9)

Worth the Risk by Karis Walsh. Investment analyst Jamie Callahan and Grand Prix show jumper Kaitlyn Brown are willing to risk it all in their careers—can they face a greater challenge and take a chance on love? (978-1-60282-587-1)

Bloody Claws by Winter Pennington. In the midst of aiding the police, Preternatural Private Investigator Kassandra Lyall finally finds herself at serious odds with Sheila Morris, the local werewolf pack's Alpha female, when Sheila abuses someone Kassandra has sworn to protect. (978-1-60282-588-8)

Awake Unto Me by Kathleen Knowles. In turn of the century San Francisco, two young women fight for love in a world where women are often invisible and passion is the privilege of the powerful. (978-1-60282-589-5)

Initiation by Desire by MJ Williamz. Jaded Sue and innocent Tulley find forbidden love and passion within the inhibiting confines of a sorority house filled with nosy sisters. (978-1-60282-590-1)

Toughskins by William Masswa. John and Bret are two twenty-something athletes who find that love can begin in the most unlikely of places, including a "mom and pop shop" wrestling league. (978-1-60282-591-8)

me@you.com by K.E. Payne. Is it possible to fall in love with someone you've never met? Imogen Summers thinks so because it's happened to her. (978-1-60282-592-5)

High Impact by Kim Baldwin. Thrill seeker Emery Lawson and Adventure Outfitter Pasha Dunn learn you can never truly appreciate what's important and what you're capable of until faced with a sudden and stark reminder of your own mortality. (978-1-60282-580-2)

Snowbound by Cari Hunter. "The policewoman got shot and she's bleeding everywhere. Get someone here in one hour or I'm going to put her out of her misery." It's an ultimatum that will forever change the lives of police officer Sam Lucas and Dr. Kate Myles. (978-1-60282-581-9)

Rescue Me by Julie Cannon. Tyler Logan reluctantly agrees to pose as the girlfriend of her in-the-closet gay BFF at his company's annual retreat, but she didn't count on falling for Kristin, the boss's wife. (978-1-60282-582-6)

Murder in the Irish Channel by Greg Herren. Chanse MacLeod investigates the disappearance of a female activist fighting the Archdiocese of New Orleans and a powerful real estate syndicate. (978-1-60282-584-0)

Franky Gets Real by Mel Bossa. A four day getaway. Five childhood friends. Five shattering confessions…and a forgotten love unearthed. (978-1-60282-585-7)

Riding the Rails: Locomotive Lust and Carnal Cabooses edited by Jerry Wheeler. Some of the hottest writers of gay erotica spin tales of Riding the Rails. (978-1-60282-586-4)

Sheltering Dunes by Radclyffe. The seventh in the award-winning Provincetown Tales. The pasts, presents, and futures of three women collide in a single moment that will alter all their lives forever. (978-1-60282-573-4)

Holy Rollers by Rob Byrnes. Partners in life and crime Grant Lambert and Chase LaMarca assemble a team of gay and lesbian criminals to steal millions from a right-wing mega-church, but the gang's plans are complicated by an "ex-gay" conference, the FBI, and a corrupt reverend with his own plans for the cash. (978-1-60282-578-9)

History's Passion: Stories of Sex Before Stonewall edited by Richard Labonté. Four acclaimed erotic authors re-imagine the past…Welcome to the hidden queer history of men loving men not so very long—and centuries—ago. (978-1-60282-576-5)